For The Last Time

Janet Kelly

A BB Fiction Paperback Original

For The Last Time

Published in 2016 by BB Fiction

www.bobaloobooks.co.uk

Copyright © Janet Kelly

Printed and bound in Great Britain by 4edge Limited

ISBN: 978-0-9935091-3-1
E-PUB ISBN: 978-0-9935091-4-8

For The Last Time

By Janet Kelly

You never really understand a person until you consider things from his point of view... Until you climb inside of his skin and walk around in it."

To Kill A Mockingbird

.

CHAPTER ONE

I've been in a high security prison for nearly half my life and certainly most of my journey as an adult. There are reasons for that, of course. Reasons I hope one day people will understand.

I hate the noise of the cell door. It always makes a harsh, brain-shattering sound however anyone pushes it open. It sums up the cacophony of what goes on in here. The slightest push on the door sounds like violence.

There it goes again. The jangle of heavy keys, indicating our warder is about to burst into our lives with all the authority our society gives him.

Brian Phillips leans forward into the dingy space that's become my home and gestures to my fellow inmate.

'Come on Trev, the bus is waiting – anyone would think you want to stay here,' he says, as cheerfully as any man could after thirty years looking after lifers in one of the country's oldest and most run-down prisons.

Trevor Mahoney, pronounced 'Marny' – for some reason I can never fathom – has been my constant companion for many years. He and Brian have been the only people I could call true friends over the years inside. Only I can't call Brian a friend in public, which is a shame as I really like the guy.

Brian, or Bony as the other inmates call him on account of his sharp features and jutting elbows – only seen when short sleeves are allowed on the staff in summer - joined the service after the Army turned him down for having flat feet. His father saw an advert in a local paper suggesting that training to be a 'screw' would offer a satisfactory career opportunity. Of course they didn't use the word 'screw' but everyone knew that's what he'd be called. Brian thought he'd stay a year or two and try orthotics or physiotherapy to sort out what had now become a disfigurement. Then he met Karen, or 'Kas', a lively and homely girl whose activity levels were such that pregnancy was the only ultimate outcome. Married by the time he was twenty-three and a father of two by twenty-five, his feet soon became the least of his worries. Years went by and so did any ambitions he had for a better job.

'Yeah, go on mate. Go and live a life. For me,' I tell Trevor, patting my friend on the shoulder as he exhales the stale smoke from a flaccid roll-up.

I'm due for parole any day soon after serving a life sentence with what I hope has been not a small amount of stoicism and little rancour, despite the injustice of my sentencing.

Trevor, his greying hair spiking through dandruff and psoriasis – testament to the gruelling diet of prison food and ill-conceived nutrition – smiles slowly back at me, no doubt thinking of the time I've still to serve before my freedom is guaranteed. Both of us have talked about the day we'd walk, and now it had come for Trevor, there's little to be said. The dream's been realised. Life has finally visited upon us everything we'd waited for. It's time.

'I will Alan my mate, thanks. Thanks for everything,' Trevor adds as he picks up the few belongings he could call his own, wrapped in a towel of indeterminate colour. He hands me a small tin, gnarled and used to the point that the lid was raised in one corner – resolutely refusing to close shut.

'Here's my baccy. Roll one for me,' he says, holding my gaze for a little longer than we both felt comfortable.

Trevor goes to say something else but hesitates, knowing any sign of emotion could open up floodgates of sorrow, anticipation – feelings that have been wrapped in the shroud of acceptance and conformity for so long neither of us know if we could ever care about anything ever again; and if we could, whether it would hurt.

'Thanks mate, I will,' I answer. 'Take care. See you on the outside, eh?'

Trevor doesn't look back. There's so much to say but so little. Maybe he thinks he won't see me again – why would he when he has his wife and family waiting at home, a job set up by his brother in law and the opportunity to forget about the years he'd spent idle as his life continued in his absence. He can pick up where he left off.

'Come on, let's get you outta here,' says Brian to Trevor in a jovial manner, knowing there's no point asserting his authority now. He never did like to pull rank, often worrying there would be a back-lash. The uniform doesn't protect you from the prejudice of being 'one of them' and popularity is important. He's always relieved when an in-mate leaves without any personal grudges. Too many of his colleagues had been on the receiving end of 'lessons' that only those from the school of criminology knew anything about.

The worst was Chris Roy's two sons. Harry Hartnell had been a former inmate who hadn't got on with Chris's way of dealing with prisoners. Once Harry was released he arranged for Chris's children to be picked up from school - pretending their mum had sent a special car for them. Harry's "apprentice" took the young teenagers, aged twelve and fourteen, on a ride they still won't talk about. Although physically unscathed, apart from the abrasions of the ropes they were tied in when found, their mental state is sufficient to require constant psychiatric care. Harry reportedly left the country shortly after and hasn't been seen since. Brian did wonder if it was a coincidence that Chris took a long journey around the same time, returning a much quieter man.

Brian pulls the door shut behind us, saying on his way out: 'I'll be back to see you in a bit, Al. See if we can sort you out a new cell mate.'

I slump onto the bottom bunk – barely covered by the thin, striped mattress that visibly curls at each corner from over-use, not unlike my tobacco tin. A thin duvet with a thick cover, streaked from necessary heavy bleaching and the care of uncaring domestic staff, lays crumpled to one side of the bed. I don't want a new cell mate.

There's nothing to do but stare at the walls. My eyes take me to the corner of the room, but there's nothing to interest me other than a worn picture of a woman I once knew. Once married, in fact. Even had children with and thought, at the time, I loved a good deal: the woman who ran off with one of the men who got me into jail in the first place, within minutes of my getting a life sentence. I don't know which was worse – the judge's comments about my cold blooded attitude to my crime, which was unfair, or watching that man walk into my life, then out of it again - with my family. I sat in the dock and watched him walk away into my future, seemingly unaffected by the pendulum of right and wrong. I often wonder if he ever had any concern that he was taking my space in my bed, in my life, while I languished under the sentence passed to me by a judge who considered my only existence should be one behind closed doors. Injustice happens on all levels and sometimes it is that within ordinary life that is the most painful. Legal anomalies happen because the law is an ass. Integrity is a choice and isn't obligatory.

I remember the sentencing with finality. There was no going back, no arguing for clemency. I'd looked back over my shoulder as I was taken down to the cells, to see my brief chatting pleasantly to the Crown Prosecutor. In the background I could see three members of The Team leaving, seemingly satisfied with the result while I felt cheated and lost. I was just another pawn– one who'd been taken off the board while everyone else played their game.

I keep the picture of my estranged wife above the small toilet, shielded for privacy only by a low wall. I could always see Trevor's knees when he was on it – we both sat down for any type of toiletry as even the tiniest bit of personal space was cherished like diamonds in the confines of our twelve by ten foot shared cell. I'd stopped looking at Marie's face which was many years younger than it would be now. I can't help but think how time, on all levels, changes everything. Often I would look at the scene behind her; my house, my garden, my kids. All distant memories since she decided I'd see none of them again. A decision she could freely make while I was locked up, out of sight, out of mind. Something must have died in me because it doesn't seem to matter to me so much now.

I've had discussions with myself about what makes a woman like Marie so different from Trevor's wife, who'd kept the home fires burning and worked three jobs to keep their kids in clothes and the mortgage paid while her husband did his time. She visited every time she could, with all the children - and even her mother on special occasions. There was no blame, no guilt, no recriminations. No affairs, and no doubts over the identity of his second child's parenting.

Marie could have had the same life and attitude but she never seemed to be happy with anything. She'd been fairly jolly when I first met her so I don't know what changed, other than our marital status. Her apparent brightness in those early days might have had something to do with her vast capacity for vodka and coke but she never moaned as much as she did after we were married. I'd like to call her an enigma but she just wasn't that interesting.

I often felt a little bit jealous of what Trevor had and think that what screws most of us up is the picture in our heads of how it's supposed to be. Marie had a different vision to me, one coloured sufficiently to hide any shadows - and doctored to exclude any unpalatable elements of what might otherwise be considered an average life. She wanted more. If anything I wanted less.

Trevor had said before he left that he had every intention of going straight. *That means he'll try not to get caught next time,* I thought when he said it but didn't voice any opinion. I wanted to believe it to be true.

He also told me he wanted a better life. We'd talked about it most days but I didn't really believe what I heard. The ones who really did go straight usually found God, but that hadn't happened to Trevor.

It's like, you come inside, get religion and it's a free God of your own choice. One provided with every prison sentence, I'd repeatedly thought when some of the cons tried to persuade me to go to the chapel and pray for God's forgiveness. I'm not so sure it's his forgiveness I want. Who is he anyway? I don't fancy my own personal deity.

'It's all I can do to live with my own conscience. Let alone someone else's,' I'd told Trevor when we'd talked about whether it was worth agreeing to visits with the prison chaplain.

'I don't piss myself off in the same way that God might - telling me to repent my sins or else it's a diet of Hail Mary's until I meet my maker,' I'd said.

'Johnny Paris found Jesus for a while, which was all well and good until he got home. His missus told him there was only room for one sanctimonious bastard in her house so he'd better make a choice. Johnny's still there. I guess his new mate got the chop.'

Trevor told me he'd repented but I told him he didn't think he knew what that meant. He agreed that he certainly wasn't furious any more although when he came in he was full of rage.

'You be great fun for the likes of Ann Widdecombe.' I told Trevor after one angry outburst.

'She thinks every con should seeth with inner rage and indignation. Then when they are full of moral decreptitude… that's a good word that…they can say they're sorry, wear sackcloth, ashes and a sensible suit before becoming fully paid up members of the rat race.'

I'd then added: 'Didn't anyone ever point out that the only winner in the rat race is a rat?'

I thoughtlessly pick at the stitching on my mattress as I look back to my time with Trevor. *I hope it isn't too much of a shock going out. It's one thing talking about it, but another actually doing it.*

We'd talk about how things might have changed. Over the years we heard about things like email, mobile phones, global warming, liposuction. We could only read about them and so they didn't mean anything. Still don't. They are just things happening in a world we weren't part of: The Millenium year was a big one for both of us. Not just for getting locked up but because it was the last time we knew who was in the Top Ten.

'Now I don't know where we are,' I'd said. 'Is Banarama still a group? And smoking in public is a crime! What next? community service for scratching your arse? Probation for singing out of tune in the car? Bloody health and safety. Most dangerous words in the English language. Bullshit.'

Trevor hadn't been so worried. He wasn't a man for great depths of thinking, preferring to swim on the surface of life, catching the sun's rays where they were and refusing to look down the dark, shadowy fathoms. He couldn't see the 'nanny state' or invasions of his privacy. Probably because he did what he liked, when he liked, anyway.

'I wonder why we call it bullshit?, he'd said to me. 'Is it any worse than any other shit? Do bulls go about their morning excrement, look around and say "that's a load of bullshit"? I don't think so..'

Trevor told me not to worry, that we would both cope. I thought back to that conversation with affection – an affection we both shared but were very careful not to display in public. We were scared of being targeted as 'poofs' or 'queer', or worse still, candidates for Brainless Boris's next 'bitch'.

'We're mates,' Trevor had told his wife on a regular visit. She'd asked kindly about his friendship with his long-term cell mate. No suspicions although Trevor felt the need to explain to her.

'Nothing more, nothing less,' he'd protested. 'You can't help it when you're banged up together night after night,' adding that he thought it was no different to being in the army.

I didn't agree, when he repeated the conversation – as he did after every visit. Any germ of any news, people, life in general could feed our discussions for hours and days.

'Soldiers kill people and get a medal. We do it and get 20 years.'

Although it was our previously long-held belief that long term prisoners bugger each other all the time, I was surprised to discover it isn't as rife as people might think. I recalled the moment with Dave the Axe. He'd got hold of some Amyl Nitrate. It put him in a rather romantic mood and a couple of the inmates said it was very seductive in its own way. I couldn't claim the same, particularly as Dave's lack of dental hygiene gave him impressively bad breath.

Dave had tried to kiss me when we were on supervised swimming sessions. He'd leaned over by the shower area, told me he thought I was attractive and then grabbed my hand, guiding it into the tight waistband of his trunks. I'd recoiled and one of the warders came past in good enough time to stop proceedings – and for me to inhale again before passing out.

It reminded me of the time when I showed my erection to Lucy

Manning in Forester's Grove Car park. She was twelve and I was fourteen. She was playing with those Ker-nackers or whatever they were called. As a toy it was like giving a kid a couple of snooker balls and a pair of socks – certainly wouldn't be allowed now. Probably gave a few of the inmates from that generation a few ideas.

What happened to Lucy? Does she ever talk about the first erection she ever saw? Was it a "seminal" moment for her? I don't suppose she would know what seminal means. She came from Hamsey Green. *Which if you know Hamsey Green, says it all*, I consider. I remember she had big tits though. Even for a twelve year old.

In terms of sexual safety I reckon prison is better than some schools. There are quite a few boys' education establishments offering 'full time boarding at very reasonable rates'. Or that's what my step-father used to tell me. Thinking about it, I expected he was being sarcastic and would have delighted at the possibility of full time babysitting even if it was provided by the criminal justice system. Kevin Johnson had been sent to such an establishment after a number of incidents involving social services – he seemed to be more prolific with his crimes than I was at school -and it took years for him to tell people what really happened to him.

'You'd think someone would work out that putting fourteen teenage boys in a dormitory every night guarantees someone gets it up the arse before half term,' I told Trevor one night when we were listening to some particularly vigorous activity from our neighbours.

In the early days we were told homosexuality wouldn't be tolerated in prison. They can't say that now so just say any sexual activity is banned among inmates. It's kind of self-regulating. If you fancy men, the opportunities are there and everyone turns a blind eye. If you don't, then as long as you avoid Dave The Axe, you remain celibate or at least untouched by human hands other than your own.

I'm going to miss him, I think as I absent-mindedly feel the raised scar above my temple. I turn on the small portable TV bolted to the corner above the door and tune in to Lorraine Kelly's discussion about pelvic floor exercises, hoping I can think of something to look forward to.

Trevor was the sort of bloke you couldn't help but miss. He was always there, even-tempered and solid – certainly in latter years. He didn't question the waste of life his 'time' involved. He counted the days off and lived from visit to visit, playing personal videos in his mind of what was going on at home – all based on received information from those who loved him. Perhaps that was what made the difference. He knew he was loved. It helps.

I wonder what he'll have for dinner tonight, I think as I place my hands behind my head and lay down to listen to another few hours of broadcasting bilge.

I bet it's steak.

CHAPTER TWO

His head hurt. It wasn't the first time he thought he was going to die from the beatings. If only he could work out what he'd done wrong.

The trouble with being hungry is it makes me do things that make him angry, thought Alan.

'You fucking little shit. Touch my bloody scran again and I'll kick your shitty little arse outta here,' Wanker had said, snatching back the piece of cold fried chicken Alan had taken from the box by the sink.

Wanker was Alan's mother's name for him. The man who wanted him to call him 'Daddy', unless he'd had too much to drink then he didn't want him to exist. She never called him that to his face. She called him 'Babes' but with an edge to her voice that anyone living a sober life would recognise as sarcasm.

Alan went to his room after the beating. The bed smelled. The sheets and duvet had never been cleaned, even after the stray cat that came in had shat on them. The curtains hung off a few hooks, most had been broken in violent attempts to block out the light – and the eyes of neighbours.

He knew there was no point arguing that he needed to eat. His mother would be home soon and hopefully she'd be able to sneak something to him – once Wanker had fallen asleep, usually after the tenth can of strong lager or a couple of spliffs, if his dealer had been round.

She thought she was good to him, when she could be. Last week she spent two quid on a second hand jumper from the school lost property bin – even though it made Wanker cross.

'We ain't made of frigging money, Shell,' he'd screamed at her. 'If they want the shit in a uniform tell 'em to buy it therselves.'

Other boys had been teasing him, calling him 'Stink' and pissing on his books. He'd try to do his homework but it became a futile battle against his home surroundings and the bullies who sought out any weakness, any frailty that would provide entertainment for their sadistic fear-seeking characters.

Alan thought he saw his mother crying after she cleared out his school bag of the soggy pages, the pages he'd spent hours over, drawing maps of foreign countries for his geography project. Lands he would rather be living in, exploring, than this hell hole of an existence. She'd wiped a tear away from her bruised cheek, wincing slightly as the pressure of her hand reminded her of the previous night's punishment. But Shelley Shoesmith – she'd always kept his father's name because she liked how it made her sound – wasn't one to complain, which was unfortunate for her sons.

Alan's two younger brothers had been taken into care. They were all only a year apart making his two siblings nine and ten - but they had a different father. Their dad had been a nice enough man and he'd included Alan in his family. Jimmy was Jamaican and proud to be family-orientated - so much so he decided he'd better go back and live with his first wife and four other children in his mother country. Things hadn't been the same since social services started asking questions about his visa applications and benefit claims. He never paid any maintenance and at first Shelley took on as many jobs as she could, all minimum wage and physically demanding. Cleaning by day and caring for the elderly – as best she could with little or no sleep – at night.

She occupied whatever spare time she had with cigarettes, alcohol and dealing with the fall-out from her dubious romantic choices. No wonder she gave in to the promise of some help from Wanker, and then finally looked for more lucrative ways of making a living, without having to leave the house.

Denny was just eight when the social services got involved. They were concerned about hospital reports regarding a fall at home, and whether or not it had caused brain damage. Wanker told them Denny had always been slow and unbalanced, eradicating any suggestion that he might have been pushed. It was a more difficult process with Martin, seven. The police held Wanker for twelve hours and asked for previous medical reports on anyone from the family, but it was difficult to prove anything untoward as Shelley had always provided a reason that if not exactly feasible, crossed the line of reasonable doubt. Alan had seen what had happened – yet another of his step-father's rages – but at the time of the initial investigation had been in detention for hitting a dinner lady. She'd refused him extra potatoes, causing an angry outburst from the normally subdued Alan Shoesmith and also his absence from the family meeting - at the one time his input might have had a real chance of bringing about some justice. Even though evidence suggested Martin's injuries were in keeping with repeated abuse, they couldn't proceed with any action.

Despite being let off the rather slippery hook of the official investigation, Wanker didn't appreciate his luck. After a night's shouting and many sounds of fists on flesh, Shelley called the police and said she couldn't cope with her domestic situation and wanted her two youngest boys taken away for their own safety. Pleased to be able to deal with a worrying situation without having to resort to lengthy negotiations, 'second chances' and periods in limbo when all agencies waited for the next horror to happen, they were quick enough to oblige and social services were on us before the next round of beatings.

Denny and Martin both went to the same foster parents and Alan couldn't help but feel a twinge of jealousy.

'Stop mithering Alan,' his mother had told him after many questions about why his brothers had been sent away, but not him.

'You can look after yerself, they can't.'

Admittedly Shelley had missed many of the attacks Alan had suffered and as he wasn't keen to 'split' on Wanker, it was as if they'd never happened. The consequences of suggesting anything violent had taken place were often worse than putting up with the first round of abuse. Sometimes a little bit of guilt on Wanker's part would make him slightly softer to his step-son for a week or two. It was a trade-off that worked in Alan's interests, given the choices.

What Alan couldn't help notice was that his brothers were escaping to what looked like the bosom of a caring and loving family. One where you didn't get your head kicked in for asking if you could eat the crusts from your step-father's pizza.

After the boys were taken away, Alan's life changed. No-one ever got him up in the morning for school or offered breakfast, even though in the past his mother had tried. The house was cold and any food that did come in was ordered late at night after heavy drinking sessions. If Shelley had seen the inside of a supermarket it would have been to buy more of the cheap white wine or own label vodka she considered an appropriate barrier to reality.

The previous evening Alan had found the remnants of the night before's take-away and didn't see the harm in eating the cold chips, or chewing the grizzly bits of fat and skin from the chicken wings. He didn't expect to get attacked for eating scraps and normally he wouldn't have been, but Wanker hadn't gone to bed as first thought. He'd crashed out on the settee and woke up to find his step-son in the kitchen, having found the box of food resting on top of their already full rubbish bin.

Alan knew there was nothing he could do to defend himself. It was a pattern. Wanker got drunk, Wanker woke up, Wanker sometimes beat up Alan – for whatever reason he could think of. The only good thing, in Alan's mind, was that Wanker wasn't as fit as he used to be and the abuse of alcohol and drugs rendered him weak and unbalanced, both physically and mentally. After a couple of ineffective punches he would reel and fall, usually to the sound of his mother's pleas for peace. They were rarely heard but did have the effect of distraction.

This time, however, he'd picked up a beer can and used it to hit Alan in the face. It had crumpled and the torn corner of metal had caught the side of his head, scratching along the top of his eye before penetrating the soft skin at his temple. It bled badly and the sight may have been enough to cause Wanker to stop before he lurched back to the settee from where he'd come. Alan managed to get to bed before any more damage could be done, although his sleep was peppered with rising fear his step-father would be roused from his drunken slumber and come to find him. He was as alert as a fox until it was time to get up.

Alan stumbled out of bed and rubbed the side of his head in memory of the previous night's violence and wondered if he would be able to get out of the house and to school without further incident. He didn't like it there much because of the boys who would add to the permanent bruising he seemed to have on his body - but it was warm and he was entitled to a free meal. He didn't care that people called him 'fleabag' or 'scuzzy'. It'd been a long time since he gave a damn about what anyone thought.

'Alan, you up?' he heard his mother shout from the bathroom. It was unusual for her to be awake at this time. He made his way quietly downstairs into the kitchen, keen to avoid any conversation and with the sole intention of getting out of the house.

There was a loud grunting as Wanker woke to the sound of Shelley's voice and started to make his way towards the stairs. For fear of another beating Alan stood flat against the wall behind the kitchen door. If it was pushed open, Wanker would think he wasn't there.

This time no-one came after him and he heard his step-father belch as he made his way to his mother's bedroom. Alan shivered as he went into the front room to collect his school bag, thinking of his attacker drunkenly pawing over his mother's body - and noted that yet again Wanker had used a beer bottle to take a piss, missing and leaving a puddle on the stained carpet. Everything about the man his mother claimed to love made him sick.

Within a few minutes the house was quiet so Alan inched the living room door open onto the hallway and stepped quietly out, carrying with him the two odd shoes that between them made up a waterproof pair. He'd learned that comfort was the easy victor over fashion, despite the teasing and looks he got for the fact the left shoe was black and the right one, brown.

He'd asked on many occasions if he could have new shoes for school but was met with an exaggerated look of sadness from his mother who said she didn't have the money. He never dared ask when Wanker was there and Alan always accepted the negative answer, even though she was able to smoke at least twenty cigarettes a day. In desperation he'd walked to a number of charity shops in town but even the cheapest, least up to date, pairs of shoes were three pounds, which he didn't have.

He got to one, however, that was throwing out odds and sods even a charity shop wouldn't want. Amongst the piles of broken toys, torn clothes and incomplete jigsaws were a number of single shoes - including two of the same size and similar style. It was fine for Alan, who'd had enough of shoving bits of Wanker's empty cigarette packets into the soles of his last pair, to stop them leaking, and dealing with the pain of blisters on the sides of his little toes where they pinched from being two sizes too small.

The air was cold but cleansing as he left the small council house which he rarely called home. Pizza boxes and empty bottles piled up outside the front door, too many for the dustmen to take in any week. The council would come round and complain but nothing was ever done. Sometimes they took a garden's worth of rubbish

– mainly to satisfy neighbour's complaints - only for it to pile up again within a matter of weeks.

Denny's rusted tricycle – a legacy from the days when Jimmy was around-rested against the back gate which hadn't opened for years and one of Martin's prized roller blades was poking out of a weed-filled plastic plant pot. It had once held three cannabis plants Wanker had tried to grow in an attempt at becoming a drug dealer. He couldn't even get that right, mainly because he couldn't be bothered to nuture the plants sufficiently to get them to the point of being worth smoking.

Alan looked around before crossing the quiet road on his way to the comprehensive school. It was a three mile walk or two and a half if he cut through the alleyway. He would always weigh up the risk before deciding which way to go. If he should come across the Boyce brothers then he was likely to be spat at, or worse. They didn't use the alley but the Williams' twins did. If his timing was right he would avoid them but often he would get delayed looking for his homework or hadn't got up in good enough time and they would capture him, push him to the floor and kick him wherever they felt like it. There were always jibes and comments about his clothes, or his haircut, or the fact his shoes were different colours.

He'd tried to get a paper round so he could pay for his own school uniform, or at least a white shirt and some decent footwear, but the local newsagent was run by the Williams' uncle who said he couldn't have a scabby mongrel like Alan representing his business. He was too young to do anything else to earn a living.

He got caught stealing a few times. Mostly he was let off once the police knew his name and on more than one occasion a kindly onlooker would offer to pay for what he'd taken, claiming it was their gift. He particularly remembered one older man who said he remembered being hungry and so paid for the pork pie Alan had taken from the corner shop. He also bought him a packet of biscuits, a chocolate bar and a can of cola – a rare treat as the only drink available in his house was either alcoholic or tap water. He didn't like either much and repeated kidney infections were put down to dehydration as well as lack of general nutrition.

Alan generally tolerated the physical and emotional deprivation. He coped with being hungry, thirsty and generally unclean. He knew other people had families who ate meals round a table, watched television together and maybe went to watch football or on holiday but didn't envy any of that.

What he hated most of all was the feeling he was totally and utterly alone in a horrible world with not one single person he could call a friend.

CHAPTER THREE

I really wish Brian wouldn't bang so loudly on the door. I always know it's him because all the other screws just walk in. I suppose it's polite but you'd think a bulldozer was belting round the corridors the way he goes about it.

'Social worker's ready for you Shoesmith,' says Brian.

'Tell her to fuck off, the useless patronising tart,' I tell him. She's the last person I want to see on my first morning without Trevor.

It's strange how much I miss him. I keep wondering what's different. For a start there's no bouncing around on the top bunk. He'd do that as he got himself into position to jump down – he never used the ladder.

'Don't you want to sort out your parole details?' asks Brian, balancing a tray of breakfast on one hand while pushing the door with the other. 'I thought you'd like to eat in your room today. My treat!'

Food is a focus of all prison life, but I'm not hungry and although Brian's trying to cheer me up I don't care less about where- or if -I have breakfast. They can feed it to the prison pigs. Those poor things brought in as an attempt to foster caring and consideration among those of us chosen to look after them. A nice idea except we end up eating the poor blighters, just as we start to get to know their personality. One thing to kill something you've never spoken to – I know all about that - but those little beasts become just about as close as you could get to family to some of us, only friendlier. I always feel a little bit sick when I eat a bacon sandwich, knowing the meat comes from the previously powerful hind quarters of the animal I've called Percy.

'I don't have to see her, don't want to see her. So unless you want me to do my impression of Hannibal Lector on a particularly peckish day, she'd be better off seeing someone who mistakes her for being any use,' I tell him.

Brian puts the tray on Trevor's empty bed. It holds a packet of cornflakes resting in a plastic bowl with a small plastic dish of sugar and a carton of semi-skimmed milk. Hardly what you'd call a full English.

'Aw come on Al. She's here to help you. You've been a long time inside. She can help you get to grips with what's going on outside these days,' adds Brian.

'All I want to get to grips with is her scrawny little neck so I can wring it until she says 'please very nicely' in order for me to let her go,' I say.

'Please yourself,' says Brian, watching me as I roll my cigarette, as if he wants to say something else but thinks better of it. 'Maybe you'll feel different tomorrow,' he adds on his way out.

I think about Trevor and what he could be up to as I light his tobacco and inhale a deep breath, hoping it will somehow bring me closer to him. I imagine myself in his place, on the way to his new life and an evening wrapped nakedly around a loving wife. Maybe she's got in some food for breakfast, so the family can eat together again. A bottle of wine? Perhaps they'll be popping into the pub later for a drink with some friends, who will welcome him home and buy him a pint.

None of that scenario is likely to sound that special to many people, but it's an entire world to those of us deprived of the luxury of freedom.

I'm out of sorts now. Trevor's leaving has taken me by surprise even though I've known about it for years. I think the word is 'discombobulated'. It sounds right anyway.

Trevor's alright. He always gave sound advice. He got on with his social worker and his parole officer. He gets on with everyone, never causing any grief or concern but telling everyone what they want to hear. Chatting through a few things so they'd let him get on his way. I wish I could be more like that. Or at least pretend to be like that. Sometimes I just say what I think. I used to believe I was being honest but honesty is a subjective opinion. Most people don't like opinions, unless they are their own.

The trouble with my social worker is she's one of those middle class women who have had little to strive for in life and think everyone ought to be like her and her husband. She's never been hungry or poor, not in the real sense, and doesn't have to work to pay her bills – her husband does all that. She comes in here from her detached house in south suburbia, with a degree in social work and a Masters in bollocks. She probably travels by train, but calls it commuting, because she has time to read the Guardian and look as important as she thinks the other passengers look. She might even manage the crossword before she comes in here to chat to a murderer or two. She always leaves early. No doubt to pick up one of her kids from advanced ballet for the exceptionally smug. I can just see her at dinner. It'll be something steamed. And a moderate glass of good wine while she spouts on about how the country should be run, or how little Fuchsia-Annabelle – her eldest daughter - has astounded the entire teaching profession with her superior intelligence. She doesn't eat much as she's watching her figure. More than anyone else will be doing to any great extent as her deprivation of calories means she has an arse like an elephant's thigh. Scrawniness only works in your twenties. By the time any woman is pulling forty, the backside needs some meat or it flattens out like a deflated tyre; while her neck would do well on a turkey. I'm not saying she hasn't been attractive or that she still isn't in her own way but she'd do better with a good meal on a regular basis. She might get into size 10 jeans but I bet she's bony in bed.

Then I have a picture of her banker of a husband. He doesn't mind going to bed with an ironing board because she looks good in the designer dresses he buys for her to wear when she accompanies him on the various dates that clog up his corporate diary – meetings with pompous twats who earn a fortune for spewing out hot air and writing reports. Their opinion matters and so does the state of their wives so it doesn't do to put on any excess weight. No good taking some lardy lump with a penchant for lager top even if she is more fun. She'd be picked on by the other women like a worm in a chicken shack. Although I'd bet my bottom dollar most of the men would harbour a secret fantasy to slap her arse and ride in on the waves.

I bet her husband nods into his Financial Times while she prattles about how much good she is doing for the lower classes. All of which is entirely academic.

What she doesn't realise is everything about prison to an outsider is academic. 'How long did they get?', 'It wasn't enough', 'They should bring back hanging!' or the classic, 'Why don't we make them look after old people?'

Because, dear middle class patronising twat, we would end up eating them.

Just wait until one of their lot finds themselves on the wrong side of the law and sees some travesty of justice. Like that bloke off the telly accused of having sex with hundreds of teenagers over thirty years ago. You see, mud sticks even when the mud wasn't meant for you. Will their comrades at the squash club be keen to get to know the real story? As hell as like! They'll be running for cover in case any of the mud-slinging leaves stains on their pristine designer suits.

It's more likely the predicament of their unfairly treated associate becomes a dinner party anecdote for a few weeks, before they bury the memory of the person they once called a friend like a cat buries its own poo. I bet none of them know anyone who has been falsely convicted of murder and had to give up half their life to a justice system that is as flawed as the instructions in a DIY store flat-pack.

There's a loud banging outside the cell, in the corridor. It sounds like John the Junkie is having another one of his episodes. They happen regularly and no-one can really work out if they are genuinely to do with having to come off Class A drugs or whether a few stints in the amateur dramatics workshop have taught him how to play up to good effect.

'Shut up you noisy bastard! Can't a man get any peace,' I shout at him.

Peace. What's that eh? The only person I knew who was totally happy with his lot had the IQ of the room temperature. And one single life-time dream to be able to watch Neighbours at least twice a day. Once he got a portable telly and a place in a home for the bewildered he was happy as Larry - whoever Larry might be. I guess he could tell us a thing or two.

I learned once about something called "Imposter Syndrome." It's the feeling that people get when they are doing something important but they think someone will find out that they aren't really very good at it.

You'd think a few more would catch on to that idea. That Liberal Democrat leader for a start – whatshisname – never would have been made to Deputy Prime Minister without the country's inability to make a proper decision.

And definitely Sally the sodding social worker with her dissertation on the effects of Pilates on the criminal mind. But no, they carry on regardless, swelling up their chest cavities with over justified pride in their own importance.

Where do people get this uncanny ability to be so confident? Do they really give themselves a pat on the back at every opportunity? All when the only real ability they've got is to be able to arse-lick their way up the greasy pole of societal mediocrity?

These people strive for what they refer to as security - and by doing so create what seems to me as a very peculiar type of hell. There are no certainties in this life but they plan their futures with precision and arrogance. They spend their time at the gym and eating properly, ensuring they will be the healthiest bodies in the morgue. Of course they don't see their own death, which is just about the one thing that can be guaranteed (although they would probably argue taxes, which they are all trying to avoid, are a certainty). The eventual mortality rate on our planet is exactly one hundred per cent. No more, no less.

I am confused by their confidence. I often have a sense of disorientation in the face of an apparently absurd world. I think it is what is called "the existential attitude".

There I go again, big words. Sometimes they just make more sense than the small ones. It astounds me how many words there are in the English language, most of which we never use. I'd love looking them up when I was a kid. We didn't have many books but I'd go to the library to read dictionaries before borrowing a novel to throw myself into, such as *Lord of The Flies*.

I absorbed that book into my very being, dreaming of the visions the words brought into my imagination - even though I read more into it now than I did then. The idea of a group of marooned boys trying to govern themselves without authority appeals to my view of our world. There has always been academic discussion about human nature versus the common good but this said it all to me. Even well-educated children will regress to a primitive state and descend into savagery if left to their own devices. Education is only of value if it can be used effectively.

It is only natural to have a dilemma between living by rules, peacefully and harmoniously, or to choose the will to power over others. We all struggle at some point between the group and the individual, between rational and emotional and between morality and immorality.

Anyone who thinks otherwise is a dick.

CHAPTER FOUR

The room smelled of prunes and old fires. The worn wooden walls were pierced with pictures of ex-headmasters and rare certificates for excellence. But however much its décor aimed at communicating authority, it was so run down and over-worked it gave little more than an air of despair and exhaustion.

Alan stood with his hands in front of him, partly to cover the fact the flies on his trousers didn't do up but also because he didn't know what else to do with them. He could feel liquid running from his knees down the side of his leg, where his trousers didn't touch the skin. He thought it might be blood.

'So, are you going to explain yourself?' said Mr Nightingale, the recently promoted Pastoral Officer for the inappropriately named Headway Comprehensive in New Beckton. No-one had made any headway in that place since the former Bursar plunged off the Bristol Suspension Bridge in a failed attempt at suicide, having embezzled most of the school's funds.

Mr Nightingale had a job on his hands according to his colleagues who'd warned him against taking on the trials and tribulations of pupils from a school in South London that had never been able to get out of Government special measures, regardless of the funds and talent thrown at it. Many thought Headway would have to be closed as its reputation had become so bad.

To the naked eye Alan stood still, although his right leg shook like a fern in a gentle breeze beneath the expanse of his trousers – taken by his mother from a recycling bin at the local supermarket after his latest, and more earnest, request for school uniform.

The words he wanted to say jumbled up in a car crash of a sentence and he stared in front of him, wishing he wasn't there and that someone could understand he wasn't as bad as they thought. His lips twitched and a desire to force his own instant death overcame any sense he was trying to make of his situation.

'Come on, boy, we haven't got all day. What on earth were you thinking of?' Mr Nightingale said, standing from his chair and perching himself down on the edge of his leathered desk, now scratched and dismembered from years of questions, discussions, decisions – and undoubtedly a fair number of canings when they were legal.

Alan raised his head and pursed his lips. He could feel bile rising to his throat – there wasn't much else he could throw up – and tried to swallow it down without being noticed. He gagged as he did so and then felt sick again at what he'd done.

The teacher took on a softer approach and moving nearer towards Alan took hold of his face with both hands, gently enough to direct the boy's gaze into his own.

'I don't believe you are a bad boy, Alan, but the way you are behaving these days is not acceptable. You have had three cautions now and no doubt many more elsewhere, from what I have heard. Is there anything you want to tell me?'

There was so much Alan wanted to tell this man, who seemed kinder than any adult human being he'd met for a very long time. He wanted to tell him he was starving, that he'd started to have wet dreams and had to sleep in the consequences, that his mother has sex with strangers for money and that his step-father watches it while she does.

Could Alan tell him about his brothers being in care and he was jealous because they won't have to do want Wanker wants him to do, the sort of things no boy should ever have to do and which he knew he would eventually have to do if he was going to be able to stay in his house?

'No sir,' Alan finally said. 'I just wanted to have a look.'

Mr Nightingale's body sagged as his shoulders dropped in the knowledge he was being fobbed off and was unlikely to get to the bottom of this boy's story. Anyone could see Alan Shoesmith was a 'problem' child, on the social services register but so far not considered to be 'at risk'.

At twenty six years old this was John Nightingale's first posting to a school after teacher training. He'd wanted a challenge but even so didn't think he could have found so many dysfunctional families in one postcode.

His friends told him he should get a job in a grammar school somewhere in Surrey, where parents supported the school rather than viewing it as a babysitting service.

Occasionally he thought about it but he found the position both interesting and challenging – in contrast to many of his more experienced colleagues who described the role as both exhausting and demoralising.

Alan, however, was one of the most intriguing pupils he'd come across. The tight-lipped interviews and lack of evidence regarding any mistreatment were difficult to overcome. When questioned, the mother seemed caring and supportive and Alan certainly seemed intelligent and receptive. His malnutrition was dismissed by his mother as a metabolic disorder and his lack of suitable clothing as Alan's own boyish and naturally uncompliant nature.

Because Alan would never say otherwise, no-one could identify the real issues behind his misbehaviour. Mr Nightingale often wondered what engendered such loyalty.

'The trouble we have with this situation, Alan, is that the girl's mother wants to press charges. And I can't say I blame her.'

He lent his body towards Alan and paused, hoping for effect but also to think carefully about what to say next.

'You've never resorted to violence before Alan. Before the police get here I want to try and understand how this could have happened. Surely you have something you want to say to me?'

Alan dropped his head. The intensity of Mr Nightingale's stare made him uneasy. Close proximity to anyone other than for reasons of violence was unusual and now he was in the spotlight - for something he wished he hadn't done.

Lucy Manning had been given a new bike for her birthday and was allowed to ride it to school. Alan had always wanted a bike because it would get him around quickly, saving him the discomfort of his worn or leaking shoes, and would also give him the ideal tool for escaping the bullies. When he saw Lucy's new Raleigh road cycle it was like a vision.

He hadn't intended to try and steal it. He used every ounce of restraint in every fibre of his body but some force made him push Lucy out of the way as she was about to padlock her bike to the posts set up for the purpose.

'Hey, get off flea brains. Take your pissy hands off me,' she shouted at him. A small crowd of school smokers, hiding in the most obvious place from teachers, had gathered and started the usual taunts, ranging from 'Stinky' to lurid descriptions of what the older boys wanted to do to his mother.

Alan held on to the handlebars and as he felt his anger pulsing through his arms and up to his head, pushed the bike first into Lucy and then into anyone else getting in his way. Using it as a battering ram he managed to floor one of her friends and keep off a few of the smaller boys who'd started to join in.

'Give me my bike back, you tiny-dick moron!' Lucy had screamed. Alan knew he was doing wrong but so desperately wanted to know how it felt to be on a bike that he climbed over the saddle and tried to ride off in the direction of the exit. Never having been near one other than to envy his neighbour's last Christmas present before it was well and truly trashed by the Adamson boys, and having been excluded from the cycling proficiency classes at his primary school for not having his own bike, he immediately fell off – to the sound of much mirth from the crowd.

'Stinky can't even ride a bike he's so crap,' said one of the boys from his class. Others joined in with cruel laughter while the girls tended to Lucy – throwing hateful looks in Alan's direction.

'What sort of a knob hurts a girl,' added the boy who he noted was wearing brand new Commando shoes, something he'd always wanted since he first saw them in the shoe shop in town.

Alan's blood rose and every disadvantage from his thirteen years of life came to the fore, acting as a force against those he saw as his enemies. As Lucy came towards him to reclaim her property he powered his right fist into the side of her face, to the sound of her screams and then the sight of blood.

Shocked by his own actions, Alan ran to the gates but was caught by two older boys who tripped him up before happily handing him in to the teachers, who had already been called by Lucy's friends to deal with the incident – once they had squashed the life out of their cigarettes.

'I can only try and help you,' said Mr Nightingale. 'But to be able to do that you need to talk to me. I need to understand what is going on in your head.'

Alan's head felt fuzzy. It often did if he hadn't eaten for a while but this felt different. Little grey dots swam around his eyes and instead of Mr Nightingale and his office he could see only white light with pink tinges around the edge. The light slipped from his vision and was replaced with an avalanche of black and an overriding sense of powerlessness.

When Alan came round, Mr Nightingale was sitting next to him on the floor, holding a hot drink to his lips, which tasted sweet.

'Try and drink some of this tea, it might make you feel a bit better,' said the teacher.

Alan couldn't remember ever having tea, certainly not hot. To him it was heavenly. He could feel the liquid sooth his throat as it wended its way to his empty stomach. Within a few minutes he felt stronger and able to sit up.

'What did you have for breakfast, lad?' asked the teacher, his brows furrowing at the question.

'Didn't have time, sir,' said Alan. He hoped he might be offered some food as well as the tea.

Mr Nightingale looked around the room and, allowing Alan to get up to a chair on his own, took out a sandwich from a lunchbox that had been sitting on his desk.

'Here, have this,' he said and as he did so, Alan had grabbed the sandwich and taken a first bite. He could barely swallow but kept folding in the bread and ham into his mouth, keen to absorb the calories offered.

'My, you're hungry aren't you? Don't your parents feed you?' Mr Nightingale watched carefully as Alan answered, hoping for some clue – a key to solving all the boy's problems and thereby gaining some personal satisfaction and possibly recognition for his self-sacrificing work.

Feeling better by the minute, as the sugar from the tea kicked in, Alan replied that of course he got fed but he'd overslept and hadn't had time for breakfast.

As Alan stood up there was a knock on the door and on the request of Mr Nightingale that the visitors should come in, two police officers – one male, the other female – walked into the room.

They looked over to Alan with no registration of any emotion. The female officer, made to look even more rotund than she already was with the addition of a flak jacket, belts and various pieces of equipment, took out a notebook and pen. Alan wondered how she was able to carry that around all day without falling over.

'I think you know why we're here,' said the male officer, lightly shaking Mr Nightingales' offered hand. 'We've had reports of a serious assault against one of your pupils – a Lucy Manning – by a boy believed to go by the name of Alan Shoesmith. Is that you?' he said.

Alan shuffled on the spot. *Hardly a serious assault*, he thought as he remembered the beatings he'd had from Wanker. He nodded to the floor, not daring to look up.

Turning to Mr Nightingale the officer added: 'Who is the appropriate adult in this case?'

'I've tried to contact the mother who's not available and we don't have any contact details for his step-father,' said Mr Nightingale adding, for the record, that the family are known to social services – to which the female officer raised one of her eyebrows and scribbled something in her notebook. 'So I'm happy to be his responsible advocate on this occasion.'

'Alan Shoesmith we are arresting you on suspicion of the assault of Lucy Manning. You do not have to say anything. But it may harm your defence if you do not mention when questioned something which you later rely on in court. Anything you do say may be given in evidence."

Alan felt more liquid run down his leg but this time it was warm. He'd not been arrested before and despite his step-father's juxtaposed opinion, he'd always had a respect for officers of the law. He wanted to cry.

'Come on lad, you're coming with us,' said the female officer as she took hold of Alan's arm and led him to the door. She looked to the wet patch on the floor and after a general appraisal of the boy's general state took a gentler approach, placing an arm round his back and edging him out of the room.

A number of teachers were on duty to protect the police vehicle which had attracted a good deal of attention from pupils. As Alan was led out to the back of the car he could hear 'woman-basher' and 'pig-fodder' being called out to him. He blanked it out as he blanked out most of the names he'd been given since starting at the school. Names were the least of his worries. Once Wanker found out he'd been involved with the cops he'd be in for a much harder time.

Once inside the station his details were written down in a big book and he was placed inside a cell. It seemed comfortable and certainly cleaner than his room at home.

'You get yourself sorted out,' said the custody officer – a large and jovial looking man who wouldn't look out of place in a Santa suit at Christmas. He'd seen that Alan's trousers were damp and had also noticed the stale and unwashed smell coming from the rest of him. On their way to the cell he'd rummaged in a black bag in a side room and found some clean track suit bottoms and a T shirt.

'Put those on and someone will be in to see you soon.'

Alan wondered if they'd contacted his mother yet. The duty sergeant had rung home but he guessed she'd have been out or busy doing whatever she does during the day. He rather hoped they hadn't. Mr Nightingale was more likely to help him out of this trouble than she was, while Wanker would just use the whole episode to deliver his own deluded form of social justice.

CHAPTER FIVE

So many people have their lives planned out. The plan doesn't just include knowing what they are doing tomorrow, next week or even next month - they even think they know what their opinions will be in every single given situation.

Take football. The entire male population, and most of the media, seems to think it's something we should all take seriously. Fans support a team that represents a geographical area but which has not a single local resident playing for it. Most are foreign with names a BBC linguist couldn't pronounce and they earn so much money they wouldn't be seen dead anywhere near the towns they claim to be playing for.

Yet your 'Average Joe', if there is such a thing, has so much knowledge about 'their' team – often hundreds of miles from their own home town – and will resort to violence for the right to defend their belief in a group of over-paid men who run about a field every other week, earning more money in a few days than would cover the entire national debt of a small African state.

The loyalty's largely unrequited. Said players will transfer at the drop of a massive salary cheque and teams will often repeatedly lose to opponents creating depths of depression unknown in the absence of an accidental royal death. Yet men across the country will remain loyal and continue with their faith in whatever colours they have nailed to their mast.

But you ask them to stay faithful to their wives or stick to one brand of aftershave and they will question their human rights and the privilege of personal choice. It's all rather astounding when looked at from the inside, out.

All that human nature comes under a spotlight here. It's quite amazing what becomes important. I like to sit in a particular place at tea time. Breakfast is always the same; toast with no butter but a little bit of marmalade. I don't much like the marmalade here because it has rind in it. So I just use a bit. Crazy Colin hates the smell of it so won't sit near me when I eat it. That's a blessing. Crazy Colin supports Chelsea. I find it's best to say I do, too.

We watch TV a lot in prison. Only between certain hours and with only four channels we all tend to watch the same thing, or the same films. Guaranteed that if there is a moral discussion, for what it is worth, about how people would or wouldn't behave if they were the main character of a film, everyone will have an opinion on what they would do. It's the same with the news, or real stories about crime. Everyone in here will tell you how they'd do something. What they would do in someone else's place. How do they know? They aren't there.

Everyone thinks they can judge a situation from the outside, as an onlooker. But how can they? It's a different view. Being there is always different. Watch any quiz show and the contestants will tell you the questions they can answer without thought from the comfort of their own armchairs become tantamount to the Spanish Inquisition when faced with the lights and camera action.

And all the while people keep planning what they would and wouldn't do at some other point other than the one they face. You only have to look at the millions of people who buy lottery tickets every week, fully expecting to win the jackpot and change their lives. They've more chance of being hit by a meteor but still live in hope. Knowing my luck I'd get hit by a meteor just on my way to cashing in the winning ticket. So many people spend their week building up to the night the numbers are drawn, daring not to think what they would do with their millions. When they lose they console themselves that there is always next week, another draw – or even the football pools.

They kill any chance of living in the moment. You have to live in the moment in prison. They call it doing time here, but I see it as having time; time to think and time to be. If you don't know who you are after a spell in solitary then you probably aren't anyone at all. When does anyone on the outside have hours every day to consider the universe and its many complexities? Prison makes time stand still and then you can see how fast the outside world is - how little opportunity anyone has to take stock, take time out. Really think about what is important.

There's a lot of talk about trust in the world of the free. But what does it mean? I'd hear Marie's friends going on about their men and how they can't trust them again because they've slept with someone else. Why not? It's only sex. What's that got to do with trust? Dogs hump old men's legs because it's an urge, not because they are consciously thinking they're going to abuse the good nature of some random pensioner while turning their back on the mother of their puppies. It isn't a matter of trust, just nature. Acts of sexual infidelity don't turn a person into a thief or someone who will con you out of your life savings. They just make you feel a bit shit if you're on the receiving end.

Trust is altogether something quite separate from those things we just can't help. For example, if I were to die could I trust Marie to give me the funeral she knows I have always wanted? A humanist reading of my favourite Larkin poem followed by a cremation and my ashes sent to the skies in the largest firework my legacy could afford?

I'm not sure I could. And if you're not sure, you can't. Trust, that is. It's got fuck all to do with who fucked who.

'What the hell is that noise?' I shout through the grill in my cell door.

There's always some kind of banging and shouting and a new sort of drama. We're all shut away. There's no society other than the one we generate for ourselves and some bastards go and destroy the peace!

'It's me, Bernie. I'm coming in with your dinner. Guess what, it's gypsy tart for pudding!'

I've been allowed to stay on my own today, at my own request, after I stated that I thought I was heading for a period of depression. I'm better off without the others around me when I'm feeling low. They know when you're down and kick you a bit harder. Nothing worse than showing weakness, it's like a fox finding a wounded rabbit. They rip you to shreds and leave you limping, bits missing but not always entirely finished.

Those who don't have depression don't get how it brings you to your knees. Trevor would often tell me to pull myself together. He didn't mean to be thoughtless but you can't pull yourself together when you don't know where 'yourself' has gone. He would try and cheer me up with lame jokes I've heard a thousand times or by telling me funny stories about the other cons. Some days I'd laugh to make him feel better. Others I'd keep sinking into the quicksand of my withering emotional stamina, leaving him to carry on in his bright, optimistic and fully-functioning world in the hope he'd get the message and shut the fuck up.

It's just the way it is in here. I don't blame anyone for feeling the way I sometimes do. Everything that happens is under the microscope. All events are fair play and all emotions are used as entertainment. The sad people offer the best fun for those feeling strong. Make them cry or feel like shit and they feel they've achieved something. There's very little else to achieve in here unless a NVQ – Not Very Qualified – certificate in painting and decorating floats your boat. When I'm feeling at my worst I couldn't give a shit what they say or do. But I never forget.

I take the tray from Bernie, which I then take over to the bed -the one that was occupied by Trevor. I'll put up a big fight if they suggest putting Sean Bates in here. Everyone in the wing can hear him snorting and spitting and his last cell mate said he spent most of the night masturbating – usually standing up in the middle of the room before ejaculating where he felt like it. Sometimes it was on the wall and sometimes on his cellmate's face.

Sean hasn't even got any conversation to make up for it – just talks about how he's going to kill the grass who fitted him up, once he's out. I don't like that kind of negativity. It makes for a poor bedfellow.

Thankfully his dirty protest after his tobacco was confiscated (because he'd taken it off one of the new boys who didn't know the score about the currency of cigarettes) has led to the possibility of a move to another prison. We might all be lifers here but we know how to behave in this system - and Sean hasn't been in long enough to understand that shitting on your own doorstep, literally, isn't the way to get on.

The word will get round, he should know that. We might have lost our freedom but we don't lose the ability to communicate. Prisoners don't like dirty boys. They get taught lessons.

Thankfully I'd not been in the block when he decided to smear his walls with excrement. I was on one of my trips to one of the various psychiatrists who have been through this place over the years. They all painfully try to extricate any information they can about our crimes and whether we have any regrets worthy of note. Those who are prepared to say they repent often get more of a chance of parole and an opportunity to leave this place a bit early. I suppose they are repenting for their leisure.

I usually tell them I can't remember much and whether they accept that as the truth or not is for them to consider. They only get thirty minutes with each of us once a week, so not enough to push the point.

I look at the meal on Trevor's bed and can't help wondering who plans our menu. Today is a sandwich containing some indeterminate meat, cheese and onion crisps – which always leave an aftertaste of vomit - and the Gypsy Tart, which looks like vomit in a pie crust.

Why is Gypsy Tart called what it is anyway? And who in their right mind decides it is the ideal pudding option for a selection of the nation's hardest criminals? I can't help but think what it would look like smeared on my cell wall, or rubbed into the blanket. I bet it would stick there for a while. It looks like it might.

To be fair, I generally quite like the food you get in prison. It's provided on the clock and is vaguely edible. I get better fed here than when I was at home – either with my mother or the wife.

In the early days when mother got round to occasional bursts of shopping, she couldn't cook. Before she was with Wanker, when food became virtually non-existent unless it came from a plastic takeaway tray - she would open a tin of Spam and if you were lucky you got chips with it. We could tell what day it was according to what we ate. Monday sausages, cooked within an inch of recognition. Mince and onions was the fare for Tuesday, Wednesday and just as likely Thursday too - if there was any left – otherwise it was whatever you could find, which might be cornflakes or toast. Fish fingers on Friday which we'd have in a sandwich with salad cream or if we were really lucky, Sandwich Spread.

Sundays was another experience altogether. She'd get up early to ensure maximum cooking time for the cabbage, the only vegetable we'd have with whatever frozen pie or bit of reconstituted meat she'd found in the market butcher's freezer cabinet. The house smelt like a tramp's fart after three hours of boiling the greens. We'd eat at noon on the dot and it didn't matter what we had it always looked the same.

My first step-father, Jimmy, covered everything he ate with mint sauce and ketchup. So it probably all tasted the same as well. I occasionally feel sorry for the poor bastard. He married my mum in the excitement of lust and ended up with little more than a life of indifference and yellow cabbage. No wonder he went back to Jamaica. Life with Shelley Shoesmith coupled with the British climate would be enough to push any hot blooded male over the top.

Now, the wife has always been far more interested in food. She'd open up a tin of Spam, eat the lot and then look in the fridge for something else to contribute to her ever-widening arse. I reckon she had that eating disorder, bulimia – it's just that in her case she forgot to throw up afterwards.

I thought I would miss the wife. God knows why. All she was ever interested in was her spray tan. That and whether or not Tom Jones' genitals had been digitally enhanced for his *Atomic* album. She didn't bother coming to court this last time. Said she couldn't bear to see me going down. Funny that.

It never bothered her before.

CHAPTER SIX

The Youth Court took just forty minutes to decide Alan's fate. In the absence of any parental support – his mother had promised to show but failed to do so and couldn't be contacted even when a police escort was sent to her house – he was sentenced to eight months detention for his first crime of assault.

The bench heard the local authority report which gave a poor account of Alan's home surroundings and school record. An official handed over piles over paper higher than any folder could hold, while Alan stared into the middle distance, not having any idea of what was going on. Mr Nightingale acted as his responsible adult, stating that he believed Alan would benefit from a custodial sentence. Alan wasn't surprised to hear this. Everyone wanted rid of him.

Mrs Stanley-Hearst, Chairman of the bench, was an authoritative figure, dressed in a slightly tight, dark green suit that buttoned up to the bottom of her long neck, abruptly meeting the sharp angle of her chin and her chiseled, almost manly facial features. A string of pearls hung loosely on top of the jacket, catching occasionally on the top button and looking more like a Christmas decoration than a piece of jewellery. Occasionally she would try and unhook the necklace from its inappropriate landing place but gave up when it took up too much of her attention.

She smiled at Alan who sat in a seat surrounded by people he'd met since his arrest, all of whom at some time had prodded and probed into every aspect of his life. No-one had ever dissected his circumstances to any level and he found it difficult to answer some of the questions about his family.

'How do you spend you evenings with your parents?' one social worker had asked. Alan had no idea what he could say that would sound appropriate so kept quiet, ensuring a diagnosis of social inadequacy that was highlighted in most of the paperwork delivered to the bench that morning.

Had someone made him run around naked in the High Street while doing unspeakable things to himself as passers-by watched he probably couldn't have felt any worse.

'I take particular note of the medical reports conducted during Shoesmith's remand to Beldown. It's quite appalling that the support systems expected to look after vulnerable young people have failed to notice his physical condition. I would like to ask our social services representative why anyone under the eye of our various agencies is not protected from extensive tooth decay, uncorrected sight issues and anaemia?'

She glared over her half-rimmed glasses at the scruffy social services officer who, attempting to associate with youth and in the interests of levity, was wearing torn jeans and a T Shirt with the name of a well-known rock band emblazoned on the front.

'Er, no, I don't think so,' said Nigel Ansell, shuffling through some files but with no clear idea of where to look. 'It's certainly not that common.'

Nigel, as he'd asked to be called, had been assigned to Alan's case as soon as he was arrested. He'd been to the house and told Shelley Shoesmith what was going on - and seemed to have gained her respect. Or so he thought until she threw him out after he went to ask some difficult questions about meal provision, abuse and unsuitable domestic behavior. Wanker had been at home and told him to 'fuck off and interfere with small girls' which didn't go down too well but Nigel seemed ineffectual in being able to deal with the 'lack of engagement in their son's welfare' – as it was told to the court.

Subsequent interviews with various people in Beldown achieved nothing. Approaches varied from sensitive to intrusive but Alan stayed quiet. He might not like what happened to him at home but he wasn't a grass. And he didn't think it was anyone else's business.

What was normal to Alan was described in serious tones to the court who reacted with various intakes of breath, utterances of 'surely not' and sad and consoling looks in his direction. He wondered what the fuss was about.

Mrs Stanley-Hearst took a deep breath and continued with her sentencing directions, addressing most of what she was saying to Alan's lawyer, a young Turkish woman with a defined accent and a recent qualification in representing young people in court. The woman looked over-earnest in her desire to appear concerned, to the point Alan had to stop himself screaming that no-one gave a toss about the real him, the boy who knew too much, too young, and had no direction or barriers to either challenge or defend him.

The lawyer turned out to be of little use in Alan's eyes. Her language was good enough to pass exams but not to communicate with a dysfunctional youth.

She's spent little more than ten minutes assessing his case and didn't ask one question of Alan, just read his notes and made her own assumptions. Her view was that teenagers are hard enough to get through to at the best of times, unless you also happen to be one, so the added complication of a reclusive, sullen and abused boy with little interest in telling any story – truth or otherwise – meant she had more or less given up on defending his actions regarding the assault. She threw in the details social services had given her on his upbringing and hoped that would finish the case so she could get on with something less likely to bring her professional status into question.

'Now, Alan,' added the chair of the bench as she took her gaze away from the lawyer, much to her apparent relief, 'you may or may not have been advised that because you have been convicted of an offence for which an older person may go to prison, we can pass a detention and training order. I feel this is of most benefit to you, bearing in mind your current home circumstances and the lack of support you have been given to date.' She glared at Nigel as she continued: 'Do you understand?'

Alan didn't understand but said he did, while doing so pushing his new glasses up his nose so he could see her properly.

When asked if he had any more to say just mumbled 'thank you' and allowed himself to be escorted back to the van that had brought him to court. He had with him the few belongings he'd taken with him from the remand unit, namely a clean track suit, some underwear and a case for the spectacles that had been prescribed for severe short-sightedness after he was given a full medical on arrival at Beldown. He also had a book, *Of Mice and Men,* which Nigel had given him, although he wasn't sure why.

Alan thanked his stars he'd gone to school enough to be able to read. Reading was the one escape he had, when he could find a book to borrow. The last one he'd read all the way through was *The Catcher In The Rye.* He'd found it in the same charity shop where he'd found his mis-matched shoes, ready to be thrown out because some of the pages were a bit torn but still readable. He'd kept it for a while before reading it and when he did, immediately identified with the character of Holden Caulfield and his extensive use of slang and profanity. It was what Alan was used to and what he felt like using at that moment. There was no clarity in his young thoughts, just anger and distress. His hormones were raging alongside his mind and he felt isolated in his inability to make sense of his uncertain life.

The discussion of adolescent sexuality also allowed him to indulge in his own natural feelings of unrest. His uncontrollable erections were disturbing because of what he'd been forced to witness at home – he gave in to nature but none of his sexuality felt natural. The book's portrayal of isolation in a heartless world and the disengagement from human connection rang bells with the socially restricted and the culturally compromised teenager.

'Where am I going now?' he asked the detention centre escort as he climbed into a large white van, taking up his place within one of the isolated cubicles. There were no windows and he would have no idea of his journey other than muffled sounds from traffic, the stops and starts of the vehicle and possibly a vague idea of where he could get to in the time he travelled.

'You'll know when you get there,' said the gruff woman as she pushed him into his place and told him to sit down.

It went dark as the back door was closed. He feared he might be on his own so settled down to his own thoughts. The engine spat into life and the smell of fumes invaded his breathing space. Alan's lungs filled with the acrid smoke and he coughed, feeling no respite from the heat and smell of the van's exhaust. He hoped the journey wouldn't be too long.

'Oy, you. Puffing Billy, Who are you?' said a voice from nearer the front of the van. Alan ignored it, despite being intrigued to discover there was another prisoner with him on the journey.

'Don't fucking ignore me you little prick. What's yer name?'

'I'm Alan. Who are you?'

'You can call me King if you like. And then you can kiss my arse,' added the voice.

Alan wondered where he was going. And what was going to happen. He knew nothing of youth detention and nobody had thought to prepare him. He shook and tried to stop the tears with sniffs and deep breaths, which he hoped would also block out the engulfing fear creeping over his skin.

'Hey, don't be making that noise, boy,' said King. 'We don't want no softies where we're going.'

Alan wiped his nose on his sleeve and held mouth tightly closed in a bid to stop a fresh sob bursting out. He knew he had to man up, but he didn't know how to. As if in answer to his thoughts, King told him not to worry and that he'd look after him.

'I've been here before, bruv. I know what goes down so stick with me and we'll be fine, right?'

Alan muttered a muffled response that suggested acknowledgement and wondered what the odds were on his fellow offender actually wanting to help him, be on his side. It would be a first.

CHAPTER SEVEN

I think being put in a detention centre at the age of fourteen was a turning point for me. That's if there is any possibility of being able to turn when you've been shoved into a corner all your life.

What was laughingly called home had little to offer and I'd blotted my copy book at school by punching Lucy Manning. I don't know why I did it as I quite liked her. She was one of the few girls who spoke to me, even if it was to call me names. It was after the erection incident. I thought she was my girlfriend but she thought otherwise but we were still mates. She offered me a puff of her fag once. Lucy is probably to blame for my tobacco addiction but maybe I should thank her. Cigarettes are not only a currency in prison but a language. Thankfully one I can understand.

The first time I was locked up was the worst. King wouldn't let up all the time we were in the van, which was about an hour and a half but felt like three weeks. He was a good six inches shorter than me but probably weighed the same. He was wearing trainers and good jeans so I guessed he fared a bit better on the home front.

He'd tried to talk to me but we didn't have much time. I can remember feeling very lost and lonely, wondering why my life had turned out the way it had while everyone else had loving families, friends and things to occupy their time that didn't involve escaping the deadly effects of alcohol, drugs and unfettered disappointment.

The school had tried with me, looking back. Mr Nightingale was not much more than a boy himself when he took me under his wing and offered some of his considered concern. It didn't feel real, though. He wanted a result but I wasn't playing ball. He didn't realise that some pain is so great it is best left buried deep, beyond any expression through words or emotion. Had he managed to dig to the very core of my sadness he would've opened up entire continents of rotting, savage rage. He'd started something he couldn't finish and my last memories of him were sadly offering a thumbs-up as I was led to the cells for my first term of imprisonment.

Coming in this last time has been routine. I've seen the inside of enough institutions, and learned enough about the social niceties, that I felt no anquish. Not like that first time. All eyes were on me, all eyes apart from my own as there were no mirrors. Just polished blocks of stainless steel. No edges, no glass, no methods of self-destruction.

As a young man I would choke back the unfairness, hoping against hope that I would be rescued from my plight and that someone would recognise, without me having to blurt out my inner core, what I'm really about.

I remember I tried to pick the thick enamel paint from the skirting boards but it wouldn't budge. The layers of dark blue, coloured against an age-long tradition of tidying up; hiding a multitude of misadventures, DNA and blood stain.

I have to look at the colour of the woodwork in my cell now as I can't remember, even after 14 years. It has no relevance and so I take no notice. Oh yes, it's a green colour against yellowing magnolia walls and lots of metal. Not anyone's obvious choice for home décor. I think it has been painted a few times since I've been in. Always the same, though.

White noise. I didn't know what it was but I do now and crave it now I'm alone again.

I'm reminded of that first night I was locked up and I couldn't sleep. They watch you eat, shit, sleep, yawn. I couldn't take the attention, I preferred being ignored. I would wait for the white noise to muffle out the hidden stories and discussions behind my back. It would keep me safe. I wanted to be left alone.

There was a screw who made it better. Can't remember his name but I think it was something like Johnson. He could hold my gaze a lot longer than I could hold his so there was no point disrespecting him and he wasn't too bad in the long run. He helped me get stuff done and got me a shower the first night I was there, which isn't always possible. He sorted out loads of other stuff, too, that no-one else had ever bothered about.

The dentist was shocked to find I only had 12 of my teeth left. Some had been punched from my jaw but the others had fallen out due to gum disease. He asked if I'd brushed my teeth as a child and I couldn't remember. I think I did have a toothbrush once, before Wanker moved in, but I don't recall toothpaste.

'I don't know how you manage to eat,' he'd said, while prodding around with a sharp instrument that made my mouth taste of metal. When I spat out the pink liquid he offered to rinse with, it was full of blood.

I rarely ate that much so it wasn't a problem. Pizza crusts and chicken wings were swallowed too quickly to be chewed. Cold chips could be sucked. It was a relief to know the pain could be alleviated with further work and antibiotics.

That's one really good thing about being held at Her Majesty's Pleasure. They are like the best family ever.

Not only do I get a shower most days and regular food, from that first time the only regular dental and other health checks I get are when I'm inside. In youth detention I was diagnosed with a blood disorder but within a few days of being given some very large pills I felt stronger than ever. Instead of waking up tired I felt like I could run for miles. Strangely I didn't want to.

Despite all that I didn't see how good I had it. Two months in to completing my first round of time, with only a few weeks to go, I ruined it all by stealing a biscuit. One lousy chocolate chip cookie cost me 21 days of incarceration. It didn't matter how much food I had then, I still thought it was in short supply.

I wouldn't do that now. I know the rules. Back then I may subconsciously have wanted to stay where I was. The routine was surprisingly comfortable once I got used to it.

The other good thing about doing time, even as a lifer, is that the screws talk to you about getting out. There's always another life waiting for you, one where you can move forward from where you have been. No-one ever wants to go back, because that's where they come from. I don't know anyone who would want to go back. We all want to start over.

Well, at the beginning we do. A foster family had been sorted out for me when I was released after the Lucy Manning incident and I was looking forward to being taken in to their care. My mother had disappeared off the face of the earth and as she hadn't visited or responded to any social services intervention it was agreed I should be looked after by the Ludlow family until I finished school.

I know they tried their best but they really got on my nerves. They had two of their own children, Lucy and Dominic, and they were at private boarding school, so were only home at the weekends. I was the family's first 'project' in fostering which came about after Mrs Ludlow read an advert in her local WI magazine looking for understanding families to help make a difference to the less fortunate.

As a teenager with little to respect I found her constant nagging about using a knife and fork to eat, and tidying my room – the box room of their five bedroom house, as the other double room was kept for guests – raged at my patience like a woodpecker at an oak tree. Tap, tap, tap. She was relentless about order and routine, going to church and being grateful for all she had.

She should be grateful. While her husband earned millions running a variety of successful engineering companies, she had access to a joint bank account, four or five unlimited credit cards and enough free time to patronise for England. When she wasn't 'fostering' (I was the only one and I only lasted six weeks) she worked for a charity that educated young, single mothers on how to bring up their children on benefits by making a chicken last for a week and giving up smoking.

'If they just learned to be more sensible then they would manage quite well on the handouts they get,' I heard her telling one of her coffee morning colleagues. She'd been on the phone for over an hour and was the one who did most of the talking.

'All they need to do is give up smoking, stop buying clothes and boil up the bones for soup. We all had to do it when we were young parents,' she'd added as if her opinions were fact.

She had no idea that for so many of these young women they'd got pregnant in the first place because they thought the sexual act led to the love of the child's father, or at very least would give them an alternative to finding work when career choices for the rigorously incompetent were limited.

Cigarettes became these young women's regular friends and a way of marking their otherwise pointless days and evenings. The clock would tick by along with their disappointed hearts, punctuated by timely breaths of nicotine. The addiction kept them going, got them up and about. I couldn't see how chicken soup could have the same effect. Not even for the Jewish among them.

There are no handbooks when you have children and although the Ludlow's seemed 'normal' in the eyes of society I bet all the kids have little bits of insecurity and instability stashed away. How can anyone get it right first, second or even third time?

There aren't any tests and if there were, the Ludlow parents would probably only get a B-plus. A mark far less than they would expect from their privately educated children in any examination of their abilities. But Mrs Ludlow thought with absolute certainty she'd got it right. Her children were as near perfect as any human could be and that was down to her upright, Christian attention to discipline, hygiene and domestic science qualifications. I just hope she never found out her fourteen year old daughter was shagging the Ludlow's thirty-five year old, pot-smoking gardener every time her back was turned.

What is frustrating, more for them than any onlookers, is why some marvelously perfect people, ideal potential parents, can't have children. They must look at those who pump out five or six sprogs without a care for their future, and wonder what they've done in a former life to face such injustice. Cap it with the fact their taxes as couples with a double income will be going to support the hapless progeny of a third generation of benefit scroungers, each of which will no doubt continue the family tradition of producing offspring as soon as is humanly possible.

Mrs Ludlow had her views on such social disorder and put them as ineloquently as possible on various occasions, between her bouts of bleaching the bathroom and ironing every item dispensed on a daily basis from her integral tumble dryer.

Dominic had some nice clothes which I borrowed when he was away at school. I'd been given some of his hand-me-downs, which were OK and even fitted. He was two years younger than me but had been well fed, presumably on chicken soup, and regularly trained for his school's rugby team.

I preferred his new stuff and didn't see how anyone could object as he wasn't there to wear them himself and his parents could afford to buy him whatever he wanted.

Mrs Ludlow got cross so I called her a slag, left home for two nights and ended up being picked up by the police after I'd sat in a pub and got propositioned by a middle aged man who asked if I was looking for business. I thought he meant he would find me a job so I could pay my own way but I was just about to get into his car, after he said he'd pay me one hundred pounds if I was as good as he thought I might be, when the cops arrested him for importuning and sent me straight back. The silly cow had reported me missing and the minute the police and social workers had left started the tap, tap, tapping again.

'Just you wait until Mr Ludlow gets back,' she'd whined on, still dressed in her sensible tweed skirt and flat shoes.

I probably came across a bit sullen although really I just wanted her to leave me alone. She got on my nerves with all that prattling. No wonder her own kids seemed eminently happy to be living somewhere else.

Mr Ludlow came home and went straight to the whisky bottle. She *tap, tap, tapped* at him until he eventually relented and came to have 'a word' with me which was little more than a tired request I didn't piss off his wife anymore – because he got it in the neck if I did.

I agreed, waited two hours until I knew they would be asleep, packed one of Dominic's bags with a load of his clothes and a few things I thought I could sell before nicking what I could from the Mother Hen's purse and leaving. I never saw any of them again.

I feel bad about that now. They were only trying to do something good but didn't get how that made me feel. I would look at everything they had and it would remind me of where I came from.

They took their privilege completely for granted. If they were hungry, they bought food. If they were cold, they put on a fire. Education was a given as was the love of two parents who might not have always had great passion for each other but at least knew the value of doing the right thing by their kids.

Their kindness brought into sharp focus the absence of what

they would call 'a good start' and just made me even more resentful of having picked the short straw.

At the time, I hated them.

CHAPTER EIGHT

King's name was Julian Redford-Kingston although he asked to be called Jules by the screws, and King by the inmates. Some people called him Julie and, if they did, got hit for it.

He was five feet four and a half - the medical officer confirmed his height every time he was admitted - but he always claimed to be five feet six. Either way he was a good number of inches shorter than Alan's six foot frame.

'You stick with me and I'll make sure you stay out of trouble,' King had said to Alan when they arrived at the reception area. 'I know the score, you know what I mean?'

Alan wondered why he spoke like a black man when he was as pale as a pint of milk and as blonde as bleached sand.

'So, we have the pleasure of entertaining you again do we, Jules? What you in for this time? Something vile, no doubt,' said the warder has he went through our belongings and took a note of anything we'd brought in. My bag was limited to what I'd been given in the police cell but King had far more to show for his previous life. His trappings of success included a nice watch, a wallet with a wad of twenty pound notes in it, some cigarettes, a lighter and an electronic organiser.

'What do we have here, then? Getting a bit technical with your methods now aren't we?' the warder smirked to King.

King's face hardened. His lips pinched in a straight line and his chin set upwards. He'd learned a long time ago not to give any back chat or he'd be up for an internal examination. Last time they'd found his drugs, tightly packed in cling film and inserted deeply into his rectum, they'd put him on a rehabilitation course, in isolation, for six weeks.

'So, Mr Shoesmith, first time guest are we?,' said the officer, turning his attention to Alan, who shuffled from foot to foot as he felt his cheeks heat and his stomach tighten.

The warder seemed nice enough, if a little annoying, but Alan guessed from King's stance it was best to keep quiet.

'Well, we'll soon have you settled in, don't you worry.'

Within a few minutes the boys were separated and Alan was being offered the chance to look round his new home, make calls to relatives and have a shower. He declined the telephone tokens but welcomed the chance for hot water and soap. Mr Nightingale was waiting for him in a side room, having established himself as the boy's legal representative.

'Must all seem a bit daunting?' he said, inviting him to sit down on the plastic bucket chair opposite him.

'Yeah, a bit,' said Alan, his voice shaking a bit as he took in the enormity of his situation. He was still shaking from the windowless journey with the intimidating King.

'Is there anything you need or want, that I can get you? Are you hungry, do you need any more clothes?'

After devouring a burger, chips and beans downed with a can

of cola, Alan felt like he'd been treated to the best hospitality in town. That and another clean tracksuit and a pair of new trainers put him in a far more appreciative mood, despite the raging pain in his mouth that pulsed to the site of scar on his temple. He held is hand to his jaw.

'Right, we're going to get you back to the dentist,' said Mr Nightingale.

On Alan's three week remand to Beldown, he'd been given a full medical and was now under observation for a number of minor health issues. There was also a programme of care written for his dental work, which he'd been warned would be extensive.

'I'm alright, I don't need to go there,' Alan said, mindful of the blood and pain he felt on the last visit – even though it had been numbed with analgesics.

'You have no choice, we have a duty of care,' added Mr Nightingale, saying that the doctors would also be looking into treating any other concerns they'd picked up.

Once Alan's needs had been communicated to the prison officer, Mr Nightingale was told his requests would be recorded. He was then asked to leave and Alan was taken on the tour of the 'facilities', which included a games room, learning centre and a gym.

It might help me beef up a bit, he thought, while fantasising about getting his own back on school bullies, Wanker – and anyone else who he felt had done him any disservice.

At the back of the centre there was also an art room and most interestingly for Alan, a library.

'When can I get a book?' he asked the warder who was showing him around. Surprised by the question, he'd replied that he wasn't sure, but said he'd find out.

'OK, thanks,' said Alan not sure why he felt so grateful for the potential access to words that were either the opinion or fantasy, often both, of people he'd never met or was ever likely to meet. All he knew was that those words helped him escape, allowed him to be the protagonist in a different story to the one he was living.

Two hours after coming in to Beldown as a sentenced prisoner, rather than on remand, Alan was taken to his cell. He was told he'd be on his own for a while, to settle in. The warder who'd escorted him through the long corridors, lined with eyes staring at the new admission and a smell of old cooking and stale cigarettes, left him to put his things away. He said he'd be back later to make sure he was OK.

'Oi. Got any fags?' said a tall lad who was standing in the gap between the door and the end of his bed. Alan hadn't heard him come in, maybe because he was busy looking around the cell and noting is meagre but seemingly adequate contents.

'You deaf or what? Got any fags,' added the boy with red-ringed eyes, dusted with the remnants of sleep he hadn't washed out. He also had acne which was barely noticeable against a back-drop of freckled skin and ginger colouring.

For once Alan, with his thick mop of black hair and pale facial sheen, didn't feel like the loser in the looks department.

'No, I don't smoke,' he replied, lying a little bit because he always took a cigarette if he could find one. When his mum didn't notice or he could nick them from an aunty or a girl at school. Lucy Manning was pretty good at letting him have a puff, before the 'incident' and he winced internally at the thought of hitting her. He shouldn't have done it and couldn't understand why he did because he really liked her.

'Great,' said the ginger boy. 'I can have your ration, then.'

Alan didn't reply but just nodded almost imperceptibly. He had the feeling it wouldn't do to make friends too quickly in this place.

'I'm Jono. If you want to know anything let me know.'

Jono told him it was tea time and so the two of them went to the canteen although Alan was still full up from the meal he had on arrival. He wasn't used to eating every day so to be offered two meals in the space of a few hours was overwhelming. Jono was delighted at his new friend's lack of appetite and ate anything Alan could bring back to the plastic table.

'Fancy a game of table tennis?'

Alan thought Jono was joking. He'd fully expected to be locked up after tea with nothing to do other than, hopefully, read a book. Just like at home. He didn't know how to respond in case he was being set up for everyone else to have a laugh at, even though no-one had taken much notice of him so far.

'Come on mate, let's show you the master at work. Follow me.'

Alan was sure a warder would come running after them and throw them both back into their rooms but as he followed his fellow inmate it became apparent there was plenty going on for entertainment and he was free to join in.

The TV room was full of boys watching some motor-racing while others were in the art room, drawing pictures of an old woman who was posing, fully clothed, for what he reckoned was some kind of proper art class. He recognized the gym and saw a couple of the boys sparring in a make-shift boxing ring, supervised by what he assumed would be a prison officer even though he was dressed in shorts and a singlet. He had a whistle and was stopping the fight to give some advice on what they were doing, which Alan thought of as rather bizarre in the circumstances. One of them, at least, was likely to be in there for violence.

This is bonkers, thought Alan as he and Jono headed towards the games room housing a full table tennis table, occupied as they went in by two youngish looking lads who immediately stood still when they saw them.

'Off, suckers,' said Jono and pushed one of the lads heavily away to the point he lost his balance.

'Jono!' boomed a voice across a tannoy a few seconds later. 'We can see you. Let the lads finish their game or you'll be losing your privileges again.'

Alan looked to where the voices came from and saw small cameras and speakers around the room, which he guessed fed back information to a central observation point. It made sense as he couldn't see how the few warders they had could monitor everyone's behaviour. Even the cameras would have a job and they have eyes everywhere.

Jono moved back and let the boys finish their game, which took less than a minute although Alan was sure their score was only four-three when they'd come in.

'Right, we're on,' said Jono and immediately belted the ping-pong ball straight into Alan's stomach.

'Hey, wait a minute,' said Alan. 'I'm not ready.'

He picked up the ball and belted it back, causing Jono to have to reach out to return the serve, which he just managed to do – straight into the line of Alan's bat so he easily scored the first point.

Alan was delighted as he'd only played a few times before but the look on Jono's face told him it would be wise to treat his apparent ability as fluke, and to lose the game in the interests of self-preservation.

After over an hour of suffering repeated losses, sometimes requiring even more skill and dexterity than winning might have done, Alan was pleased to see the arrival of a new officer who said he'd been sent to sort him out with his schedule and to talk to him about procedures while he was in their detention.

Jono skulked off, scuppered in his plans to reign over the new boy, and Alan was led back to his room by Alfie Johnson, a kindly man with a large belly brought on by good food, good humour and a good few beers at his local pub which he frequented as regularly as his homely wife visited bingo or her mother.

'Don't you be thinking you're on our own in this place,' said Mr Johnson, tucking down the bedding for Alan, having unfolded the clean sheets and grey blankets and placing them expertly in position in readiness for his charge's first night.

'I'm assigned to look after you and make sure you get back on the straight and narrow. If you use your noodle you can learn a lot in here and live a decent life when you get out. There's lots here to help you. No need to go back to your old ways,' he added.

He closed the door behind him and as he did the noise of Beldown filled Alan's ears. Inmates protested at being sent to bed, kicked doors and shouted abuse. Already Alan thought it was unfair to speak to the nice Mr Johnson the way they did.

Alan looked around his new living quarters. He'd been told lights would be going out in a few minutes and he fully expected he'd be in the dark, so took the opportunity to observe his surroundings. The room had been recently painted, he could smell it. He went to the window and looked through the bars, set in place to prevent escape or – if on a higher floor – jumping for other reasons.

Picking at the paint on the sill to see if he could peel it off, Alan soon found it was like concrete and couldn't be penetrated or moved. He found something quite reassuring about its permanence as he climbed into his bed wearing just his new underpants and socks.

When the lights were turned off there was a certain type of quiet – apart from the persistence of those inmates who wanted to make sure everyone could hear their voice and opinion. Alan tried to cover his ears but it made no difference.

He willed himself into a trance where he could block out all sound other than that of blood rushing through the veins in his head. It didn't take long before he could control the internal noise and make it so loud it became strong and white, a force in its own right. It was a trick he learned at an early age.

As Alan went to sleep he could smell metal, taste blood and feel the springs of the mattress push gently into his meatless bones.

It felt like home.

CHAPTER NINE

Even though I'd been kept in longer than sentenced, because of the biscuit incident, I was sorry to leave Beldown.

Not least because I was handed straight into the care of Mrs Ludlow, a woman who could do nothing to dilute my instant and unswerving dislike of her.

I don't know if it was the starchy, short hair which reminded me of Denny's long-dead guinea pig or the incessant desire to rabbit on as if she was my best mate which irritated me most. She was so different to my own mother that it was difficult to believe they were from the same species.

The fact she greeted me with 'I'm sure we are going to have such fun getting to know each other' put the hairs up on my neck and they've never really recovered.

Occasionally I tried to play things her way and even had a couple of good games of scrabble although when she banned me from using 'frig' – which is a genuine word – when I had the F on a triple letter score, I was so pissed off I threw the board at her. I caught her looking the word up after I screamed she was an ignorant whore and she never asked me to play again.

I regret running away because I could have saved myself a whole load of grief had I stayed. She was the type of woman who would have put up with anything in pursuit of a good deed, even if it caused her great personal discomfort.

More interested in what the church and the WI thought of her various unpaid occupations than being true to herself, I could have made mincemeat of her. Having been brought up to speak when spoken to and keep her opinions to herself, she dragged this sense of propriety into middle age. I could have punched her and she would apologise. She may well have thought me a good-for-nothing low life of inferior breeding to her own, but she would never say. She wouldn't ever say anything of any interest; just utterances of general good behavior and polite nature. Dull, dull, dull.

Better still I could have pretended she'd had a great, lasting social effect on me and she'd probably have burst with pride and self-congratulation. For that alone I could have baited her but I just didn't have the gall or commitment to manipulate the situation to my needs. To be honest, I've never really been able to lie to any great extent, despite what magistrates, judges and prosecution lawyers might believe.

Of course I've told the lies you need to tell. Like when I met Marie and said she was beautiful. I said it because I wanted to fuck her. She was as fat as a toby jug and had a green line running across the bottom of her teeth which her mother told her was from drinking juice from a baby bottle until she was four. She'd told Marie that as if it was her own fault, and we all believed it.

I was sixteen when we met and had been given a job, through a youth offenders' rehabilitation scheme, working with some roofers. I lived in hostel accommodation with four other boys who'd been through similar criminal proceedings to myself. Mikey was older at nineteen and took it upon himself to tell the rest of us it was important we toed the line, kept our noses clean and worked for a wage.

'Eventually we'll have families and homes of our own and we'll be glad we didn't go back to crime,' he would say with a conviction that was so set it was hard not to trust his judgement.

Regardless of Marie's faults, which increased daily after our hasty marriage – her willingness to believe my lie led to the birth of our first child within ten months of us meeting – she was attractive enough to a young lad who'd been devoid of human touch for so long. I had nothing, or nobody, to compare her with. I'd tried getting lucky a few times, with girls I thought might give out, but my bad teeth, shabby skin and lack of muscle tone put most of them off me at first sight. That and the fact I had no social skills whatsoever so would often come straight out and ask if they fancied a shag, wondering why they were disgusted by what I thought was my ability to cut to the chase.

Marie didn't do preamble either and surprised me when she agreed to sleep with me, just because I asked. In hindsight I don't think it occurred to her to say no but at the time it was the greatest thrill of my short life.

Believing that pregnancy automatically led to marriage, we got hitched at a south London register office. She wore a dress from Sussex Street market that cost half her week's wages as a trainee hairdresser. It wasn't a maternity dress and although she was only three months gone, the front rode up above her knees and slanted out from her belly, rounded more by the recent introduction of McDonald's to Croydon than our foetal child.

It was around then I met up with King again. He'd been inside a lot longer than I had and was released three or four weeks after Shannon was born. She was a sickly baby and living with her crying, coupled with Marie's television addiction was driving me crazy. We were living with the mother-in-law and her constant criticism in her spare room, for which she charged most of what I earned in a week as well as a portion of the child allowance. I wanted a place of my own, some pride in myself and a job I enjoyed.

Roofing was OK, I suppose, and I was glad of the work if only for the fact it got me out of the house. I couldn't be like other blokes on the estate who sat around in tracksuit bottoms and vests all day, drinking their way through their benefits until they got bitter, emotional and frustrated.

But we were exploited because of our criminal records. They could treat us like dirt, pay us like monkeys and make us work long and dangerous hours because our employers knew we had no other choice. One lad broke his back after being sent up a ladder with a pile of bricks and no harness or supervision. He'll never walk again but the bosses said he was negligent and no-one cared to challenge that claim, although health and safety was tightened a little after a local newspaper reported the accident – to a vague sense of disapproval from the immediate community.

It was winter and I was on top of a scaffolding rig outside a large industrial unit near Thornton Heath. It was so cold my childhood chilblains had returned and I couldn't feel my feet even though I was wearing industrial boots and thick socks, bought from Millets as a Christmas present from Marie. I'd saved up for an eternity ring for her, as she'd been banging on about one since the birth of Shannon, but it didn't fit her sausage-like fingers. I'd gone without lunch and beer for weeks to afford the payments. It was only a ten minute walk to the shop to get it exchanged but in three months she hadn't bothered. I'd a sneaky suspicion she'd lost it.

I heard hooting, which wasn't unusual for the area, but it invaded my conscience with its persistence. I was about to shout an obscenity at the perpetrator when I saw a familiar face leering up at me from the window of a black BMW car. Dance music was booming from the stereo, much to the consternation of passers-by who gave King their best disapproving looks before marching quickly past the vehicle, which he'd half parked behind the skip we'd been using for old tiles. Other drivers hooted to suggest he might like to straighten up his bonnet so it wasn't jutting into their pathway, but they were mostly met with two fingers.

'Oi, there you old faggot!' shouted King. 'Get down here and see your favourite bruv!'

Our relationship had been difficult to begin with. He was three years older and just for that tried to control me in Beldown - but I had the support of Jono who, despite his strange way of showing it, took a liking to me. He became my protector against any aggression from King who, in the end, showed an enviable ability to get people on his side.

What King lacked in stature he made up for with poise and personality. If he spotted weakness he'd be on you like a shot but anyone standing up to him presented a challenge. At first any of my own bravado was down to the fact I had my back covered but after a while King and I managed our battles with words.

He wasn't stupid and, like me, had read many books which gave us a shared, possibly imagined, superiority over our contemporaries, who we dismissed as ignorant oafs.

While I fell into fiction to escape reality, King was more interested in psychology and the power of persuasion. He read about great influencers and often hypothetically modelled himself on world leaders. His intelligence was such that he knew that the ability to lead and gain respect was of considerable value to anyone wanting any kind of power or control, of any situation. He knew then, even if the rest of us didn't, that becoming a leader meant having the resources to get other people to do your dirty work.

Despite my admiration for his desire to better his position through influence, I was always a little scared of King. He was prone to outbursts of extreme violence, undoubtedly brought on by frustration but also in response to any situation where he couldn't get to go his own way.

No-one ever asks what anyone is inside for but I'd heard his latest offence was for biting the nipple off a girlfriend who'd turned down sex. By all accounts he said he would never rape a woman but he had to 'teach her a lesson'. His defence, that she'd wanted it 'rough', was blown away by the fact he'd had the nipple preserved in resin and made into a necklace.

I thought it might have been a prison myth – there were plenty of them – but always suspected it was most likely to be true.

The hooting continued so I asked my boss if I could take a break, even though a proper lunchtime was usually denied us, and was granted ten minutes which I used to clamber down to street level and say 'hello' to King. It wouldn't do to ignore him and in some ways it was good to see him.

'What shite is this, man?' he said, clearly not having dropped the black accent since his release. 'You need to get yerself some better gig, not going up these ladders to do hard labour!'

King was dressed in expensive clothes including a good leather jacket. He balanced sunglasses on top of his head and I noticed his car was newer than I first thought. I wondered how he'd ended up looking like he'd done something right while I looked like I'd done everything wrong.

'Hey, King. What are you doing?' I asked, knowing it was best to be friendly and approachable. He didn't respond well to anyone who wasn't.

'Get in, man, hear the sounds,' said King, gesturing to me to climb inside his BMW. It smelled sweet and sickly and the music pounded so loudly the seats made my arse reverberate.

'Great car,' I said. 'How come you got this?'

King winked, locked the doors and drove off as I protested I only had ten minutes break. He said I wasn't going back there as he had other ideas for me. As much as I tried to tell him I needed the job to pay for nappies, milk and a never ending supply of trashy magazines and fast food, he took no notice – laughing as he sped faster and faster through the congested roads of south London and into Brixton.

'You ain't never going to have to work like a dog again, dude,' he said and his demeanour was so convincing I was pulled along with the belief my life was about to take a turn for the better.

It's funny looking back to that day. Had I stayed on the roof a little longer King wouldn't have taken me on the ride into the rest of my life, because one thing he was known for was his impatience. I might not have been given the ten minutes break to go and see him, or might not have heard him hooting. Loads of things conspired to put me in that place at that time, which then led to a chain of circumstances culminating in one life-changing event.

I often wonder what my life would have been like had I ignored him and just carried on carrying on, bringing home my miserly wage and putting up with my lot.

I might not have murdered Julie Gill.

CHAPTER TEN

'The delivery is to Teacake Tony in Smitham Lane,' said Eddie, placing a bag about the size of a packet of fish-fingers in Alan's hand.

Since working for King and The Team, as his former inmate liked to call his 'business', Alan had been set up with a small scooter and the promise of regular wages – twice what he was earning as a roofer and more than enough to keep the wife happy and the kid in dummies - the only thing that would stop the little mite crying. Alan's only instruction was that he asked no questions and told nobody anything, not even lies.

Marie was bored with parenting and Alan had become bored with the constant jibes from her and the rest of her family. A matriarchal environment, Alan was referred to as 'the thing with the dick' or 'the useless pratt' and rarely given any words of appreciation, tenderness or kindness. Just the odd civil exchange would have been enough, particularly since the comfort of regular human contact, albeit in the form of rushed and unsatisfactory sex, had started to wane. He couldn't even take pleasure in reading.

'What the fuck you doing with that book under yer nose. If you've got time on your hands, deal with Shannon,' Marie had said when he'd taken up Catch 22 to read one Sunday afternoon.

'What do you mean, deal with her?' Alan had asked. The child had been asleep and Marie and her mother were watching some game show, both wittering away about the contestants' choice of clothing while they ate their way through two packets of ginger creams and a Crunchie each. Marie would occasionally prod a finger into her mouth to dislodge the bits that got stuck in the gaps between her teeth. That was something the two of them once thought they had in common before separately concluding that dental loss was not the glue to hold a marriage together.

When King told Alan he could change his life for him, he would have liked the chance to think long and hard, but he didn't get time to breathe let alone weigh up any pros and cons.

Not only that, going straight was tough, not because he didn't want to work for a fair day's wage, but getting a reasonably paid job, where the shackles of his criminal record weren't taken into consideration, was nigh on impossible.

He'd gone to the job centre, as his probation officer had told him. He'd been for interviews and taken exams which he passed easily. He even bought a suit that almost fitted. So when he went for a job in a bank, he thought he looked the part. Even Marie had said he looked like a 'posh twat' which was praise indeed from her.

'I would love to work for a bank,' he told the interviewer who reclined back in her seat while looking at the young man as she might judge a tramp who'd asked for a seat at the Royal Opera House.

'Why on earth would you want to do that?' she'd asked, picking something out from underneath her nails. 'Surely we'd be far too boring for the kind of life you've been leading?'

She smiled unconvincingly and threw the application form onto a pile on the table in front of her. She was conducting the interviews in the open plan area of the bank's reception and Alan's face reddened as people looked around to see where the woman's loud voice was coming from.

Alan wanted to tell her that being in a place that was an accepted part of everyday life was all he wanted. That he thought he was bright enough to work with money and that he would like to meet different types of people. That it would offer a chance to be part of normality.

'I think it would be interesting,' was all he could manage to say and although he barely whispered, he really meant it. Three weeks later he got a letter to say the bank didn't consider Alan to be a suitable candidate for them and wished him luck finding employment.

'Bastards,' he said to Marie. 'Didn't give me a chance. Stuck up bitch looking down on me.'

'Get over yourself Al. What do you wanna work in a bank for anyway? Bloody tossers in suits telling people they can't have an overdraft. Bet they love saying that to people they know is on their uppers. All power crazy cos the rest of their life sucks.'

Alan conceded Marie might have had a point. Maybe banks weren't for him. Not in the traditional sense anyway. He went back to his roofing job and spent most of the day thinking about what he could do to break the pattern so he could do something worthwhile with his life.

The journey through south London on that first fateful day of his employment with The Team was one of the most exciting things Alan had ever done. He was scared but intrigued, particularly after the repeated rejection he'd received for every job application.

'So, what do you do, then?' he asked King when they got to a flat above a kebab shop, ironically in good view of the local police station opposite.

King sucked his teeth and gave the question some time to filter before answering.

'Let's call it investment,' he'd said. 'You don't need to know any more than that. Cup of tea?'

He gestured to Alan to sit on the brown leather settee, which was new enough to still smell of leather. His mother-in-law's second hand mock-hide couch – he thought the fashionable name for it was 'pleather' - smelled of hair that needs washing and stale sheets. In fact the whole house did, when it didn't stink of nappies, fags or chips.

A small woman appeared in the kitchen door. She looked to be in her forties and well-dressed until you saw her feet, which were clad in novelty slippers in the design of two crocodiles. Alan wondered if they ever tripped her up.

'Did I hear you say tea, Julian?' she asked. 'And who is your friend, I don't think we've been introduced.'

'This is Goose,' said King. 'As in Mother Goose. This, Mum, is Alan. A friend from my school days.'

Goose raised her eyebrows at him, complicit in the knowledge that the two had met while in Beldown. The only length of time King had ever spent in one place long enough to make a friend would be in detention of some kind, not education.

'Hello, pleased to meet you,' said Alan and she nodded in reply.

'So why you all posh then, bollock brains?' King said. 'You been going to those electrocution lessons or summat?'

Alan looked puzzled and then worked out he probably meant elocution lessons.

'No, mate. Just trying to be polite.'

Goose came over and smacked King gently round the head.

'Don't you be so rude to your guest. It's a fine thing he takes care to mind his Ps and Qs,' she said in a clipped and controlled voice meant to have anyone believe she came from a good background. She wore bright pink lipstick that bled outside her natural, oval, lips, giving her the look of a blow-up doll.

The doorbell went but before anyone could answer, two men let themselves in – both wearing smart suits and highly polished shoes.

'Bro!' said King, getting up to greet them and throwing his arms round the taller of the two, in what could have been a bear hug had he been able to reach. The man in question was at least six feet three and nearly as wide.

'Meet the new man on The Team,' he said to them. 'Doc, Tommy: Alan is going to be our events manager,' he added laughing loudly but mainly to himself as no-one else joined in. 'Alan, meet my personal assistants, Doc and Tommy'

'Um, I didn't know I was going to be your new man,' Alan said nervously, noticing that Doc had the most incredibly piercing and immediately noticeable pale blue eyes, striking against his olive-coloured skin.

King had talked about him working with The Team all the way to the flat but he hadn't agreed to take him up on the offer. If anything he'd spoken about how he'd like to get onto an evening class, get some qualifications and then get a 'proper' job. King smirked and

Alan just thought he was jealous of his ambition to do well, regardless of the odds.

'You don't get no choice, bruv. Not if you know what is good for you. Isn't that right boys?'

King looked over and the 'suits' nodded before sitting down on chairs either side of the settee.

By the time Alan left the flat he was told he was a paid up member of The Team. Initial hesitation was met with a roll of ten pound notes and an invitation to report for work at 12 noon the following Monday. It was the sort of invitation Alan knew would be difficult, if not unwise, to decline.

'So I'll be working with some friends who have started a business since coming out,' Alan told Marie. 'I will be doing some kind of deliveries and organising stuff.'

'What's the money like?' she asked and Alan said it was a little more than the roofing job. He didn't want to suggest there'd be plenty of cash about as she'd want it.

'Look, they've given me an advance,' he said, thrusting three of the ten pounds notes into her hand. 'Go and buy you and Shannon something nice.'

'And what do you think will be nice with thirty quid? By the time I've got the basics there'll be nothing left,' Marie said as she pulled herself tight up to the sofa and searched for the remote control, which had dropped to the floor.

Alan pulled out another twenty pounds and handed it over, telling his wife there was nothing left for him although the truth was he'd not even given her half. He was only grateful the mother-in-law wasn't there otherwise she'd be going through his pockets.

Marie couldn't help but smile. She'd had her eye on a jumper down Sussex Market but had spent what was left of the week's child allowance on a bottle of supermarket vodka, twenty Benson and Hedges and a family bag of cheese and onion crisps.

Alan liked the feeling of freedom and power having some money gave him, so after the inevitable argument about who was going to sort Shannon's bedtime, he went to the pub on the pretext of having to meet King to discuss the finer details of his employment contract.

Something very close to satisfaction stirred deep within him as he walked out of the door leaving his wife clearly considering what to do with the fifty quid he'd just been able to give her.

For once in his life he felt like a man.

CHAPTER ELEVEN

G etting married is a strange thing to do when you think about it. It isn't even restricted to the banality of the Christian church – people do it everywhere.

Historically it was just a way of gaining land and power. Marry one posh family into another and they could take over the world. On a social level it makes sense if you stick to the rules and stay together to give kids a stable background. Give them emotional and financial support until they can stand on their own two feet. I don't suppose many people think like that these days and I know Marie and I didn't. We just got hitched because we didn't know what else to do. It was like that *Third World* song; '*Now That We've Found Love What Are We Going To Do With It?*'.

We'd done the going out, shagging and getting used to each other farting. We'd stopped pretending to be interested in each other's lives and spent much of our time arguing about what to watch on telly, what pub to go to and whose friends we should spend time with. The last bit was easy because I didn't have any friends. Those I made inside were shunned by Marie's family as 'no good' even though all of her relatives, bar none, were on benefits because they couldn't be arsed to get a job.

'Why should they when they don't have to?' Marie's mother

would say should I suggest that working for minimum wage was better than no wage at all. At least they would be doing something with their day rather than thinking up ways of convincing the dole officers that they had bad backs or psychological disorders that made them prone to having to stay in bed all day and drinking all night.

I should have left at that point, despite the kid on the way. Plenty of blokes do just bugger off when it gets complicated. It's nature, isn't it? Impregnate the female and look for another to do just the same with. Women don't always get it, but it's in our genes. To be able to control that takes some adjustment and understanding of social responsibility. In my case the whole situation was self-regulating because even if I did want to go out and procreate with various women at the same time, the chance of finding enough of them to agree would be beyond a miracle.

Marie wasn't the love of my life but she was there. She wasn't so much Mrs Right as the 'Mrs Right Now' - and she set me a challenge. You know when you're at that moment, the one where there is no turning back if full release is to be found, and then she asks if you love her. You have to say "yes" don't you?

But it was a trap. She said the next morning if I really loved her I'd marry her. She'd always wanted to get married and didn't seem to mind who to.

Not keen to be seen as a predictable male I got my own back. Eight days later we were married in Croydon register office. Then we had an "eat all you can for five pounds" reception at the *Khyber Pass*. That showed the silly bitch.

We had two kids in the end. Funny little creatures; parasitic, noisy and bloody expensive but you just keep on loving them. Every time I looked at them I thought of my own parents. Does my own father think of me ever? If he does would he know, or care, that my life has gone the way it has? Worse still, in my opinion anyway, would he think he might have been able to do something that would have produced a more positive outcome for his son?

I can almost forgive him because maybe he didn't know. He may have walked off into the distance thinking my mother was nothing more than a one night stand, a shag with no consequences. She never talked about him and never told me his name. I could walk past him in the street and not know his loins spawned my very being. It makes me feel a bit lop-sided, to be honest. I know everything I want to know about my mother, more's the pity.

It's more difficult to forgive her. Once I saw my own kids I just wanted to look after them and protect them, whatever it took. How can you not want to give them everything you can lay your hands on? How my mother could sit back and watch my life pan out the way it did without doing something confuses me. That isn't love. That's laziness, neglect and a terrible waste.

Although there is no doubting that being a parent is the most difficult job in the world and nobody gets it right. You can only do the best you can with the resources and opportunities you have at the time. People have called me a thief or a murderer but surely you'd steal or kill to save the life of your own flesh and blood? Tell me you wouldn't and I'll tell you you're a liar, or a selfish bastard.

Even with my new job with King, the wife and kids absorbed every bit of anything I could give to them. I didn't mind, it made me feel useful. Every time I went home I was reminded of fledgling sparrows with their beaks permanently stretched open -anticipating the next tasty morsel, all provided by an exhausted and demoralised father.

Every Spring after I first became a father I thought of those poor daddy birds, no time to look at their offspring and admire their beauty. They'd be in and out of that nest, finding whatever food they could for their constantly open and demanding beaks. In the case of the cuckoo, the poor old chap would be finding grub for a massive great addition to the family that was nothing to do with him.

I feel for Daddy bird. He never gets a moment to sit down and eat his own hearty meal of worms. When does he get a chance to take the world in?

You can do that here. You can take the world in. The world is, after all, only our interpretation of our individual experiences. It is just what we see through our own eyes, information that we evaluate and filter. Set the right parameters and you can have a wild time – free to roam the inner reaches of your own imagination. You can lie around and contemplate your navel, or anyone else's. No-one will ask if you have done the washing up, or what you want to be when you grow up. I still don't know the answer to that.

It's possible to get on OK here. You do have to be careful of the beds though. They offer a threat that goes way beyond the power of a man-made weapon. Billy no-balls sat on the top bunk without any pants. His giblets dropped below the springs. All fine until he decided to jump off in a hurry. He got to the floor, but his testicles didn't. The picture of them, like ripened figs bursting in the sunshine, still brings a tear to my eye.

It's amazing he survived. At first there was an investigation but Billy told them what happened once he'd been brought round and had regained some degree of comfort. The questioning didn't last very long because the interviewing police officer couldn't stop giggling at Billy's new voice. He's a male soprano in his local community choir now and living with a woman who has enough balls for the two of them.

Just follow a few rules and you can do well in this place, considering. I've been in worse hotels and it beats working in a job you hate day in day out. One of the reasons I took up the work with King, apart from the fact I had no real choice, was because it meant I could stay away all night and be asleep all day. I'd like to say it kept me out of trouble but clearly it didn't.

The first real job I did for The Team involved a retail store. When the plan was unveiled to me it seemed like an adventure, not a crime. It was all part of getting me more involved with their 'business' and for once I was given information they wouldn't normally pass on to someone like me.

We didn't use real weapons and I couldn't see anything wrong with taking away some of the profits of a burger house that had bled the masses dry by feeding them nothing short of cow's knees and sugar.

It's not like we hurt anyone. OK they were a bit frightened because they thought the gun was real, but it wasn't.

It scared them all enough and so the outcome for us was success, mainly judged by the financial spoils. I got over three thousand pounds for that day's work and bought myself the best pair of shoes I could find -real leather brogues with proper stitching and both the same colour. I felt as high as a kite for months after that.

The whole event bred a confidence I'd not known before - but also a laxity in terms of looking after my own welfare.

More jobs followed, mostly the same scenario. There was always a discussion about moving up the criminal ladder and pulling off the big heist.

And of course there was always talk about buying some guns.

They say love conquers all. But a fully loaded Smith and Wesson can be fairly persuasive.

CHAPTER TWELVE

Alan retched at the sight of the blood. The Team had been sent to teach Jimmy Cartwright some lessons about grassing up King to the police and it hadn't been very pretty.

'We've come to see Jimmy,' said Doc, known for his pleasure in using his boots to square up grievances. They were standing outside the front of a small terraced house in a run-down area of one of the many 1960s council estates of South London.

'He ain't here,' replied the short, puffy-faced blonde woman as she tried to push the door closed on Doc's foot.

'Well, we think he is, don't we Al?' said Doc as he pushed her back into her hallway and into the bannister, only a few feet into the house.

At that point Alan's stomach lurched as he knew Doc didn't like being given the run-around. He'd already seen how he'd behaved when Ken the Kebab gave him too much chilli sauce on his doner and chips.

'What's going on Vee?' said a voice from the kitchen, giving Doc clear directions for the whereabouts of his victim. As Jimmy came to the door, holding a sandwich, his face dropped and he went to run – losing his lunch as he tried to get away through the back.

'So, what do we have here then Mr Cartwright?' Doc grabbed

him, pulling him sharply back. 'I think you might be ready to come with us for a little ride, don't you?' he said.

Jimmy looked at his sandwich, as Doc ground it into the floor with his massive black, steel-capped boots, and then to his wife who'd followed the men into the kitchen.

'Leave us alone you thugs,' said Vee, tucking back some stray strands of straw-like hair into the elastic band that held a ponytail so tightly her face looked like it had been in a wind tunnel.

'Mrs Cartwright. We've some business with your husband that doesn't concern you and would be most grateful if you could find something else to do, out of my sight. Alan, make sure she understands will you?'

Alan took his cue to escort Vee into her own front room, being careful not to hurt her. He didn't mind being involved in the 'education' of those men who'd been paid by King and then betrayed him – they deserved it – but he didn't see the need for innocent people to pay for their partner's cock-ups.

'Just sit yourself down and don't you go worrying about anything,' Alan said to her as he gently eased her down into the sofa. Finding the remote control he turned up the television volume to drown out the sounds of shouting coming from the kitchen.

'So, how long have you lived here?' he asked Vee nervously, checking his watch and looking to the mantel piece which was covered in photos – mainly of children but also of Jimmy and Vee at what looked like their wedding. The colours were faded and Alan guessed it was some time ago.

'None of your fucking business,' said Vee as she turned the

volume down and went to listen at the door. Alan jumped up and immediately stood in her way.

'Just let them sort out their business,' said Alan. 'It won't take long,' he added, looking again at his watch and then around the room which, on close inspection, showed the signs of the good life. An expensive stereo, leather furniture, collectible ornaments and what looked like an original Rolex watch lying on the coffee table. Alan pointed at the pictures of the children.

'How many do you have? How old are they?'

As he finished his question there was a loud crash and the sound of breaking glass. Jimmy could be heard shouting that he hadn't done anything wrong and didn't know why King had it in for him.

Alan kept on talking to Vee, listening to her tell him that Jimmy just wanted to go straight and have a normal life.

'He's fed up with jumping every time the phone or door goes and wondering what he's going to be asked to do next. He just wants out. Why won't they leave him be?'

Alan nodded and said little. He didn't want to commit to any opinions on the matter. He also didn't want to frighten her with what he knew about King: that he doesn't let anyone be. Once you're in The Team, there's no going back. The only way you leave, without running away, is in a box.

'Come on, Al, we've got a job to do,' said Doc, kicking open the lounge door and indicating to Alan they were on their way out. He had Jimmy in an arm lock and was frog-marching him forward, threatening to break his arms if he didn't do as he was told.

Vee screamed. 'Let him go, he ain't done nuffin. He just wants a quiet life away from you bunch of bastards.'

Doc tightened his grip on Jimmy who winced and told Alan to hurry up.

'Let's get this job done then we can go home,' he said, growling under his breath with the effort of carrying a fully grown man through a hallway littered with kids toys, clothes and a large radiator.

'Don't go worrying, now' said Alan to Vee. 'He'll be back in no time. Just got a few things to sort out and then he'll be home, you see.'

'Cut the fucking phone and stop whimpering to the silly bitch. She's been happy enough to live off The Team for years so deserves to worry,' said Doc, kicking back the front door and nodding his head to where the telephone box was sited.

'Don't want her doing anything silly, now, do we?'

Alan went to the box and cut the wires, testing the line to make sure Vee couldn't make any calls in a hurry – certainly in the time it took to get Jimmy into the car. He blocked her exit from the house until Doc hooted, indicating it was time to go.

'Nice to meet you, Vee' said Alan as he ran down the path with his coat hood up, taking care not to be identified by the neighbours who weren't hiding the fact they were intrigued by the commotion.

'Get in the back and deal with the idiot,' said Doc who had already tied Jimmy up with strong rope to stop him trying to escape.

Alan gave a nervous smile which was met with a mouthful of spit in his direction.

'Who's this fucking monkey? Being all nice and polite and then fucking smiling while he watches me being kidnapped by thugs. Arse-wipe psychopath. Get your kicks like this do you?'

No. I get a living, thought Alan.

They arrived at the hall of the Two Hundred Club. King had a room which he used to deal with his 'staff' – knowing that any blood stains could be melded into those often created on a Saturday night between opposing gangs.

The room was at the back of the old 1950s dance hall, frequented regularly by mods, rockers, bikers, dancers, lovers – anyone who wanted a good night out at the weekends, where the bar was open late and drugs were readily available. King was a 'director' which meant he was paid for ensuring there was never any trouble. Or more like he was paid so that he wouldn't cause the trouble himself. He offered to 'keep an eye' on the premises during the day, which meant he could use it as a kind of office and court room.

Alan was often asked to deliver parcels to the back entrance and the bar manager would offer him coffee and maybe discuss something meaningful like the effects of the pill on women's emancipation, or the rise in immigration and how it might affect relationships in the future.

'Will our kids and their kids be marrying blacks and so we all end up chocolate colour? Can't say I'd mind, like, as it is so much prettier than pale and pasty,' he said on one occasion. Alan wasn't sure if the reference was personal.

On another he wanted to discuss how south London was controlled by the gangs in cahoots with the police, but Alan knew better than to discuss this in any detail. He thought the manager might have been fishing for information but even if Alan had known what was going on, he'd promised faithfully to tell nothing to anyone.

A bag was always passed back to Alan for him to take back on his motorbike to King's flat. Sometimes King, sometimes Goose, would gratefully reach inside and give Alan his 'wages' and thank him for his good work. Often they were in excess of two or three hundred pounds, for what amounted to less than a day's work. What was more important to Alan was being appreciated, although the money was nice too.

As a result Alan had a better life than he could anywhere else, particularly with his record and lack of formal education. He could take the family on holidays abroad. They went to Benidorm twice and even managed to buy a second hand caravan which they parked in Southend.

Sometimes Alan had to go away on King's business. If he did he was always booked into the best hotels – all in the name of someone called Simon Devlin. King had even provided ID in that name for him, in case he was asked for it - although he never was.

If Alan expressed concern about leaving his family for any length of time, he was assured by King that one of The Team would look after them. That's what The Team did – looked after the family of their 'absents' which was also a euphemism for those who'd been caught doing King's work and ended up jailed. As long as they'd kept their mouths shut, their family would be provided for. Men would turn up with money and, if required, some male company for the otherwise lonely wives. This was all above board and not meant for any purpose other than to offer stern words for anyone interfering with the smooth flow of family life.

Alan enjoyed the privacy of going away on these deliveries more than the luxury. He'd have a bath, using the hotel shampoo and shower gel. Sometimes he'd read for hours or maybe watch some TV and ask for room service. He rarely ate in the dining rooms despite having carte blanche to order anything he liked, even wine. Alan was a beer man and could have ordered a pint but didn't like to take advantage. He also felt uncomfortable eating and drinking in places where people he considered to be far above his social standing would be next to him. Worse still, was the questions they would inevitably ask about what he was doing there, what he did for a living, and what was the scar on the side of his face. Only a few people asked the last question but the fear of having to think of anything to say in response to any of them was enough to keep him living in a blessed kind of solitary confinement.

'I don't do much,' he told Marie when she asked what he got up to, in one of the rare occasions she showed any interest in Alan's life. It was a few weeks after she'd announced she was pregnant with their second child. He was surprised because they hardly went near each other these days, but vaguely remembered a midnight coupling where she took control and ended up on top for a very short and unfeeling few minutes of frantic pumping. It had left him feeling used and somewhat puzzled even though the physical need had been met.

'I just get the job done and come home,' Alan answered.

'So you don't meet any women or anything, then?' Marie asked.

'Why would I want to do that, when I'm married to you?' he replied, genuinely shocked by the suggestion.

'Well, some men would use the opportunity for a bit of something on the side,' she said.

'Not me,' said Alan. 'I'm faithful to the core. You should know that by now. And we've another babe on the way so I've responsibilities. I just get on with my work.'

She sniffed and looked away: 'Cuppa?'

Alan noted it was the first time she'd offered to make him a cup of tea since they first met.

'Yeah, why not,' he replied, settling down into the sofa and thinking that maybe life hadn't turned out too bad.

CHAPTER THIRTEEN

I can remember that first taste of violence. We'd been to Jimmy's house and took him back to the room at the Two Hundred Club – named because it could hold two hundred people – and he was placed in front of King for his 'court martial' from The Team.

He'd been sick in the car, claiming he couldn't travel well in the back although I suspect he was shit scared. Everyone knew Doc's reputation and it didn't bode well if you were told you were on a 'ride' with him to see King.

When we got there King was counting out a pile of money behind a big table pushed at right angles to a closed bar. The shutters were loose and wind from an open window juddered them into life, creating a disturbing metallic chiming that echoed through the entire dance area. A slot machine stood to one side, its front door flapping open and a metal box thrown to one side.

Jimmy's legs had been untied but his arms remained behind his back, while Doc pushed him along the room in the direction of the makeshift desk.

King, dressed in a smart suit and a neatly ironed white shirt with a thin blue tie, carried on counting. After a few minutes he folded the paper money and placed it in a metal filing case before locking it with a padlock attached to a key ring. He pushed a number of piles of coins to one side.

'Think we'll leave those to later,' he'd said as he stood up and held his right hand out to Jimmy.

'Oh, of course. You can't shake my hand can you?' he said through a forced smile.

King punched Jimmy hard in the stomach while Doc caught him from the rebound, pulling his hair as he did so.

'Is that because your hands are tied or because your handshake means nothing?'

King hit him again, only this time to the side. I suspect he got him somewhere that impacted the bladder because he cried out and then wet himself.

I wanted to look away for the next bit but knew that if I did King would think less of me. It never paid to look like a wimp or that you didn't approve of his methods. I thought he went over the top sometimes but the rules of The Team are clear. Anyone who doesn't abide by them knows what happens.

King took out a long hunting knife from inside his suit jacket. He held it to Jimmy's face while Doc pushed him against the blade, catching his skin enough to produce droplets of blood each peeking out from the face as if ready to run but too scared to make an entrance. One by one they oozed into a line of perfectly formed circles, eventually falling slowly either to the floor or onto his shirt.

Jimmy tried to scream and every time he did, Doc would put a cloth in his mouth.

'Make that noise again, dickhead, and you'll be taped' said King who delivered a slice about four inches long with the knife

- sufficiently high on the neck line to ensure pain but to avoid immediate death.

When Jimmy cried out at the pain, he was shoved into a chair in the middle of the dance floor where he was tied by his hands and his ankles before gaffer tape was swirled around his head, capturing the cloth and imprisoning it into Jimmy's mouth making him gag.

His eyes bulged as he tried to gulp for air but King sat back down and shouted orders back to Doc to 'teach him a lesson' which didn't appear to involve any words, just acts of physical violence including setting fire to his groin with petrol and smashing his thumbs with a hammer.

Just as I – and presumably Jimmy – had thought they'd finished, King would think of some other crime that had been committed and asked Doc to think up a new punishment.

After two hours Jimmy was barely conscious and he was surrounded by blood. The air smelled of shit which I could only assume came from him as he whimpered and gasped until eventually the tape was removed.

I hadn't eaten that day or the one previously, but still wanted to retch up the contents of my stomach. Instead I stared at a wasp trying to make its way through a net curtain to the outer world, and identified with its frustration. It could see where it wanted to go, but was prevented by an almost invisible barrier.

I needed to witness everything as if it were normal, not reacting or responding. The occasional growl I offered up kept King's belief I was on his side and I showed no relief at being asked to fetch lunch and cups of coffee while the 'judges' considered their next move.

This gave me a chance to breathe and also to wonder whether to run – run away from all this madness and dark control.

It was hard not to cry out for the man's release. He'd been stupid but I didn't think he deserved to be put through so much pain when what he'd told police had led to nothing. He'd given the weakest information to get himself off a minor charge and in the end the police couldn't be bothered with such small fry. Not only that, King's contacts had been sufficient to get rid of any investigation very quickly and the leader of The Team was free to continue, unabated, without any tarnish to his local reputation.

But King didn't like to feel he was losing any control and needed to make an example of Jimmy. You don't join The Team, take the spoils and then expect to leave whenever you've had enough. It's like joining the Masons. Once you're in, you're in for life.

'You've taken something of a liberty, James my old boy,' King had said to him in the middle of the punishment. 'Now it would be no good if word got round that I let you get away with it, would it?'

That's certainly how I saw it. It would never pay to let King down. He was good to those on this side and The Team offered me far more than anyone else in society did. We were like family only better. You knew the rules. Play fair, be fair, don't cheat and all will be well. King was good to those who were on his side. He had an incredible sense of loyalty and expected it from those he worked with. As long as you played by his rules, he'd be there for you. It was easier than marriage and far more rewarding.

It was still all quite bizarre how King, Doc and I ate our sandwiches while Jimmy's almost lifeless body hung from the chair, still bound from the rope. Blood had dried around his neck and the bruising on his side could be seen where his shirt gaped open. I was surprised he was still alive after the beating he'd got.

'Go and clean him up, Al. Then get yourselves both home,' King had told me after he'd finished his lunch. He'd wiped his hands against each other to remove the crumbs and started to count the coins in front of him, seemingly oblivious to the pain and fear around him.

At the time I wondered why he let Jimmy go home as he usually 'got rid' but of course it was to be sure that word got round. Jimmy was a bigmouth and would whine to anyone that he'd been beaten by The Team. It would serve as a perfect warning to anyone else who thought they could get away with being cheeky to King.

I was never really sure what he meant when he told me he was getting rid of somebody. Did it mean taking them home and making sure they had nothing more to do with The Team or was the rumour about the funeral director and the farmer true?

I'd been told that body parts had been added to a few coffins over the years as a way of disposing of people who hadn't learned from the lessons imparted by King.

Initially whole bodies had been thrown in on top of loved ones cadavers until one family complained that their father was only nine stone eight pounds all his life yet the six male children, two of which were champion weightlifters, couldn't manage to carry their loved one up the aisle of the crematorium without their knees buckling.

It was all the funeral director could do to stop them opening up the coffin there and then and it was only a story about weighting the body to stop it exploding once in the furnace that placating them sufficiently to allow the ceremony to continue. After that the risk to all involved was too much so the funeral director was released from most of his services.

After that, I was informed, King engaged the services of a farming butcher who would dismember victims and then put all the pieces into different coffins – feeding leftovers and offal to his pigs while simultaneously advertising his pork joints as the best organically-reared meat in the south. I would imagine the Food Standards Authority would struggle to argue with that statement on the basis there are unlikely to be any appropriate guidelines. And we all know that without written guidelines government officials are entirely devoid of decision-making capabilities.

CHAPTER FOURTEEN

'You done good,' said King as they sat around the Burnham Bar in broad daylight, avoiding the sticky beer patches of the table from the previous night's entertainment.

The dust motes drifted aimlessly through the shards of light that forced their way through the basement window bars, seeking out the smoke-filled romance of midnight trysts and expectation.

Alan sat at one end of the table with a roll of twenty pound notes in front of him – reward for mopping up Jimmy Cartwright's broken body and getting him back to Streatham High Street, where he was left to limp his own way home without a penny to his name or any treatment for his injuries.

Alan had stayed with him for the day, buying him some lunch – even though he could barely eat it – and a number of pints of beer to stall the pain.

At the end of the evening he gave him some of the cash he had left in his pocket and wished him well, turning as quickly away from him as he could before sympathy set in.

'I won't forget this,' said Jimmy as he grimaced his way in the direction of the cab firm littered with drunks, prostitutes and late-night workers all wishing their driver would turn up sooner rather than later.

'I hope you do,' answered Alan and headed off back to his home where the lights were on, but nobody was in. He didn't have the energy to question the whereabouts of his family and went straight to bed, only to be woken at 3am by his drunken mother-in-law. By what he could make out from her slurring, Marie had given birth while he'd been looking after Jimmy. It was a boy.

'We've called him Shane,' she told him, exhaling the stale fumes of wine, fags and some kind of fish.

He couldn't remember anyone asking him what he thought about names.

Turning in his sleep his dreams involved theft, false identity and small children floating away on a stream running faster than he could. However hard he tried he could never catch up.

When he went to collect his wife from hospital, Alan wanted to tell the world he'd fathered a son. He walked past an elderly couple sitting on a bench outside the drop-off area. They were sharing a cigarette despite the woman being attached to some unhealthy looking tubes.

He couldn't work out why he didn't tell them he had a new baby boy. He wanted to, but the words caught in his mouth.

Alan found Marie, picked up the new bundle and cradled it while she had a cigarette before getting into the cab he'd booked. He noticed the paleness of the child's blue eyes.

There was no sense of familiarity, just an overwhelming feeling of responsibility. His world closed tighter and all he could think of was how he'd started that size and only got to where he was through a peculiar kind of luck.

Once home it wasn't long before he was called to see his boss.

Doc came round with the message, flowers and chocolates for Marie and a huge blue teddy bear with a blue scarf and hat. He asked numerous questions about Shane; how much he weighed at birth, whether it all went well and if he was proclaimed fit and healthy. He cast a watery-eyed smile at Marie before summoning Alan to his meeting.

As they drove to King's flat Doc spoke about the new baby and how proud Alan must be.

'Yeah,' said Alan feeling that something must be missing from his paternal genes. He'd never felt ready to be a father and now he'd two kids to bring into the world. 'It's good.'

He felt differently about Shannon. After her birth he thought he'd just been invited to a club that he never knew existed. Where everything took on a new light and the reason for life was obvious – to create and nurture. It got him thinking about his mother and his absent father. Alan couldn't imagine not wanting to do anything he could to be with his child. Shane's arrival hadn't had the same impact. The romance of human creation had been dulled by sleep-deprivation and the seemingly endless task of provision. There was also something nagging at the back of his mind that wouldn't shift.

Doc parked in a disabled parking space outside the health clinic near King's flat, disregarding Alan's objections and comment that someone with difficulty walking might need the space.

'You'll have difficulty walking in a minute if you don't hurry up,' said Doc, uncharacteristically aggressive.

Doc had a key and let himself into King's place, where they found him in a fluffy pink dressing gown, playing a game of *Solitaire,* using playing cards with a picture of London's Routemaster on the back. Alan couldn't imagine King on a bus.

'So, we are thinking of promoting you,' said King, smiling broadly in a way that could be construed as genuine.

'What do you mean by promoting?' said Alan, aware that he had to appear to be grateful. King's job descriptions didn't exactly fall in with Human Resources regulations or thought-leadership but everyone in The Team – from Chief Executive Officer (King) to Events Manager (Alan) and Head of Security and Team Personal Assistant (Doc) – had to accept their titles without question. The fact the titles bore no relation to what they were asked to do was irrelevant.

'Well, my young man. I've seen your potential and now you have another mouth to feed, I think it's time to up our game a little.'

He stood up and walked around the room, smoking and sighing heavily as if in deep contemplation.

'What would you most like in the world? Just think about it for a minute,' said King, breathing out a circle of smoke into the light where it mixed with the dust and mingled ghost-like until the particles couldn't be defined from each other.

A quiet life, a good book, regular sex with someone I love and a still mind, thought Alan.

'I guess a house of my own, a nice car, a villa in Spain. And a Rolex watch,' he finally answered after leaving a reasonable gap for his 'consideration' to the matter. He knew what King wanted to hear.

'And my boy, how do we get these things? Through hard work, speculation and accumulation. We need to *invest*.'

King leaned over and placed the palms of his hands on the table. He moved them slightly to avoid a circle of stickiness. Alan noticed how clean they were. No traces of blood.

'My investment is about to come to fruition and I want you to be our Chief Operations Manager for the project,' he added, standing up and rubbing his hands down his trousers to remove any alcoholic residue he'd picked up.

'So, are you in?'

Like I've a choice, thought Alan. 'Yes, of course.'

'Good man. You need to make sure you keep Friday week free. Go home, get some rest and make sure you are fit for the job. No drinking or drugs for two days before. I'll be sending over your instructions in a few days.'

Alan lifted his chin slightly, as a boxer might before waiting for an inevitable punch. He knew the stakes were rising but he'd no choice but to keep playing the game. He'd never seen himself as a gambler, thief or cheat even though he'd had to undertake some actions under all of those headings in the interests of personal survival.

'I look forward to it,' said Alan, rising from the table and lifting his leather jacket – a recent purchase – from the back of his wooden chair.

'Good boy. I'll be in touch,' shouted King to Alan's back as he headed for the door. 'And you don't want a Rolex. You want a Patek Phillipe - far more classy.'

Marie wanted to know why he was always at home these days but used the opportunity to leave him with the two children as often as she could. For someone with minimal fitness and a BMI a good ten points over what it should be, she recovered exceptionally well from the birthing process and was soon back to her usual ways – mostly outside of the house, thanks to the introduction of bottled milk at birth.

Alan was fine with the feeding and nappies but struggled to find things to do with such small children. Apart from the fact they were too young to talk to about anything he knew about, he had no experience of family life.

On his own with them he would read to Shannon and Shane. Not kids' books but the books he wanted to read but was always shouted down by everyone else in his house.

Might as well kill two birds with one stone, he would think, rationalising his decision to choose something of his own liking by believing it would satisfy everyone concerned; and possibly educating, albeit subliminally, his charges. *Crime and Punishment* was an excellent read in Alan's view and, more to the point, reading it out loud sent the children to sleep within minutes. He concluded all they wanted was a recognisable and friendly voice. The rest took care of itself.

It was quiet when he was left to babysit. When Marie was there with him, she filled any silence with loud television, Kiss FM and her various loud Lambrusco-drinking friends.

Doc came round a few times to see 'how things were going' and he always seemed to be surprised to find Alan in.

'What did you expect me to be doing?' Alan asked, puzzled that anyone should give a damn how he spent his time.

'Living it up with your latest bonus,' said Doc. 'That's for starters,' he added as he leaned round to watch Marie as she left the kitchen with a glass for another friend who'd turned up to drink and be merry. Until they'd all drunk too much and started to argue.

'Nice arse,' he commented. 'Nice and meaty. Not one of those scrawny birds you get about these days.'

'Thanks for the compliment,' said Alan. 'But she has only just had a baby,' although he was thinking that even before children she'd have difficulty getting that rear out of any plastic garden chair.

'You need to do a bit of woo-ing, my mate. Take her out, tell her who's boss. She doesn't seem to know.'

Alan shook his head and felt something had been left unsaid as Doc headed off in his latest car, a BMW Series 5 with black metallic paint.

Who is he to tell me how to treat my wife?

Alan still hadn't learned to drive anything but the scooter that he was required to use for The Team's deliveries, and had no desire for cars at all. Not that he'd tell King that. As far as his boss was concerned, Alan hankered after an Aston Martin DB7 and was prepared to wait a long time for it. He wouldn't be able to understand anything else.

On the Wednesday prior to the Friday booked for his 'promotion', Kevin Hart arrived on his doorstep. Alan had only met him once but knew him to be The Team's 'Research Manager'.

Marie let him in and then put on her coat to leave. Alan didn't ask where she was going as it was probably best she wasn't in the house when 'business' was being discussed. The mother-in-law had gone to one of the neighbours with the kids and there seemed to be no sign of her imminent return.

'So, Al. You ready for Friday?' said Kevin.

'Well, I think so although it would help to know what I'll be doing.'

Kevin unveiled a map of a fast food outlet in a major shopping centre south of the M25. He explained that their takings in a day would exceed £25,000 in cash and that they only had a security collection three times a week – the last being on a Friday night.

'We're going to be there before the final collection. This will be a big haul but we need to work with precision. Understand?'

The plans had been drawn up and there would be three of them taking part. Alan would be working with two others who report directly to King – one being the driver.

'You get yourself a licence and you could be the getaway boy, but I guess you want to see a bit of the action?'

Alan felt his heart racing. His pulse beat so hard he could watch the blood travel in a blue frenzy beneath the stretched skin of his wrist.

'What sort of action are you talking about?' he asked. To this point he'd never had to take part in any violence, just witness it.

'Well, it only makes sense to be tooled up. We don't want you getting hurt. Just a knife and a large hammer should do it. The others will have the same but the key is to get away quickly. Tell them you've got a gun if you need to. They won't know the difference, they'll be shitting themselves.'

Alan felt cold, as if he were getting a fever. His mind's eye worked overtime with people being hurt, screaming for their loved ones and being terrified to the point no therapy could ever help them. He made a vow then and there that he wouldn't do any more than he had to, to get what King wanted.

'There's big money in this for you, Al. Take it seriously and there'll be plenty more where that came from.'

As Kevin went to leave he threw down three hundred pounds in cash and gave orders to get himself some suitable disguise. He explained the procedures and what Alan was expected to do.

'Try to be a bit original. Balaclavas and women's tights are a bit Laurel and Hardy for The Team. And buy a hammer. The biggest you can find,' he said. 'Although maybe not too big, as not sure you'd be able to carry it with those arms!'

Alan had tried to build up some muscles but since he'd stopped the roofing had lost tone. He'd tried the gym but found it boring and could barely manage a press-up without feeling intimidated by the gorillas lifting weights heavier than his wife. And that was a challenge he didn't feel up to.

He sat with his head in his hands as he contemplated what he needed to do, failing to hear Marie coming through into the kitchen.

Picking up the roll of notes, Marie whooped with joy and told him she was going out shopping. Alan tried to retrieve some of it but it was too late –she was making plans for a day out on the basis that the kids needed clothes and she needed some 'me' time.

At no point had she thought to invite him.

CHAPTER FIFTEEN

I t's a wise man that knows his own father, so the saying goes. But I think Shakespeare had it right when he said it is a wise father that knows his own child. *The Merchant of Venice II*, I think it was.

My wisdom has been well and truly tested throughout my life. But then the truly wise man is the one who knows he knows nothing. Wiser still is the one who knows stuff but keeps his mouth shut.

I heard my mother once talking about my biological father. I think he might have been my uncle. I know there was a lot of tension and we never mentioned her family. I'd ask about my Grandparents, but was told they weren't worth knowing. Once, when she was with my first step-father I heard them talking late into the night, working out that if my uncle was my dad, then did that also make my mother my aunty. It was confusing and I was too young to take it in. Every now and then I relive the conversation I heard and it has a different meaning. It's often best not to think about these things. They can drive you mad.

'You coming out?' says Brian, looking through the peep hole that invites voyeurism on a number of levels. Many was the time Trevor or I would have to tell one of the screws to fuck off listening to our conversations – or sometimes watching while one of us was having a wank.

We had a kind of code about that. Trevor usually needed to 'let off steam' after a visit from his wife so I would always try and get to sleep in good time to give him the privacy his fantasies would require. In my case it was more animal and just a requirement to prevent pent-up frustration and tended to be early in the morning. The 'dawn horn' I called it until Marie thought I was referring to her friend, Dawn, and hit me round the face before banning all sexual activity for a good three months. I wouldn't have minded but Dawn was a minger. I'd have to date rape myself to go anywhere near her – and wear a bag over my head. It's not even as if I'm fussy, either.

'No. Not today,' I say to Brian and so walks off, hopefully to leave me alone. He knows I'm not a great socialiser at the best of times. I still have my lunch to occupy me, not that I'm a great eater. I can go three or four days without food, which is not something the wife ever understood. It was a miracle if she could go three hours without eating.

She wanted a gastric band once. The doctor said she wasn't fat enough so she went on a diet to put on the extra three stone she needed to qualify. It didn't make sense to me but anyway she got what she wanted. After the operation she couldn't eat and the weight dropped off her, although the skin didn't. Her belly ended up looking like those curtains that people ruffle up on bits of string. I never minded what size she was and was quite happy to let her keep complaining that her obesity was down to having children, and not to having fifteen burgers a week and a virtual drip-feed of vodka, cola and cake. It seemed a bit unfair on the kids though, when she'd lift up her belly-flap, point to them, and tell them it was their fault.

Shane was a good baby. Always quiet but maybe that is something to do with being a boy and the second born. His sister loved him and despite trying to shove spoons down his throat until he choked she was a natural carer, which is surprising given her bloodline.

My own mother wasn't terribly interested in being a grandparent. I traced her to a flat in Penge, after Shannon was born, but she wasn't in. There was a familiar smell of old cabbage and cat wee. Wanker was off the scene by all accounts as a neighbour told me he thought she lived alone but 'had a lot of visitors'.

I suppose I'd hoped the news of being a grandparent might have woken her up to a different level of responsibility but of course that was me being optimistic. I've learned not to take on too much hope now. It saves on disappointment.

Not that I really wanted her involved. She was hardly a model of childcare excellence. But for a while I would feel compelled to try and contact her on what you'd think were important occasions such as my marriage or the births of Shannon and Shane. Looking back I was foolish to be surprised she didn't respond to the letters I hand posted through the letterbox of her latest social housing address.

I later heard she'd been in and out of rehab and even spent a short spell in a women's prison in Surrey for fraud – something to do with benefit cheating - and had got rid of Wanker after a particularly sound beating. It was all hearsay, so I had no direct proof of any of it. No doubt Wanker would have been replaced by a Tosspot anyway, so it was unlikely conditions or attitude had improved to any worthwhile degree.

Shannon had the look of her grandma – a sort of far-away 'no-one can touch me' air about her. But she was a baby, yet to be addled by the dubious comforts of all-you-can-drink 'white spirit' from the

Polish supermarket, or the cynicism of a life addled by an inherent lack of ambition or passion.

Occasionally I would think she was dead and then I'd get a letter, pleading for forgiveness and to understand why she was such a crap mother. They didn't move me. I was too far away from my childhood to respond emotionally.

I suspect she's dead now as I haven't heard anything for over two years. One of Trevor's mates made some inquiries and found out the house we lived in when I was a kid is now occupied by some Bengalese who own a restaurant in Tundren Lane. There was no forwarding address although the mother of the house handed a huge pile of letters over, all addressed to Mrs S Shoesmith, which turned out to be nothing but bills, credit card statements and county court summonses for non-payment of court fines. Either she'd done a runner or her liver had finally copped it after a lifetime of abuse. I know the feeling…

'Shut that bloody noise up!' I shout. We've a new intake of particularly disrespectful criminals – not the type that I would associate with.

Those who have never been part of the justice system have a tendency to lump us all together, but they really shouldn't. Like outside, we have our own morals and an internal society that deems – through peer pressure – what is right and what is wrong.

The nonces never get past any of us. One sniff of child pornography or abuse and they are 'dealt with'. The thought of any of those evil bastards touching either of my kids makes me sick. I'd kill for real then. Not by accident.

This lot are from a travelling community and have been stealing from old people's homes, preying on those with Alzheimers or who are so critically lonely they are willing to trust anyone who'll give them the time of day. It goes beyond anything I have ever read or seen – even *Clockwork Orange* – so I just don't understand where they get their ideas from.

I don't often use the word 'cunt' but it comes to mind only too quickly when describing the main perpetrator of their crime. He befriends an elderly person in one of those homes where there is an emergency key outside. He offers to do their shopping and give them a bit of company. After a few weeks they get to trust the only person who has shown them any real interest for some time, and so willingly hand over the code for the key box.

Lo and behold within a matter of days all the residents in the block have been burgled. In this case one of them was ninety-one and in a wheelchair with cerebral palsy. They took all his life savings and his wife's jewels. She'd been dead ten years and he kept them wrapped in a scarf. He would show off the engagement ring she'd worn for sixty two years, as a mark of their love and commitment despite all the ills they'd carried in their long lives. Even in extreme poverty, neither of them would part with it in exchange for cash, whether it be the lure of the pawn shop, or the willing pounds of a travelling gold merchant.

Not only did these vile criminals break the man's heart - which had survived every blow from disability at birth to two wars, recessions, strikes, grief and the general ignominy of getting too old for anyone to care – they left him a note which read: '*Got you, you old fukker. We'll be back for more.*' They couldn't even spell.

He died two days after the burglary, leaving his own note telling any judge that finally found the thieves to forgive them, as they did not know what they had done.

Local outrage, and CCTV, was all that was required to find the tricksters and they were caught and sentenced quickly.

The judge in question refused to take too much note of the old man's wishes and banged up the whole lot for every crime he could think of, stating to the press and the public that none of them should see freedom for a very long time.

It was a good move talking to the papers as we all got to read about it. Nothing's been done about them in here yet and they are all cock-a-hoop with the joy of their human rights and the opportunity to play pool and watch TV all day, at the taxpayer's expense.

'Go fuck yourself, stick insect,' called out one of them, in response to my request that they should keep the noise down. I could hear them laughing amongst themselves and oh I how I remember the saying; 'He who laughs last laughs longest'.

Just wait until the internal management get to issue their own verdict and punishment on the idiots. Those bastards will not only know what has hit them but they will also know who hit them and how often they will continue to do so.

You can get away with a lot on the outside. Not once you're in here. Everyone says they're innocent, for a while anyway, but people know right from wrong. Most of us are sorry for anything that has upset anyone else. Few prisoners are inside because they got up one day and thought they were going to hurt someone. They just saw a means to an end, or they were on a path they couldn't get off. Survival mechanisms kick in some strange behaviours – all of which seem perfectly acceptable at the time.

I look around the cell again. It's so empty without Trevor. He's a good guy, caught up with the wrong crowd and doing the wrong things. That's why we got on so well and people left us alone, mainly. Neither of us felt sorry for ourselves but we know if we had our life again we wouldn't cause the pain or distress we have. Both of us are truly sorry.

I wasn't totally sure of the details of his history but from what he told me, he'd been heavily into drugs and broke into a vet's surgery to get hold of ketamine – a drug used to tranquilise horses. What he didn't realise was that someone slept there at night to keep an eye on animals recovering from extensive surgery. It was a middle-aged woman, desperate for the extra cash after her husband left her with five kids to bring up on her own. The court was told how she would leave her fifteen year old home alone with the others and bed down at the surgery for the night, hoping against hope that none of the cats or dogs would need her attention, otherwise it would deprive her of much-needed sleep. I wonder if she ever hoped she wouldn't have to deal with the fall out of a bungled burglary and the totally random injury sustained as a result?

When Trevor broke into the building at the back, it was close to the small recovery room full of animals, where the woman had camped for the night.

She got up to see what the noise was and he was taken by surprise – lashing out immediately and pushing her against the cages in his panic to escape. The one she fell against had a glass bottle attached to it, filled with fluids for a rabbit recovering from a tumour operation. It broke and as it did so, pierced her flesh as might a knife, slicing up one of her kidneys and cutting an artery. Trevor saw the blood and ran, although he did stop at a telephone box to call for help. There's no way he wanted anything to happen to her and told me many times he wished he'd just stayed and taken the consequences as he got caught anyway. And he wouldn't have done the job in the first place had he known someone might have been there, forgetting that CCTV is just as good a witness.

By the time the ambulance came she was in a critical condition and her daughter was left to look after her kids for five weeks before her mother made it home.

The woman failed to identify Trevor in a parade he was obliged to take part in after an anonymous tip off cited him as the offender. But he confessed anyway because at the time he thought the woman might die and he felt so bad about what he'd done, despite it being an accident.

Trevor said he felt the verdict was unfair but never claimed innocence as such. He did, however, claim repentance and that is what many victims – and their families- require.

I should know.

CHAPTER SIXTEEN

The final details were sketchy. Alan had been told to wait with Eddie outside the restaurant at four-fifteen. The final security pick up of the week was due around five-thirty so they had to be out and gone by then.

Kevin told them that Tommy would be inside. King would be monitoring the situation, and would give the cue to follow him in.

'Alan, you will need to be ready to go straight in once Tommy has controlled the staff. Take no prisoners and frighten the shit out of all of them. You will need to control the customers. Any looking like they're getting moody, do what you have to do.'

According to Kevin's 'research' the timing was to coincide with the start of a film in the nearby multiplex cinema and so the restaurant wouldn't be as full as normal – but it would have plenty of cash.

Eddie had turned up in a grey Audi A4. It's roof was down and he was wearing dark sunglasses and a scarf, despite the searing heat of an exceptional summer day.

'Where's your disguise, dude?' he'd asked Alan, using the same fake Caribbean lilt that King adopted somewhere between Peckham and Streatham during his late teens.

Alan showed him the bag he was carrying – an old football holdall he'd picked up in a charity shop the day before. Inside was a black walking hat – the type with flap down sides and a peak. He had taken the comments about balaclavas to heart and thought it was far from conventional as a robber's disguise could be.

His bag also contained the biggest hammer he could find - and a toy gun also purchased from the Oxfam shop.

'Jeez, man,' said Eddie. 'You want these guys to think you're taking them on a hike! What you thinking?'

He laughed quickly and then dropped his head so he looked over his glasses.

'You need to be careful, you know. We don't want no-one seeing you, right? Cover yourself up.'

Eddie handed Alan a woman's scarf from the glove compartment of the Audi. It was floral pink and frayed at the ends.

'I'm not wearing that!' said Alan. 'Whose is it anyway?'

'I dunno. It was in the wheels when I lifted them. Smells of expensive perfume so I'm guessing it weren't cheap.'

Eddie grinned widely at Alan, exposing a gold tooth and a gap on both sides of his left incisor. He threw the scarf at him.

'Cover yourself. Or else I'll be telling King you ain't been playing nice.'

Alan had never been on the receiving end of King's punishment techniques but had seen enough of them to know he'd rather do as he was told, wherever the instructions came from in The Team.

The car sped off in the direction of the retail park while Alan tried to find a way to hide the scarf under his bomber jacket. At least until he needed it.

They parked up and waited. By twenty past four Alan was sweating. The scarf was building up heat around his neck and his lips twitched in the corners. A heady mix of excitement and nerves built up and he started to shake his leg up and down.

'Stop that would you? You're making me nervous,' said Eddie.' Where the fuck is King? Let's get out the car so he can see us.'

'I just hope this is going to work. What if everyone ignores us and just carries on eating their burgers?'

Eddie roared with laughter.

'Well I guess you'd better make sure they don't!' He carried on laughing to himself.

'Glad you find it funny,' said Alan. 'But I've not done anything like this before.'

Eddie stifled his giggles and turned the car's radio down.

'Look, Al. All you've got to do is believe that you are carrying a gun. Then everyone else will. Would you keep eating your chips if you faced a bullet?'

Alan frowned as he placed himself in the position of the customers. He wanted to back out when he visualised his own puny body brandishing a toy shop BB revolver which had little more power than a potato pistol.

'Just believe in this and it will go like a breeze. I promise,' added Eddie. 'Let's get out and wait for our orders. It'll all be over in a bit then you'll have a good wedge coming to you.'

Alan and Eddie hovered around the Audi, looking at the wheels and peering through the cars' windows in a bid to look like men distracted by their motor rather than robbers in waiting.

Alan checked his belt for the positioning of his hammer and gun repeatedly until Eddie told him he looked about as suspicious as a cat in a cream factory.

They'd just about run out of things to do to occupy themselves when they heard a whistle from the car park of the restaurant. Looking towards the source of the sound, Alan saw King waving to them.

'There he is,' said Alan, making to run towards his boss.

'Take it easy, boy, we don't want to get anyone's gander up. It will be mayhem in there so we want to be able to get in nice and quietly,' Eddie said, pulling down his hat to just above his eyes and hitching the roll neck from his jumper up towards his mouth.

'Put your stuff on, too, twat!'

Alan did as he was told and followed Eddie towards King's car. As they made their way they could see women and children running from the restaurant. King waved frantically at them, indicating he wanted them to go in, and quickly.

'Get the fuck in there,' he shouted over the roof of his BMW before jumping in and driving off.

'Where's he going?' Alan asked but was met with no response other than a tug on his arm to get moving.

'You remember what you were told? Go in and frighten the shit out of anyone in there. Cover yourself up and act quickly. Once I know you're in control, I'll leave you to it and bring the car over.'

When they got to the doors Alan could see Tommy waving a gun – also imitation - at a group of staff, huddled together to the side of the serving bar. The customers who hadn't got away quickly enough were stunned into silence, telling their children whatever they could to comfort them in what many thought could be their final hours.

'Get in there boy, come on. You know what to do,' added Eddie by way of final encouragement.

Alan pushed his way in, pulling his scarf up to cover the lower part of his face and feeling self-conscious in his walking hat, which he realised at the last minute had straps with bobbles. How anyone could be scared of him, he didn't know, but as he pushed his way through the doors, brandishing the heavy hammer, he could see woman moving in front of their children to protect them and men staring blankly in his direction with looks of abject terror in their eyes. His heart was powering its way through his chest cavity, threatening to give up on the person putting it through such tension.

'Don't worry, darling. It's all for a new film,' he heard a nervous woman say to the three primary-aged children at the table. One of them was crying but the other two continued to eat their chips while simultaneously watching the activity going on around them, every now and then stalling with a chip half way to their mouths.

'Get down, all of you,' said Alan, waving the hammer about and trying to keep the bobbles from his hat hitting him in the eye. 'Do as you are told and you won't be hurt.'

He noticed that the so-called security guard was hunched in the corner of the room, clutching his knees to his chest and crying for his mother.

'Over here,' shouted Tommy from beneath his balaclava. 'They've opened the tills. You'll have to smash the safe.'

One of the few men among the customers stood up from a table occupied for a child's birthday party and went to block Alan's way. The man was small, dressed in what looked like a new designer sweatshirt and ironed jeans. He looked out of place in a casual environment and not comfortable with the role he'd just given himself as protector. His face was bright red and droplets of sweat threatened to blind him on their journey down the front of his face. He raised a shaking hand as if to push Alan back, no doubt testing his luck and hoping to be the have-a-go-hero for the day.

'Get out of my way. I've got a gun,' said Alan, swinging back his coat to reveal the realistic looking toy tucked into his trouser belt.

Alan was relieved beyond his own belief when the man immediately sat down and took the hand of the woman opposite him. As he did she crossed herself and held on to a crucifix necklace with her spare hand.

'Our father, who art in heaven, hallowed be thy…'

'SHUT THE FUCK UP!' shouted Tommy. 'Give it to 'em, Al. Just bloody give it to 'em?'

Alan remembered his instructions to scare the shit out of the customers and it seemed he was doing a good job. Against the odds he found his voice.

'Don't annoy me, mister, or you'll cause a lot of trouble,' said Alan, lifting the gun out of his belt with his left hand – the right was still brandishing the hammer, which he used to smash down on the table in front of him, causing immediate cries from the children around it.

Other customers let out a communal gasp and Alan was confident he'd done as ordered. His concerns about being able to act the part diminished as his audience saw the weapon, not taking any risks on its authenticity. For good measure he threatened to smash the hammer on another table but seeing the crumpled face of a young, breast-feeding mother in front of him he decided against the need to confirm his power.

Walking backwards to behind the tills and into an office, he saw the safe. His instructions were to smash it open with the hammer but Alan had enough sense to know he was ill-equipped for the job.

'OK, who's the manager here,' he said to the group of uniformed staff still in the huddle under Tommy's watchful eye.

'He's not here,' one spiky-haired girl said after a few moments silence. 'He don't work Fridays.'

Alan shot a look at Tommy and looked directly at the open tills. He went over and took out what he could. He pulled out the charity holdall he'd stuffed into the back of trousers and starting filling it with cash, spilling coins to the floor and letting them roll noisily into the legs of the seated staff.

'So, how do I open the safe?' said Alan to the spiky haired girl, quietly and gently.

She looked around at her colleagues and then up to Tommy.

'Can I get up?' she asked and Tommy nodded.

'Come with me,' she said, indicating that she could take Alan into the office.

Within minutes she'd undone the locks and opened the safe to reveal what looked to Alan like an incredible amount of cash.

'There hasn't been a collection this week because of some strike. You're in luck,' she said.

Alan stuffed the holdall with all the notes and coins, struggling to get it all into the various pockets of the bag. He heard Tommy shouting at some of the customers who'd started to get restless.

'You've been very helpful,' said Alan, who was confused by the girl's willingness to pass on information about the safe. She could easily have kept quiet and they'd be none the wiser.

'Sorry to do this to you. I hope you don't get into trouble,' said Alan, pulling down his scarf slightly so he could make himself clear. The spiky-haired girl stopped for a moment as she met Alan's gaze.

'I hate this place,' she said. 'Run by capitalist bastards who don't give a shit about the welfare of the animals reared for their crappy meals or the people who eat them. I'm only here until I get to Thailand.'

Alan slowed down to take in what she said.

'Wow, what will you be doing there?'

'Looking after orphaned animals and working in a school for disadvantaged children. Better than this dump.'

The girl looked out through the office window and moved over to Alan so she was close enough to whisper.

'I shouldn't be telling you this, but the assistant manager has pressed our security button. The police will be here any minute.'

'Shit!' said Alan. 'I didn't even think of that. Look, thanks for everything. You've been a great help.'

'Get a move on, cretin,' shouted Tommy. Some of the customers were starting to mumble loudly in dissent.

Alan stuffed the last pack of notes into his bag and ran out of the office, brandishing his weapons. By doing so he brought about a renewed atmosphere of unease which kept the customers from building their dissent to the point that it caused a problem.

'Right, we're getting out of here. Don't anyone move until we're gone,' said Tommy as he pulled Alan by the sleeve to move along with him.

They headed to the doors, walking backwards to make sure no-one made any moves towards them, and waved out to Eddie who, by then, had driven the car to just a few yards from the restaurant's entrance.

As Alan and Tommy made their way out, sirens could be heard in the distance.

Within seconds four marked police vehicles, including an armed response unit, had cornered the car park and were shouting that anybody in the vicinity should keep still.

The Audi, which had been waiting quietly among other parked cars, roared into the space in front of the doors and skidded to a halt. Eddie gestured out the window to Tommy and Alan to get in.

'Quick, you arseholes, unless you want to be caught?'

Alan looked back at the girl with the spiky hair and gave her the thumbs up. He was going to mouth 'thank you' but knew she wouldn't be able to see it through the scarf he'd pulled back up over his facce.

They jumped in the car, Tommy scrambling into the back seat as Alan tried to get his seat belt locked while also trying to close the door, which got heavier the faster the Audi moved.

Eddie raced off, blasting his way over the colourfully-planted concrete beds edging the parking area and screeching his way past the police, who'd tried to cordon the Audi off but didn't account for Eddie's lack of concern for crashing his way through small spaces. He broke wing mirrors off as he scraped his way through the gap left between a police car and a wooden-slatted outbuilding housing rubbish containers for the estate.

Eddie had done his homework and also enjoyed a good race

through the streets of south London, which he knew better than the back of his hand – particularly since the burning incident which left a scar from his knuckles to the third mole half way up his forearm.

'Jesus, they are coming after us,' said Alan, holding the bag of money as tightly as he could to his chest.

'Don't worry. I know just how to get rid of them,' said Eddie as he put his foot down and drove at considerable speed through a maze of side streets before reaching an industrial estate about three miles from the shopping area.

On the way he'd hit four parked cars, two other vehicles that were getting in his way and narrowly missed running over three cats, a dog and two pedestrians.

By the time the car came to a crunching halt, having lost most of its hub cabs, both bumpers and wing mirrors and various unessential attachments, Alan and Tommy were shell-shocked.

Neither had ever taken part in a robbery before.

CHAPTER SEVENTEEN

Brian's been really kind. He brought me a copy of *To Kill A Mockingbird* last week. Not from the library but from home. He told me the story reminded him of me and that I should think about that while I read it.

'People aren't always what they seem,' he said as he threw the earmarked paperback onto my bed. 'That's something I've learned while doing this job. Let me know what you think.'

At first I didn't know what he was going on about but I had a dream I was back at school and had been caught stealing. When I woke up I remembered what one of the teachers had said – as if it'd been yesterday.

'Once a thief, always a thief, there's no doubt about it. Leopards don't change their spots and if something goes missing the first person I will look to is Alan Shoesmith,' said the weasel-like Harriet Shawcross, who'd taken a dislike to me the day I told her I thought our cat had fleas. She'd asked why I was scratching, so I answered truthfully. Well, apart from the fact it wasn't actually our cat, just one that would sleep on my bed when it felt like it.

The comment she made about me always being a thief was referring to an incident where I was caught for stealing Kathy Lake's lunchbox. She was a fat girl and always had twice the amount of food anyone else brought in to school – and it showed. I figured that I was doing her a favour by eating half of it. I ate two of the four sandwiches, the crisps and one of the five chocolate biscuits. I left the yogurt as I felt it was appropriate to do so, given her nutritional challenges.

Her parents were massive - and clearly thought the theft of food from their daughter was the ultimate treachery. Being food junkies they all went bonkers and complained to everyone they could.

The reaction to taking a few bits of food astounded me and I would wonder how they could find the time to buy, prepare and eat enough calories to maintain their lardy, uncomfortable looking bodies. It must have taken up most of the waking hours.

As a result of reducing Kathy's intake for that day, I was called into the head teacher's office to explain myself. It seemed fitting that I was sick as a dog splashing bits of cheese and pickle onto the front of Miss Shawcross's dainty, flat shoes.

She'd cried in disgust before rushing from the room to 'clean herself up' and I was given a detention and banned from the packed lunch area for a month. Every time anything went missing from anywhere, even sports kit from the girls' changing room, she would come and find me. Never once did she believe me when I said I hadn't taken a thing since being caught over the sandwich incident. I wasn't a thief. I was hungry.

Give the dog a bad name, then. All I was doing, metaphorically, from that day was waiting for the petard – and a good crowd to see my death by hanging, purely for the sport of it. Miss Shawcross never looked me in the eye again but I did catch her glaring at me from a distance on occasion, as if she was willing me to self-combust and disappear from her life in a puff of smoke.

Once I'd finished reading *To Kill A Mockingbird* I got what Brian saw in the story and the sub text. How people judge others without knowing anything about what makes them tick, or the reasons for their actions.

Dogs get a bad name for biting but if you keep hitting them, what else do you expect them to do? Their teeth are their only weapons. They can't explain, over a coffee and a currant bun, that they find being hit with sticks an 'unacceptable affront to their human rights.' They don't explain anything. They just think. 'That hurts, bite the bastard.'

Perhaps that is why they are called canines? The dogs, that is.

You see, Atticus was deemed a good man until he defended a black man called Tom, innocent of the rape of which he was accused. Those who thought they knew better, judged him to be another 'dog' – ironically 'blackening' his name just for his colour.

'He's black so he must be a rapist. He's poor, so he must be a thief.'

How silly of me not to have thought that. Perhaps it is my lack of education?

Then there's Boo Radley, a recluse who kept himself to himself. Because of that he was deemed a child-stealing ogre. Atticus was attacked for his ideals in saving the innocent and all in all everyone had got the whole bloody thing arse about tit. Both Boo and Atticus were good folks but they challenged what the unthinking masses considered to be 'normal'.

I spent my childhood in bewilderment. Not understanding

the rules by which we should identify each other or why we had to behave in certain ways at certain times.

Even stupid things like someone saying: 'How are you?'

Don't try telling them – they'll walk off in boredom because they never wanted to know in the first place. So what you have to do, apparently, is say that you're very well and thank the person for asking even though you feel like crap and have a sneaking suspicion you might have a serious illness. No-one wants that answer, it's just one of those questions you have to ask, and you have to answer, never truthfully but just because it is polite.

The other one is; "if there's anything I can do to help." Try calling and they'll be out, or they'll have a sick aunty they need to visit, or a diary full of dental appointments. Or they didn't really mean it anyway…

I know I'm not an academic but I love reading. It gives me an idea of other people's worlds. Of course it is all subjective but a hundred people could write about the same thing and come up with a different story. All, in their own way, the "truth".

Another book I thought of, thanks to Harper Lee's vivid observation of a society I know nothing about, is Shakespeare's *Othello*.

He didn't really write books as such, more plays and poems, and they're quite difficult to read with all that flowery language. But his plays! They're bloody good when you get the hang of it.

"Reputation, reputation, reputation! O, I have lost my reputation! I have lost the immortal part of myself, and what remains is bestial." That's what Cassio says and I get what he means. Once that woman said I'd be a thief for the rest of my life, I believed her. And if I'd

wanted to be anything else her opinion of me wasn't going to change – and she'd tell everyone about one, small incident and they would all think the same of me.

It takes a long time to realise that other people's opinions are their own business. They have a view of the world that is based on seeing your face, your actions and making an evaluation of your very soul because of them - when all the time you were just trying to go about your own stuff.

I saw a man waiting at Earls Court for a tube once. We were both waiting at the front end of the platform – me because I could keep away from the crowds, all jostling for position in their daily monotony. He was dressed in the uniform of the professional commuter: bowler hat, Crombie coat with briefcase and umbrella. In my memory I have him carrying a copy of the *Financial Times* although I think he was actually carrying a down market tabloid, no doubt for a cheeky look at a pair of tits on his way to work. I'd made my mind up about the type of person he was, what he valued, and – probably more importantly what he was likely to think of me - and the result of that was instant dislike.

Works in an office, wears a suit, loads of money, nice house, wife and kids. Possibly a bit of a fling with the secretary. Two holidays a year. Thinks people like me are scum. Arsehole.

I just caught the look in his eye as he threw everything he was holding to the floor and leaped in front of the Upminster train as it powered its way in to platform. It took seconds but I watched the tiniest movements in slow motion. The driver was screaming at the body flying towards his windscreen and onlookers took their time to realise what was happening. When they did they also started to scream. The man's sadness was physical and just before the impact he closed his eyes and shouted: 'Goodbye cruel world.'

Someone actually laughed when they caught what he said. Now I know it might have sounded like a cliché to anyone not seeing how his body relaxed in the very brief knowledge his fight for sanity was over. To me, it said it all. The tube train's front bumper hit him in the side, bending his nearly lifeless body into a shape not fit for human use. There was little sound other than a soft, bumping crunch as the driver tried, but failed, to slow his cab's transit along the tracks sufficiently to prevent running him completely over. I saw blood trickle along the tracks and settle thickly against the stump of a severed arm. I will never forget the smell of blood, sweat, tears – and shit.

By the time I'd returned from my trip, the track had been cleared and trains were moving as normal but the smell remained. If you looked closely you could see staining on the gravel between the rails. There was also a strong odour of bleach, disinfectant and death. A few people commented there'd been what I thought they said was a 'wunnunder' which I later found out translated to being a 'one-under' – the corporate slang for someone who'd been selfish enough to delay their timetable by ending their life on their shift.

The "cruel world" that took shape in that man's bowler-hatted head, was certainly over and I wondered how many people actually gave a damn.

CHAPTER EIGHTEEN

'Hurrah, the spoils of good fortune,' said King as he tipped out the cash and unwrapped the bundles of notes.

The television was on in the background and Goose was flicking channels until she stopped on a news report.

'Police are now looking for three men who escaped in a silver Audi and headed for the Columbus Estate, where the car was later found dumped. They are believed to be in their twenties and one was wearing a deerstalker hat,' said the newsreader.

'So that's what it's bloody called,' said Eddie as he kept one eye on the money and the other in the vicinity of the television. 'Stupid thing. Makes you look like something out of a Sherlock Holmes' film. Wrong bloody side of the fence, mate!'

Alan's thought process jumped into the here and now as the reality of what he'd done came into focus. Even his choice of disguise had become part of a national police hunt. He wondered if Marie would notice but remembered she never watched the news and if she did barely cared what was going on.

His concentration sharpened considerably when an interview with the spiky-haired girl came into life on the screen.

'They didn't say anything to me,' she was telling the camera with a face that no-one could believe was a lie – apart from Alan who was fondly remembering their short, conversation and her views on her employers. She was someone he would really like to get to know but apart from the fact she met him in circumstances not entirely conducive to romance, she'd told him she was going to Thailand. *She might have already gone.*

He thought more fondly of her as she said she didn't get to see what the robbers looked like as they'd had their faces covered up and she was too scared to look at them for any length of time. Her name came up at the bottom of the screen – Zara Button – and he thought she sounded quite posh.

'I think one of them might be black,' she added. 'And the one who took the money from the safe was big and broad. I think he had a northern accent.'

I like her, Alan thought before his thoughts were punctured by a shrill voice very close to his right ear.

'Ere, that you lot, then?' said Goose, laughing as she walked over to her son while he separated different amounts of cash into different piles.

'Best I go and put some dinner on as you'll be keeping yourselves off the streets for a while,' she said, shuffling in her slippers to the kitchen. She rummaged through her freezer before shouting out: 'Fish Fingers, chips and I've got some baked beans and eggs. OK?'

Alan didn't think he'd be able to eat. His stomach was awash with adrenalin and his throat thought it was trying to swallow a golf ball. He was hungry but had a constant urge to get up and run away. *What am I turning into?*

'That would be great,' they all mumbled in a kind of unison.

'Take that hat off, Al. Time we gave it the send-off it deserves,'

For the Last Time

King said as he leaned back into his chair, seemingly satisfied that his latest project had completed according to his instructions.

'We've done better than I thought. Thirty thousand pounds and some,' he said, snatching the hat from Alan's head and setting fire to one of the bobbles with a lighter he retrieved from the coffee table.

'I'll have the "and some" for all I do for you,' said Goose as she came out of the kitchen, now dressed in an apron with a picture of a nearly naked woman on the front – fashioned to make it look like she was walking around in nothing but knickers and her alligator slippers. Alan mentally undressed her, then retched but covered up his mouth and pretended he'd burped.

'You'll get your share, mother,' said King desperately trying to manage the fire he'd created with Alan's hat. It has burst into a ball of flames once the first sparks met the ear flap and they were licking up in the air, catching King's wrist as they did so. He jumped up and down, throwing the hat in the air then catching it before it hit the ground.

'Jesus, this thing's alive,' he said, running into the kitchen chucking the offending item into the kitchen sink, on top of a pile of unwashed plates.

'Don't do that, silly,' said Goose after she'd used the mayhem to surreptitiously help herself to a wad of the notes on the table and shoved them down her front. 'Put it in the bin.'

King went to the backdoor of the flat, behind which the fire escape staircase held a large metallic bin with a lid. He did what he was told.

'That's got rid of that. Stupid bloody thing.'

All the news pictures could show were shady CCTV images of

Tommy and Alan brandishing what the police described as 'firearms' . What was showing of their faces from behind their hats and scarves were barely visible, not least because the quality of the camera had been affected by chip grease and dust that had accumulated on the lenses. Alan was pleased with the effect of the deerstalker. It might have been a laughing stock but everyone seemed to be focusing on that, rather than him. *It did the trick*, he thought.

Eddie had dumped the Audi in the industrial estate and they waited for what Kevin had described as their 'transfer' – another stolen car, driven by Doc, so he could take them all straight back to King's flat.

The sounds of sirens could be heard as they waited. Sometimes distant and then sometimes near enough to make Alan think they were bound to be caught. His nerves got the better of him and made his hands shake, so he had to hide them from the others for fear of being branded a coward.

'That was close,' he said at one point as a patrol car drove slowly past the unit they were hiding in. Alan had seen one of the officers staring straight through the grid of the door they'd forced to gain access. He thought they must be able to see anyone could get into the barely-secured warehouse. The car had continued to crawl along the road which was a dead-end. A few minutes later the car came back the other way, but the officers didn't bother to look back towards the warehouse door.

Alan's breathing had got fast and his head was light. *How could they not see us, or at least where the door had been forced?*

Doc laughed. 'Silly wankers haven't got a clue. We've lost them now so they'll never find us.'

Throughout the whole experience Alan couldn't think of getting away with what he'd done. *It's daylight robbery*, he'd said to himself, smiling as he thought how many people use that phrase in response to situations that were nothing like daylight robbery – like Marie when finding out the corner shop charges two pounds for a lighter when you can get them for sixty pence in the market.

Real daylight robbery, in his mind, was scary and ruthless. It took no prisoners and operated without a care for what anyone thought. What he'd been involved with was about as far removed from the over-pricing policy of Mr Shah's grocery store as it could be.

A bit of Alan wanted to be caught so he could confess his sins, do his time and escape from the clutches of King and The Team.

When he tried to discuss whether or not he should get a 'proper' job with wages, set hours and a pension, Marie would ask him what he was worried about. She didn't really know what he got up to but if she'd guessed most of it was illegal she hadn't voiced any particular concern.

'If you don't like it find something else to do,' she'd said. 'As long as me and the kids are OK you can do what you like.'

Her tone wasn't so much supportive as dismissive, particularly when she suggested Alan take up his issues with Doc, who was spending more and more time at their place for reasons he couldn't quite understand.

'Doc could sort it out for you, if you want out,' she said, munching through a bag of Quavers she'd dipped in the vinegar from a pickled onion jar.

Alan thought she knew far more than she should from someone who was supposed to be close to King and keep all his team members happy. He felt uncomfortable about how much Doc seemed to be sharing with his wife and wondered what else he'd suggested he could do for her.

Goose brought out plates of grease-laden food on chipped white plates, each balanced on their own tray fixed with a cushion at the bottom.

'So you can rest it on your lap,' she'd explained when Alan tried to work out what to do with it.

When they'd finished – and Alan was surprised how delicious the egg and chips were once he started to eat them – King handed Alan, Tommy, Kevin and Eddie their share of the robbery takings. There were six piles in all and Alan couldn't help wondering where the other two were going, although he appreciated that King would – of course – have the lion's share.

'Pretty generous if I say so myself,' said King, packing the remaining two piles of money back into the bag and kicking it under his chair.

Alan felt the weight and the thickness of the notes he'd been given and started to feel a surge of excitement. It was similar to the feeling he got as a child, when the old man who he used to see in the corner shop would see him looking at a bag of crisps, or some chocolate biscuits, and without any expectation on Alan's part would buy them for him.

He felt the same surge of appreciation for King as he did for that crooked and toothless man. It wasn't for the sake of the cash alone. It was what he could do with it.

Alan anticipated handing over a large lump to Marie. She was bound to see him in a new light and give him a bit more attention than she had. They might even have sex, although he wasn't sure this was necessarily the effect he was after.

'It's a lot of money, Alan. It will see you good for a while yet. All you need to do now is lie low for a bit then we'll sort out what we are going to do next. If anything goes down, you know how to get in touch.'

There was a code for any problems they might face with police questioning which involved sending a note or a message to King about the Two Hundred Club's maintenance contract. Different levels of urgency were indicated by suggesting there was a bathroom, kitchen or roof leak. At which point, it was promised, something would be done to clear up any issues.

'I'm pretty sure we've got away with it guys, but be careful how you spend. Nothing too flash for a few months yet, at least until the pigs are off the scent and using their fat, pink snouts to dig away at some other project they'll fail to understand,' King said.

They had another cup of tea and a cursory glance at the next news bulletin, which had relegated the daylight robbery to the third item on the list and reduced the time of the item to just twenty seconds of bare fact.

Alan was disappointed to note that the spiky-haired girl's interview wasn't repeated.

He was missing her already.

CHAPTER NINETEEN

I've an appointment with the psychotherapist today. Someone, somewhere, has decided I might be a risk to myself.

I'm astounded how they've come to that conclusion when I've not spoken to a soul about my thoughts. I only speak to the staff when I have to, and barely speak to the do-gooders who come in here in their bid to make our lives better.

The times I've been set up with various types of visitors in the belief I want to spend time talking to what are usually silly, otherwise bored women who get a thrill from spending a day or two a month with people who, basically, scare them. It's so tempting to snarl, make them jump or say entirely inappropriate things to them, just to justify the knowledge they think all of us are capable of biting off their heads at a moment's notice. But I don't want to do that as I know they are doing their best, in their minds, with the limited resources they have available to them. They could choose to be 'ladies who lunch', contributing nothing to society other than keeping coffee shops and cheap Italian restaurants in a meagre business, certainly not buoyed by generous tips or extravagant patronage.

I suppose the edgy world of prison visiting makes a change from housework and is something to talk about to their husbands, in the absence of anything else after twenty five years of marital routine. It probably gives them something to talk about with the neighbours, or at family parties, when discussions about bin collection day and the state of the potholes have worn their way through their interest.

It is easy to frighten the wits out of these types of amateurs although I've found it can be much the same with those who have been trained to work with the likes of me. It's quite astounding how many people want to get involved in a con's life. Or lack of it.

The list includes various occupational and other therapists, a Shamanic Meditation Master, a couple of university students studying various aspects of law and on one occasion a masseur who thought she could bring inner peace to my otherwise troubled mind with lavender oil and hot stone therapy.

That went a bit wrong on account of the erection she aroused. I didn't do anything with it, of course, but suggested that inner peace was hardly going to be achieved when I'd not seen or touched a woman for some years and she'd decided to 'work' on my gluteus maximus with a decidedly erotic touch.

The screw who'd been in the room with us just raised his eyebrows at the woman's complaint of my indecency, no doubt having 'seen it all' in his career, including the various well-meaning practitioners of all-things-lovely who believed they could wipe out the nastiness in all us killers with a nice smelling oil and heartfelt enthusiasm.

She left hurriedly, leaving me shame-faced and hard-dicked on a massage table just about wide enough for a filleted anchovy. No wonder I fell off the bloody thing when I tried to sit up.

The latest attack on my sensibilities is because I told Brian I'm really missing Trevor and that not having him to talk to makes the day much longer and somewhat pointless. I expect he thought he's being helpful thinking that talking to someone from a mental health unit would make me feel better about being locked up.

'I'm not sick, I'm just bloody bored,' I told him but he raised an eyebrow in the way people in authority do when they think they know better.

I can't really see me talking to Sally the 'concerned-face' social worker about my thoughts, which she seems to assume are predominantly murderous. She forgets that behind the very slightly twisted mind of an accidental killer lies the personality of a man who also thinks of other things like music, wildlife, peace and quiet, women, books, morality and the meaning of life. In fact I don't think I've ever had serious murderous intentions, but everybody assumes I have.

There've been times I've wanted to bash Wanker's brains in, or punch a bully in the mouth - but not to the point I'd wipe out their life. That takes guts - and responsibility. Anyone who thinks about murder generally does so in an abstract way. Those who kill in cold blood are rare. Believe me I've spent enough time with people who have taken a life to know most of them didn't mean it – and would change the circumstances of their imprisonment if they could.

Of course we have people like Ian Brady, The Yorkshire Ripper and Mr and Mrs West but they serve as the exception to prove the rule. Their depravity and total lack of remorse for causing so much ongoing heartache is unusual enough to make continually good reading, so we hear of them time and again. We don't hear so much about those who run people over when drunk, or doctors who overdose their patients and send them to an early grave. That is because they didn't *mean* it.

(blank)

I could tell anyone what goes on in our heads and they'd soon work out most of life is based on accidental chaos. The authorities, however, prefer to send in 'professionals' – or in other words those people who have been so protected from society they have been able to gain degree level qualifications so they can get paid to make stuff up on a daily basis.

You only have to look at the word psychotherapist to know it's all wrong. Psycho: The Rapist. They rape your mind, take intimate bits of your very soul and play with it, like a toddler plays with clay.

Whatever I say has its own meaning to me but they'll give it a new spin. Rarely does anything we discuss have anything to do with my crime or how I came to commit it.

'So, what do you feel about your mother?' they ask and then write copious notes when I say I think she's a whore who'll do anything to maintain a sexual relationship with a man while totally disregarding the needs of anyone who relies on her for their safety or sanity.

'Do you have sexual feelings for her?' one silly cow asked once.

'Yeah of course I do. Doesn't everyone?' I'd replied, in a bid to throw the shrink out and get her confused in her judgment of my mental health. I'd read enough to know about the Oedipus complex and the importance it plays in psycho-evaluation.

The comment back-fired because I was then sent on some intensive, Freudian-style workshop full of skeletal woman in flat shoes with brown rice stuck in their teeth, talking about letting go of the umbilical cord. Me and Dangerous Denzil, reportedly in for life for murdering his parents before cutting them into pieces and eating them, over a period of months as a Sunday lunchtime ritual – were given plastic scissors and told to enact the physical actions of cutting our own cords as if they were still attached. We were expected to imagine being back at our own birth and then were asked to speak to our newborn selves, as adults. It was confusing for anyone who likes to live a linear life.

'This ain't right,' said Denzil. 'You want me to talk to myself when I know I've just had my mother's fanny found my fucking neck. No wonder I've got issues, man!'

He refused to take part in any further rituals and I had to agree that it all seemed a bit pointless.

After that the sessions got a bit milder. We had an ex copper trying to do 'hard man, soft man' all by himself and so coming across as a schizophrenic plus a couple of former armed forces officers who thought they could bully their way into the more malleable aspects of our personalities.

None of it works because you have to want to change to be able to change. The clever ones among us pretend to be conforming to all the authority requirements. We make the right noises and say the right things. We can do that because we've time to think about it all in here from what they want to happen to how we can make them believe they are getting somewhere.

Then just as they are reporting great success to their superiors we crash their world by telling them we couldn't give a toss about what we've done and are just as likely to do it again on the outside.

I've stopped doing that and just tell people what I really think, which can change on a daily basis. It isn't as much fun but at least I can go to sleep at night knowing, if nothing else, I've been true to myself.

I might be a murderer but it has nothing to do with my mother.

Yes, she was a useless tart with a limited sense of responsibility but I can't blame her for me pulling a trigger when I shouldn't have.

She was probably down the Bingo at the time.

CHAPTER TWENTY

Alan had been asleep when the knock on the door came. Marie had screamed up the stairs at him to come down and woken him from a dream about the spiky-haired girl.

They were riding elephants through a forest and she was feeding him chips covered in tomato sauce, which morphed into blood every time he went to take a bite. She called him 'hun' and made him feel like a million dollars but every time he went to kiss her, she evaporated – returning to sit next to him only when he thought she'd gone for good. Her fragility and elusiveness left him wanting, in a way he half enjoyed. Expectation and hope mingled with delayed gratification and the promise of things to come. Hope wasn't something he had a lot of, but Alan could feel it in his dreams.

As he walked into the kitchen he saw the back of a large woman in a tight shirt and manly trousers, which dug into her broad waist. He immediately noticed how the straps of her bra cut into her shoulders, dividing the fat on them into distinctly separate lumps. *She needs to get herself measured properly*, he thought.

'DC Farrow,' she said, turning round to offer her hand. 'I'm hoping you can help me with a few inquiries.'

Marie glared across the table at Alan while he mentally ran through all the things he'd been told to say. He remembered his alibi and also the programmes that had been on the television the afternoon of the restaurant robbery.

'Your wife has been very helpful,' the officer added as she sat down at the table, a cup of tea in front of her.

Alan felt his knees give. *What's the silly bitch been saying now?* Pictures raced through his head as he, firstly, thought how his wife would love to see him arrested, but then how she'd moan at his absence as he'd no longer be around for babysitting.

'Has she?' Alan said, rubbing the palms of his hands through his hair, ruffled from a bad night's sleep. He didn't dare to look at anyone in case his eyes gave away his guilt. He was still half in his dream and didn't want to get out of it.

'Mrs Wesson at number 35 was burgled last Friday evening and also attacked by two men who broke in through her kitchen window. We are making inquiries to see if anyone heard or saw anything.'

Alan hoped no-one heard the breath race through his lungs and out of his mouth as if he'd been punched.

'I was just telling the detective how we thought we heard a noise when we were watching telly on Friday. You remember? It was about five o'clock,' said Marie.

About the time I was committing a robbery at the burger place, thought Alan who instantaneously felt a surge of love and affection for the woman who was normally only too pleased to land him in the shit.

'Oh yes, I do remember now. Thought it was breaking glass,' he added as he went to switch the kettle on, trying to calm down from the initial shock of thinking his time was up.

Marie shifted in her seat to see round to him as she added: 'Alan went out to have a look. We saw an unusual car parked in the road – a Ford Mondeo I think - but didn't see anything so we just thought everything was alright. Didn't we?'

She smiled sweetly and added: 'I do hope Mrs Wesson is OK. Her old fella pegged it recently didn't he? Was she hurt?'

Alan was pleased of the questions because it gave him time to compose himself while the detective answered.

'Unfortunately she was asleep on her settee when they broke in. She'd just been to her husband's grave and the men probably thought she was out. When she woke up she challenged them so they bound and gagged her. One of them also punched and kicked her while she was tied to a chair.'

As the detective continued to tell them further details which she described as 'grotesque' Alan's adrenalin started to subside and he wanted to laugh.

'She's a bit battered and bruised but otherwise seems to have coped with her ordeal well.'

'Well thank goodness she's OK,' Alan said, as his sense of euphoria at not being found out rose in equal measure to his disgust at putting his neighbour's torment so far down his list of priorities. He wondered how well Mrs Wesson would do if she had to cope with one of King's punishment rituals.

'Please let us know if there's anything we can do,' he added, hoping against hope he'd have no reason whatsoever to be in contact with this woman or any of her colleagues again.

DC Farrow thanked Marie for the tea and nodded in Alan's direction. As she did so she looked to the corner of the kitchen, where the empty holdall remained following the robbery. Her eyes focused on it for a second as if she was trying to remember a forgotten memory.

'If you remember anything else please let us know,' she said, shaking herself out of thought and making her way out of the house to a dark green Rover car where another woman – presumably also a detective – was waiting in the driver's seat.

Marie shut the door behind her as the car drove off and marched past Alan in the hallway. When she got to the kitchen she moved the detective's mug to the sink and banged it down loudly on the draining unit.

'Don't expect me to keep doing that. I got the fright of my life when I saw her card. Fucking pigs round here. I thought they were going to arrest you.'

'What for?' said Alan. He'd not said a word about the robbery although she'd looked at him sideways when a news report had come on the radio while they were having breakfast on Saturday morning.

'You think I'm stupid do you?' she said. 'Don't think I don't know what you get up to. Just don't get yourself bloody arrested or me and the kids will suffer.'

Then after a pause: 'I saw that stupid hat you were wearing. I saw it in that bag. You'll get yourself caught going around like that, idiot.'

Alan was taken aback she'd put two and two together and for once her arithmetic was right. He refrained from any admission or telling her that The Team would look after her. If she knew she'd be OK financially without him, he couldn't guarantee he'd know she'd keep her mouth shut.

'Don't know what you're talking about,' said Alan as he made his way upstairs and into the sanctuary of the bathroom.

'Yes you fucking do, you bag of shite!' she screamed up after him. He locked the door behind him, sat on the loo and masturbated while thinking of the spiky haired girl he couldn't get out of his mind.

Nothing more was said that morning and, as usual, Marie went out and left the children with Alan, claiming she couldn't be doing with them as she had stuff to do.

Alan didn't think much of her excuses and set up the video player to play *Close Encounters of The Third Kind*. As he watched, the kids played happily with various toys on the floor in front of him. He noted how much bigger Shane was than Shannon and how much darker in skin tone.

Every now and then Shannon would climb up on his lap and he felt undeniably satisfied with his role as her father. Her soft blond hair would no doubt turn as mousey as his own in years to come and he pitied her sunburned skin once she got the chance to enjoy long, hazy summers outside with friends, maybe a boyfriend.

Alan hated that idea - the thought that someone like him could come along and just be looking to screw his daughter. He tried to quell the rising feeling of anguish and held her tight enough to elicit a small squeal. He kissed her on top of her head, creating static electricity which made her fine, babyish hair stand on end. Alan wanted to laugh as the upright frond waved about as he placed her back next to her brother. Shane glowered at him and Alan noted how he didn't have anything like the animal instincts to protect him like he did his daughter. *Perhaps it is just a dad-daughter thing*, he thought.

As the film came towards its end, Alan felt undeniably drawn to his own isolation. Despite his love for his children and his desire to give them a far better start in life than he had, Alan believed he was in his own wilderness, where he couldn't help but always think something spectacular was about to happen. He'd often wake at night in a cold sweat and expectation that he'd either died and gone to hell or he was in hospital after an accident where all his limbs had been cut off. Once awake none of it would make sense but the underlying fear of being totally alone in the world remained throughout his waking hours.

He sat for a while and wondered what it could be that triggered the sense of doom but when no thoughts came to his mind other than being hungry, he made lunch for the three of them – mashed potato with an egg on top – and tried to read out bits of the novel he'd started the night before.

It was *Tom Jones* by Henry Fielding. Alan had been drawn to it because he'd heard it was about the adventures of a high-spirited orphan boy with an unbeatable plot and 'a lot of sex ending in a blissful marriage'. He'd hoped he could fall into it and live vicariously through the story of another man's creation.

By the second paragraph Shane and Shannon were flicking their potato at each other. Shannon screamed it was in her hair so Alan took them upstairs and got them dressed.

He planned to take them to the park as he didn't know what else do to with them.

Plus he always felt so much better when he was outside.

CHAPTER TWENTY ONE

I've just had a visitor. Zara comes in every now and then, when she's not travelling somewhere exotic.

She found where I was after seeing a news report about my conviction and tracked me down through the court system. Well, it was big news and so most people in the country would have heard about my crime. Julie Gill's family weren't the type to sit back and accept their fate and they had plenty to say to the press about me, what should be done in the name of justice, and that they hoped I would rot in jail. The notoriety wasn't something I would have wanted, but was genuinely pleased that it had resulted in such a positive outcome.

Zara's a funny little thing. Her spiky hair has grown a bit and now she dyes it bright red. It suits her, except when she's been crying or got hay fever and then the colour matches the rims of her eyes. It makes her look a bit like one of those white hamsters with pink noses and see-through ears.

I was shocked when she first asked for a visiting order. I couldn't work out who she was although the name was very familiar.

That seems so ironic now. Zara was the subject of my fantasies for so many years that I'd forgotten she was a real human being. Many times I thought of that feisty young girl who helped me get into the safe and take the money from Burgerland. Without her I could easily have failed in the task and come up against the wrath of King and The Team. I'm still not sure how I was supposed to smash a safe open with nothing but a hammer from the local DIY store.

She was my refuge when married life was stifling; the ideal partner in a world I might have chosen for myself, rather than the one I just let happen to me without any care or consideration for the trajectory I was on.

Of course we could never be together because we met just after I got my life sentence, fourteen years ago. She told me she'd been living with someone but when they left to pursue a celibate life in a Nepalese yoga retreat, eschewing all wordly goods, she decided to do a few things for herself.

She didn't complain when it happened. She said people are free to do as they please and that karma would put everything right. Her resilience to challenges meant she flourished on her own and she has many stories about her work in Third World countries, helping children who had very little in terms of a life and even less in terms of hope. She taught English and Art, created choirs so they could sing and helped them understand that there was a world beyond their own.

'Many of the women have child after child, not knowing why. We try and offer sex education but so many are powerless to stop what is really socially acceptable rape. Then of course they all get left on their own to bring up the kids,' she told me.

Zara would often berate the reports about the poor behaviour of children from single parent families, her experience in Africa fuelling such opinions as maliciously narrow-minded.

'The Virgin Mary was a single parent, for Christ sake!' she said, somewhat ironically, on one occasion. 'I don't recall God being around for the nappies and the health care visits. And I don't see any Father Nature. It's just the mother.. always the mother.'

I'd never known such passionate care. She was a lioness, looking after her cubs against the terrors and challenges of an unfriendly world. She'd claw at anyone causing them danger, meanwhile nurturing those around her with a gentleness only the female of the species can muster.

She was similar with me. Standing my ground when I couldn't stand it for myself, and treating me with such understanding it made me feel weak with gratitude and humility. If only I'd known her from birth.

'You're the only constant in my life,' I told Zara on one visit. I told her I loved her but she said I wasn't in a position to make a judgement about love.

'You don't have much to love in here,' she said. 'Faced with more of a choice I doubt I'd be the one for you.'

I suppose she's right. When you're locked up with no possibility of normal, healthy relationships, it is easy to focus on the one thing you can look forward to. Even if I'd only see Zara three or four times a year it magnifies into something bordering on a long term relationship. I stopped thinking about her sexually years ago. I love her far too much to want to deprave her with the sorts of things that go through my mind.

Sex is weird really. It seems so important at the time but really is almost irrelevant. I can almost see why some religions say it should only be there for procreation. The trouble is the natural drive to procreate is what causes all the problems. Mainly because we can't identify that is what we are trying to do. We've turned the act of reproduction into a hobby without any thought for a desired outcome – other than the obvious.

Men and women, usually, want totally different things from physical relationships and that is the biggest problem for most of the world. I can see why gay people tend to have better – and seemingly more exciting – partnerships. Men tend to understand men and women understand women. Mixing it up just causes problems that would so easily be remedied if we didn't all keep trying to live with each other on a long term basis.

Zara has been keeping me up to date with her world and her passions. More recently she's been studying cognitive behavourial therapy and tried to use me as a bit of a guinea pig - but couldn't get clearance to do so as part of her course. She didn't say why but I suspect that murderers aren't a great addition to a professional CV and so she ended up with a couple of depressives and a compulsive gambler to work on.

One of them committed suicide, the other got so happy she decided to emigrate to New Zealand and work on a sheep farm with her neighbour's eighteen year old son and the gambler couldn't afford to come because he'd sold his car to pay a debt and it was three trains and a bus ride to get to her college.

I asked her how she knew it was me when she read that Alan Shoesmith had been sentenced to life for the murder of Julie Gill.

She said it was my scar, and my eyes. When she saw the picture in the *Daily Express*, she just knew.

'Apart from that red line on your temple, you've a funny little grey bit in one corner of your left eye,' she said. 'I remember it from the robbery. At first I thought it was a bit of fluff but it didn't move when you blinked.'

It confounded me that she not only recognised me but wanted to visit me. At first I said no because I was still trying to pretend that I was a married man. Women often say they are moving on because they can't face being the wife of a lifer. But after three years and nothing but the occasional picture of the kids, alongside their new 'daddy' I gave in to Zara's requests.

I was nervous at first. I thought she was going to come in and tell me what I already knew about myself. That I was a weak, low life piece of scum who'd taken the life of an innocent woman because of a drive towards greed and easy money. I'd have been happy to take that off her, but she couldn't have been more different to my expectations.

When I asked her why she'd come she told me that she didn't believe I was capable of murder and that she wanted to support me. I'd been banging on about my innocence and regret to anyone who'd listen and most of the media ignored my pleas – quoting only the judge and the prosecutors in the case. The *Daily Mail* did run a short profile of the life of a nobody – meaning me – and how neglect and lack of proper parenting can foster criminality. They'd a picture of Julie and another of her family, all looking vengeful as if they would happily cut off my balls and shove them down my throat if they were given the chance. A chance that the reporter seemed to think should be their legal right.

I wasn't given the opportunity to reply and they misquoted everything I'd said in court. But Zara said she read between the lines and, hating The *Daily Mail* anyway, for being a 'dangerous experiment in middle class propaganda serving only to inflame the prejudices of the narrow-minded and bigoted people who live in glass houses but still throw stones' said I'd been unfairly represented.

Even all these years on, Zara is something of an idealist. She fights against injustice with a faith that sheer force of will brings about change. She thinks there is no such thing as evil people, just evil actions.

I laughed when she first said that, thinking of some of the people who are locked up in here. She told me I was cynical and needed to think more of myself if I was going to live a useful life.

What Zara has given me over the time I've been in here is unconditional love. If you've never had it, it's very easy to miss. She doesn't care what I've done or even what I've thought about doing to her, Zara forgives – and understands – everything.

I did tell her I've had many fantasies about her. I romanticised them, in honour of the differences between gender sexuality, but she didn't flinch. She said it was far easier to enjoy eroticism in your own head rather than in someone else's bed.

'You can control what goes on then. It's just as you want it and doesn't involve shifting around in sweaty sheets, jostling for position or ensuring a satisfactory outcome for all concerned,' she said.

As ever, she'd hit the nail on the head. It was about then I stopped the physical fantasy and expanded my appreciation of this short, dumpy but immensely attractive woman into an ethereal level. I wanted to protect her and carry her with me always and certainly didn't want to sully what we had with my sleazy and self-satisfying thoughts.

She never seeks anything from me but my friendship and that's a gift so rare and precious, it is as heavy with meaning as the brush of a butterfly's wing. I have always been scared of saying the wrong thing or doing anything that would make her think less of me, even though she makes it seem like that's impossible.

Zara has always made me feel good. Her vibrancy and willingness to share whatever she has connects me with a life outside. She represents endless possibilities of a future filled with good things, purpose and people to share it with.

That was until today. The news she brought has changed the way I think about everything. Just a few, short sentences, however nicely presented, have the power to turn the entire world on its axis, snuffing out a future that had, until this point, been so vital, so real; and so necessary.

I can still see the back of her coat as she was leaving – the red one with the zig zag stripes on the front and the big circles at the back. It makes her look like a moving target which has always worried me. The image burned against my retinas ensuring my memory will never be unreliable enough to forget her, however hard I might try.

She's gone. And the chances are I'll never see her again.

CHAPTER TWENTY TWO

Alan had only had to use the code a couple of times. Once when he got stopped in the street by a beat bobby and asked if he'd been at the retail park the day of the robbery - and another when DC Farrow had come back to the house, using a spurious excuse about needing a few more details about the night his neighbour was burgled.

He spotted the detective looking intently where the holdall had been. He'd since thrown it in a river and its absence seemed to annoy her – after staring at the corner of the kitchen she then held his gaze for just a little too long.

'Well if you think of anything else you might like to tell me, please get in touch,' she said on her way out - in what he thought was supposed to be a friendly tone but came out more as a threat.

'Sure thing,' he'd replied, closing the front door on DC Farrow probably more quickly than was polite.

Nothing came of either incident and Alan never knew if that was coincidence or King's intervention. He was always led to believe it was the latter, if not directly then by inference. Every time he thought that maybe, just maybe, his boss's power and control was just smoke and mirrors, he ended up concluding it wasn't worth taking any risks by challenging the status quo. Alan had seen what happened to other people who'd gambled on King's ability to wreak havoc on any doubters.

'Goose is in hospital' said Doc when he came to pick Alan up for one of the smaller collection jobs that were becoming regular work for The Team.

'She tripped over her slippers and has broken her ankle. We've got to take on King's visits while he looks after her.'

'I can't imagine him looking after her,' said Alan. 'I've never seen him so much as pick up a plate.'

Doc shot him a look which suggested it was best Alan's opinions weren't voiced out loud.

'If he says he is going to look after his mother then we must assume that he will,' he warned. 'He wouldn't take kindly to knowing that people might think he isn't capable.'

Alan nodded and looked at the map. They were on their way to a snooker hall further west than they normally travelled in London.

'Aren't we a bit out of our territory?' asked Alan as Doc sped his way across a zebra crossing, narrowly missing a pram being pushed by a girl who looked no more than fourteen. She swore loudly at him and threw two fingers in the air which Alan caught sight of in the wing mirror of the BMW. He wondered how Doc would've felt had he hit her or the child.

'King wants to expand the territory. There are some players around here who've been left alone for two long. They've been getting a bit cheeky with our patch. They need to be taught a lesson.'

Doc swerved through some back-doubles then pulled up outside a second hand car showroom. The pavement in front was littered with cars all over ten year's old, mostly Audi, BMW and Mercedes. They'd been driven to their last miles but shined with spit and polish to be sold to those who could never afford the newer versions, but wanted to be part of the group of people who could.

Trading on the reputation of the brands they sold, two men stood at the front talking to prospective buyers, knowing they had every chance of selling dud or dying vehicles on the back of names emblazoned across the boots.

'Don't say anything. Just look mean,' said Doc as he flicked off his seat belt and jumped out of his seat.

Alan wondered what looking mean was like. Still only a little over ten stone wet through, he was hardly a man to be reckoned with on a physical level. Although the scar on his temple and a permanent frown made him look unwittingly brave.

'I'll do my best,' said Alan, adopting a saunter as he followed Doc into a small, scruffy looking office where a short man in a shiny, grey suit sat smoking a small cigar while writing notes on paperwork.

He looked up and immediately put on a salesman's grin – all teeth and no lips. His eyes didn't match the flow of the smile which made him look as insincere as a nun in a sex shop.

'Got your eye on the Jag, have you boys?' said the man as she stood, reaching out his right hand, which Alan noticed was short of a little finger.

Doc ignored the invitation to shake which the man seemed to take no offence at – maybe, thought Alan, because many people do the same once they see his deformity.

'Maybe one of my boys can help,' he continued, pointing to the pavement area where a man with a black leather jacket was showing a customer how the convertible roof worked on a twelve year old Mercedes sports car. Another salesman, wearing a faded blue polo shirt and badly fitting Chinos, was leaning against a Land Rover while talking animatedly to a blonde woman and her young child, even though they were both clearly trying to get away from the 'perfect pitch' – the patter he gave every female in the hope they were gullible enough to believe it, and hand over cash for a car that was unlikely to work for more than two months after the expiry of the warranty offered with every vehicle.

'We've come with a message for you,' said Doc. 'It's from someone who isn't very happy with the way you are doing business.'

'Now, who might that be?' asked the man whose name, Alan had established from the pile of business cards on his desk, was Percy Virtue. He thought it was probably quite unsuitable but possibly had a subliminal effect on unsuspecting customers.

'Let's just say you don't need to know his name. Just the fact you won't be doing any more of your deals with the Valentine brothers or there will be consequences. You wouldn't want that would you?'

Alan hadn't heard of the Valentine brothers and didn't know what business they were in. He'd tried to find out a bit more but King's view is that the less people knew about what The Team was involved with, the less they could give away - accidentally, or otherwise.

'Now listen here,' said Percy as he drew on the last few drags of the cigar which had infused the office with a low level smog. 'We don't need any trouble, do we?'

He pulled a wad of notes out of his back pocket and started separating out a handful to offer Doc.

'I think we both understand that nothing more needs to be said. You just go back to your boss and tell him I wasn't in, or that everything has been satisfactorily discussed. How about that?'

Percy pushed the cash in Doc's direction and as he did so was met with a powerful kick to his lower leg. The cash dropped into a neat pile which Doc collected and put straight into his pocket.

Screaming and hopping around the office, Percy then went to pick up his phone which Doc swiped to the floor where it smashed into a number of pieces before emitting a dial tone from somewhere in its depths.

Alan looked around and spotted a wheel clamp resting on top of a large, metal filing cabinet. He picked it up and dropped it deliberately on the desk, sending Percy's pile of business cards flying in the air from where they floated and glided, like snowflakes, onto various parts of the carpet-tiled floor.

'There's no need for all of this,' said Percy. 'I'm not doing anyone any harm. Just doing a bit of business, like we're all trying to do,' he said, rubbing his leg and stubbing out the remains of his cigar into an already overloaded ashtray.

'I don't think you understand,' said Doc, nodding to Alan to pick up a heavy lorry jack he'd spotted in the corner of the office. 'We work for King and The Team. We choose what business with you, so if you value your life I suggest you think carefully about your early retirement or playing the game by our rules.'

Percy pulled out a mobile phone from his jacket pocket and Doc immediately kicked it out of his hands. He pushed the salesman against the plastic sheeting which posed as a window to the showroom and pulled out a small knife which he used to slowly and carefully draw blood from just behind Percy's ear. When it started to drip he caught a trickle on the blade and smeared it down his blue-striped shirt, rubbing the red into the front where it spread and stained instantly. Percy whimpered but was given no mercy.

'Sort the cars,' shouted Doc to Alan. 'You've got what it takes,' he added, nodding to the jack.

Alan took his cue and went out to the showroom. The man with the leather jacket had disappeared into a back area to show his customer more cars while the other one, with the ill-fitting trousers, couldn't be seen.

The BMW crumpled with the weight of the jack. The glass barely made a sound as the windscreen shattered, loosening the price tickets indicating that £3500 was a 'real bargain' considering it only had one careful owner. Alan wondered if there'd also been five or six not-so-careful owners as the bodywork was visibly dull from years of environmental erosion and the brake pedal was showing so much sign of wear that the rubber coating had virtually disappeared, leaving only a wedge-shaped lump of metal exposed for any driver hoping to be able to make the thing stop.

He took more pleasure hammering dents into the Land Rover which epitomised to Alan everything he hated about the middle classes in London. He recalled the times he'd watch mothers take their children less than half a mile to school, driving down the middle of the road and then parking where they felt like it before leaning over open doors for a chat to the other 'school-run mummies'. He often wondered why he'd get so angry because he wasn't even a driver; but for some reason he felt for every person on an important or necessary journey who'd have their day hampered by the 'Chelsea Tractors' and their owners, whose sense of entitlement overtook any instincts of consideration.

Alan was satisfied he'd done what he needed to do to look 'mean' and was also concerned he'd attracted a bit of attention from passers-by with his attack on the Land Rover. No-one had said anything but one old lady carrying two carrier bags laden with windfall apples muttered that he was a disgrace. She threw one of the apples at Alan but it missed and landed on the roof of a Golf GTi outside the kebab shop next door to the showroom. He went back into the office where Doc continued with Percy, nicking a few more cuts around his throat and neck for good measure.

'I hope you understand the message we've been sent to tell you?' he finally said, after enjoying himself a little too much for Alan's comfort.

'I think so,' said Percy. 'Could you put the knife away?' he stammered.

'Now now. Where are your manners?' said Doc. 'Did your mummy not teach you anything?' he added as he brought the tip of the knife to Percy's nose.

'I don't know what you mean. Let me go.'

'I think we need to remember the magic word, don't we?' said Doc.

Alan shifted on his feet. He was concerned at the amount of blood extracted from one small man, even recalling how a small amount can look like a body's full quota.

'We'd better get going,' he said to Doc, hoping to shake him out of his reverie.

'Please, please,' said Percy. 'Let me go. You'll hear no more about me. I promise.'

Doc lowered the knife and stepped back, placing it in an inside pocket. He smoothed over his jacket and patted his pockets.

'I think we have everything, comrade,' he said to Alan, who threw Percy a box of tissues that had been sitting on a table near the entrance to the office. 'Clean yourself up, it looks worse than it is.'

Doc up-ended the desk while Percy stood in the corner of his own office, blotting up trickles of blood that continued to run down his neck and onto his shirt. He looked nervously through the office window but neither of his staff could be seen.

Alan saw both of the other salesmen at the back entrance of the showroom, taking it in turns to look and see what was going on without offering to help.

'Not much of a team, are they?' Alan commented to Doc as they made their way back to their car.

'No, they don't seem to be. Thank goodness, because that made the visit easy -very easy indeed.'

When they got to King's flat to report their news for the day he was wearing Goose's apron, while she lay flat out on the settee covered in a quilt and watching a quiz programme at full volume.

'Hello boys,' she said joyfully when Doc and Alan came in to the lounge. 'Long time no see. I hope you've been keeping yourself out of trouble!' She laughed so loudly it reminded Alan of a documentary he'd seen about hyenas. The memories came back stronger when she lifted her head up from the cushion and her hair had shaped into a Mohican-style, with the longest bit leaning heavily forward in one sweep.

'How do you cook spaghetti?' asked King as he waved about a wooden spoon and looked sheepishly at the packet of pasta in his other hand.

'Just read the instructions,' said Goose impatiently.

'I can't,' said King. 'They're in Polish.'

CHAPTER TWENTY THREE

I've got quite a lot in common with Nelson Mandela. The obvious fact is that we've both spent a long time in prison.

What people don't often know about him was that he was brought up by someone other than his father - and that he was given a name he lived up to. I was called a thief and he was called Rolihlahla, which means 'troublemaker'. We must both have been influenced by what our elders thought of us.

On his first day at school he wore a pair of his father's trousers, far too big and cut off at the knee to make shorts. The difference between us there is that he was proud to be wearing cast offs and no-one noticed his poverty. He didn't seem to mind the fact his teacher decided to call him 'Nelson' for no reason other than it was easy to pronounce. I didn't really have that problem but was given other names.

I've read a bit about him, particularly after his death, which moved nations. The pictures that came out at his funeral were nothing short of bizarre. Obama's wife wasn't too happy with him, taking all those 'selfies' with Cameron and that attractive German politician. I notice she soon got him to swap seats so he wasn't so close to the blonde doodle-bug shell.

Then there was that signer for the deaf. He just made it up!

Proving that with enough gall or insensitivity you can get away with anything. It's like the Emperor's New Clothes. Walk around, with nothing, and as long as you have enough arrogance to believe you know better than anyone else you are on to a winner. I don't think the bloke was particularly arrogant though. We've all pretended to be able to sign after a few drinks. I tried it with Marie once on a train, after we'd been up town to see the Christmas lights. We'd got most of our carriage convinced until she gave the game away by answering her phone, which had made the gentlest of sounds inside her handbag.

Mandela started off as a pacifist, you know. Something else we have in common. He didn't take up arms until he decided to support a sabotage campaign against the government in the sixties. I didn't take them up until I thought I had no choice. I often think it would be so much better if I'd had an understandable reason for being a murderer, rather than gross stupidity and social incompetence. There's a big difference between being a criminal and a saint. I suppose it is to do with the quality of people you kill to reach your goals.

Of course he didn't get away with it forever – another connection between us. He was dressed in a chauffeur's outfit when he was finally arrested. He gave a good speech about being prepared to die and by all academic accounts it helped save his life. I've often said I'm prepared to die but all they do is send me off to the doc's for more happy pills and numerous appointments with various counsellors.

He was a principled man and maybe that's where our similarity ends. I would have probably negotiated a release on any terms but he refused, claiming that only free men can negotiate and I suppose he had a point.

'Anyone there?' says Brian, peering through the spyhole. 'Can I come in?'

I'm not sure when screws became so polite they asked permission to enter a cell. In the early days they'd barge in and shout regardless of the time of day or what you were doing.

'You still feeling sorry for yourself?' Brian adds, pushing through the door and leaning against the small cupboard in the corner of the room which housed the few belongings I could call my own – three pairs of pants, some socks, not necessarily in the same pairs they were intended, four books, a writing pad and a blunt pencil. I have to ask if I want it sharpened.

'Why don't you join the others for some exercise?' His eyebrows move upwards in a quizzical fashion, supposedly to indicate he's hoping for an answer. I ignore him as I always do when questioned about joining in the routine of prison life.

'That book,' I say. 'It's got some good stuff in it.'

'Ah, I hoped you would read it, ' says Brian. 'What did you think of it?'

I've been thinking about *To Kill A Mockingbird* ever since I'd read it. After thinking about Mandela and his name, meaning 'troublemaker' and my various names, including 'thief' or 'stinky' I re-read it to find the quote I was looking for.

"It's never an insult to be called what somebody thinks is a bad name. It just shows you how poor that person is, it doesn't hurt you."

Harper Lee was right about many things but wrong about the fact a name doesn't hurt you. I think it does. Who likes being called 'fat' or 'ugly' or 'stupid'? Those names really hurt, far worse than a beating or falling down the stairs.

'Yeah, it's good,' I say to Brian, not wanting to go any deeper into my thoughts.

'It reminds me of you,' he adds.

'What, the bit about being born good at getting progressively worse?' I say, remembering how that bit resonated with me. My first step-father would always call me a good boy, my mum did, too. I used to try and analyse where it all went wrong, or where I went all wrong. But I gave up after a few years inside. It just all goes round and round.

'No,' says Brian emphatically. 'I was thinking more that you deal with your fights with your head. You know violence isn't the answer to anything. You're a bright man, Alan. Not many inside have your brains or conscience. There's plenty of people here who know you're not a bad man.'

I think again of the book and agree that while those people are entitled to full respect for their opinions, I need to believe that for myself.

'The one thing that doesn't abide by majority rule is a person's conscience, I think is the quote,' I say to Brian. 'But thanks for the vote of confidence.'

'So, can I persuade you to come out and talk to someone for a bit? There's a new lad in for the first time. He might need some guidance from an old timer.'

I consider it. Can I really be bothered with someone who was starting a long sentence and going to have to live through the boring, banal and soul-destroying existence that makes up prison life? Do I tell him to watch his back, tell no-one anything and make sure you find out who you can trust before you let anyone into your space – particularly the space you occupy in your head, day in day out.

To quote Larkin, what are days for? He was right when he said: *"Days are where we live. They come, they wake us, time and time over."* Although it isn't just the days that wake us, it is the screws, or the screams of the troubled, or Operatic Ozzie with his latest rendition of *Nessun Dorma*.

Larkin was optimistic by suggesting that days are to be happy in, although where else can we live? It's about learning to exist in our minds without trying to solve any questions. Trying to, as the poet accurately explains, "brings the priest and the doctor in their long coats."

I agree to meet the new guy even though I'm not feeling up to it. My release has been drawing me to another world, despite the devastating news brought to me by Zara. It had changed my view of the future and left it bleak and empty. Like a TV screen when you haven't selected a channel, or a DVD that won't play.

His name is Charlie. He has a tattoo of a spider on his neck and the words 'Fuck' and 'Shag' etched onto his otherwise blue knuckles. Around twenty five years old he's already balding and is so thin his track suit bottoms rest loosely on the bones of his hips, allowing a space between his concave stomach and the waistband.

'Alright?'

As soon as he speaks he gets my back up. You don't speak unless spoken to when you are new. It's the prisoner's law. *This place will soon knock that out of him.* I think, consciously trying not to display my irritation.

'Charlie's going to be here for a while, Alan, so maybe you could show him the ropes?,' says Brian, adding: 'He's one of our better ones is Alan. But he's out soon so make the most of him, Charlie. He could teach you a lot to help make your time better.'

Brian walks away and leaves me with my new charge. I don't know where to start with him so take him to the games room, show him where the telly is and give him a few clues about how to cope.

On our way round the wing I see he's already a target for Dave the Axe, who has been looking for a new 'bitch' since Ron (known as Ron and On because he would never stop droning on about anything that came into his mind) got a bad case of piles and had to be hospitalised. Once he was out he had to use a particularly strong pessary cream every day which, according to Trevor, acted as the ideal barrier against any of Dave's advances.

'This is better than being at home,' says Charlie and I stop myself from making any judgements. There are certainly a number of elements which are a good deal better than the type of homes I knew. Maybe he'd had similar experiences.

We go through prison routines and I ask him where he's been before. It's his first long sentence and apart from a few short spells in youth institutions hasn't experienced the 'big boys' jail before.

My heart was about to go out to him when he spits on the floor in front of me. It's clearly a habit of the streets but he is mistaken in thinking he could bring it into the very private, and very intimate, lives of my fellow inmates.

'I suggest you clear that up,' I say, stopping and standing by the offending mucus, which I notice is -yellow and frothy suggesting not only a smoker but one with a long-term chest infection.

'Go fuck yerself,' Charlie answers. 'That's what the cleaners are for.'

At that point four prisoners advance towards us. They surround Charlie and push him around between them.

'Think you've got a personal cleaner, do you?' says Marty the Maths. He used to be an accountant but embezzled most of the funds from the residents of a home for the mentally ill.

'I think you should know that me and my friends are the cleaners here and we don't take kindly to anyone making our job any harder than it is. Get it?'

Charlie carries on with his bravado for a little while longer, although I sense he may have been told to hold his head high and stand his ground to make life comfortable.

I let the boys get on with whatever it they need to do and when I turn back to see what is happening, Charlie is licking up his own spit from the floor of the corridor while Marty and his friends hold him down with a combination of strong arm tactics and a boot to his back. I suspect there will be a new era of respect from the young man once he's had time to reflect on his approach.

Back in the cell I'm thankful for my time with King. He taught me enough about keeping my head down and my thoughts to myself.

CHAPTER TWENTY FOUR

Plans were underway for the big heist. King had given the matter a lot of thought since being stuck at home, looking after Goose.

She didn't require much in the way of attention but required him there for making cups of tea, constant bits of toast with jam or peanut butter and also helping her to the loo.

Six weeks it took to get her back and walking and by that time King had formulated every detail of his plan.

Once he was sure he'd put the final touches to the blueprint he called a meeting of The Team.

'I've thought of a hundred different scams,' he said. 'But this one's never been done before.'

King paused for effect before he announced The Team would be turning over a forensics van, on its way from a London police station, to an incinerator out of town.

'This van will contain hundreds of thousands of pounds worth of goods,' said King, being careful not to explain in too much detail what the goods would be, particularly in what he saw as his motivational speech to his employees. Also his mother was listening.

As if trying to be as conscientious as possible he added: 'These are valuable goods that the authorities think no-one should have. By my estimation more people want them than don't, and will pay top price for them – something in excess of one million pounds.

King paused for effect and smiled at the response. Alan gasped at the prospect of that sort of money and Doc snapped his fingers in front of his face. 'Yeah, man!' he said and jumped up from his chair. Tommy and Kevin looked similarly pleased.

'That's a lot of money, Julian,' said Goose, still reclining on the settee despite the removal of her plaster cast.

'What sort of things do the police throw away that are worth that amount?'

The Team members looked around and Alan frowned.

'Never you mind, mother,' said King as he passed round pieces of paper showing a route from south London to a place in Hertfordshire, marked with four crosses along the way.

'Doc, I need you and Alan to check out all these points for their viability. We need to establish likely traffic, stopping points, clearances, exit routes, access to B roads and plenty more.'

Doc shifted in the seat he'd just reclaimed and straightened his back. He looked over the map and ran his index finger along the markings King had made.

'Yo, this looks good,' he said, thumping Alan on the back hard enough to make him cough.

'So how do we know when we can do this?' asked Alan. 'Surely they'll have some kind of security with them?'

King moved to the centre of the room and wobbled his head slightly to suggest a superior knowledge.

'Let's just say I've been going to the sauna up the road lately. There are some very interesting people in there.'

He explained that he got a tip off about corrupt police officers meeting at a rundown health club two roads up from King's flat. They went there on the excuse of using the gym but would generally discuss what opportunities might arise through the privilege of their position. Three of them had been overly enthusiastic about the van, not because they thought they would be able to do anything with it but because no-one had ever tried to rob it before.

'It seems it is an open secret but in more than twenty years they've not had a sniff of trouble. By all accounts they are quite complacent now. They even let women drive it!' sniffed King.

Alan said: 'But they can't possibly take the same route every time? That would be security madness? And don't their vehicles have some kind of cameras or tracking devices so they can be monitored?'

Again King looked smug. 'That's the beauty of it my boys. Same route, same times and often the same drivers. It's gone so well for them for so long they don't even think about it. Even our local police think it would serve them right to get done.'

Goose lifted herself up from the settee onto her hands, holding her weight so she was in a half-sitting, half-lying position.

'Now you know what I've told you about women, Jules. We don't want you going around and frightening them.'

'Leave us be, mother. I know what I'm doing. Why don't you go and have a nap or something?'

Goose flopped back down and picked up a magazine, calling out clues when she couldn't answer the crossword questions.

'Twelve across. When the sun's up, time for robbery?' she said, laughing. 'That's appropriate isn't it?!'

Alan picked up his bit of paper and chewed his lip while he studied the markings King had placed.

'It all sounds too easy,' he said. 'There must be a catch somewhere.'

'Don't be so negative. We've someone on the inside prepared to play ball. He's been on the payroll a while and always gets a good share of our proceeds. He does well from us. He won't let us down. What could possibly go wrong?'

Well, we could get caught for a start, thought Alan, noting that he was due to be playing a major part in the heist. 'Daylight' he added.

'What?' said King.

'Daylight. The answer to the clue,' Alan said.

'Thanks babe,' said Goose, scribbling the answer into the grid.

'So what's this note about weapons?' Tommy asked, not having taking any part in discussions to that point. Kevin, also quiet, had been leaning back and watching King through screwed up eyes.

'You needn't worry about it. Only Doc and Alan will have guns. The rest of you will be support and getaway. I need some brains on this.'

'But that's a lacky's job, ' said Kevin. 'I'm usually the brains, not the back-up!'

'Aha, Kev. That is why you are now in charge of distribution. You will be responsible for making sure that whatever we gain from this job, we get to our customers as soon as possible.'

'We don't normally have such a high demand,' said Kevin.

'I think we will find the outlets soon enough,' King replied. 'Its not like we're selling a load of second hand shoes. This stuff will be good and there'll be plenty of it.'

'But a million's worth, King? That's a whole lot of hooch'

'Come on then, we're off! Four and two,' said Goose.

'Where are you off to?' said King, looking over to his mother with a vague look of disdain.

'Let's Go,' said Alan.

'Don't you bloody start,' said Doc. 'We've got enough going on with her,' nodding towards Goose.

'Respect for my mother, please,' said King. 'And hold your horses Alan, we've a few weeks planning yet.'

'No, let's go is the answer to the clue,' said Alan.

King sighed and resumed his directions for the heist.

'You two,' he said, pointing at Alan and Doc, 'will need to follow the van a couple of times so we're sure they take the same route each time. We can then organise the back-up and the transfer of the goods to other vehicles. Then if one gets caught we will still have other produce to sell on.'

'What do you mean if one gets caught?' said Kevin. 'If we're putting brains behind this then it shouldn't be an issue.'

'Just covering all eventualities Kev. It's better to be safe than sorry.

'Who's for tea?' said Goose. The room went quiet.

'Golfers,' said Alan.

'No, who's for tea?' Goose repeated.

'Yes, golfers. They use a tee.' Alan said.

'Oh, you're so funny Alan. I'm just asking if you want a cup of tea!'

Everyone laughed in a sudden and welcome air of levity.

'Oh, yes. I see. OK,' said Alan.

'Well put the kettle on. Don't just sit there!' said Goose as she plumped up her cushions and settled down to read her horoscope.

'Today things will go well with family and people will be around to tend to your needs. Enjoy the small things and take it easy,' she said, reading aloud.

'Best bring out the biscuits then,' she shouted out to Alan.

'You'll find some ginger snaps in the tin marked "drugs",' she added.

CHAPTER TWENTY FIVE

Why do people say such silly things without thinking about it? Like "better be safe than sorry". What does that mean?

I suppose the cliché means one should act cautiously in advance of any situation rather than have to apologise afterwards. But sometimes all you can do is say sorry -and being sorry is about meaning it. You should never ruin it with excuses or self-pity. A good apology can put right so many things, answer so many questions and superglue back that which has been broken.

I played a game with myself once. I used a Monopoly board and every time I landed on a yellow or green property it was time to think about something I'd done wrong and offer up an apology. I'd say sorry in my head to whoever I've hurt and every time I did so I hoped I'd one day pluck up courage to make a call or a visit – so I could make my apology happen for someone else.

I saw it all in my mind, where I would get them to understand what I did wrong or why I did what I did. Then if they forgave me I could move forward, collect my £200 for passing 'Go' and then everyone cheers.

I couldn't imagine what it would be like if I didn't get the forgiveness. It wasn't an option.

But then there's a twist. If I landed on a utility I'd call up a person who'd hurt me in the past. They would realise what they had done to me, what harm they'd caused and so say sorry and everything would be OK. Game Over. Get Out of Jail Free.

I only played the game once. I suppose that's like life. You get one chance to get things right. People say "there's always time" and of course they're right. There is time. I'm doing it right now.

There are other clichés like "Time Heals". But does it? Does it really? Ask a man who has lost his legs in a pointless war if he feels totally normal a few years after getting used to his prosthetics. Does he say all is well and he can hardly remember having his limbs blown off with a device that could only be devised by the sickest minds on earth? I don't think so.

It was Rose Kennedy who said she didn't agree with the sentiment either. She said that the wounds remain, adding: '*In time, the mind, protecting its sanity, covers them with scar tissue and the pain lessens. But it is never gone.*'

You can hear people giving advice to those who have just lost their husband, wife or kid. We get comments here all the time; well-meaning people suggesting that all you have to do is sit back and wait and eventually all the sadness, guilt, anger, wanting and fear will just drift out of your life like tumbleweed across a desert.

Trevor went to a bereavement support group last year. It was three years after his Dad died. He wasn't allowed out to the funeral which upset him more than anything. He only went to the group once. He said he was embarrassed that that he was still crying so far on, when there were other people who'd just heard their children had died -one from a car accident, the other through a stab wound inflicted by a stranger in a pub.

'I'm stuck, Al,' he'd said to me one night after lights out. 'I can't see how time can get rid of this feeling. Time's done nothing for me. It's not my friend.'

Six months later he told me he'd sort of stopped thinking about his father and how he'd let him down. Whether Trevor had taken on board some of the words of the bereavement counsellor or time had just slipped in and did what it needed to do, if a tad late, neither of us voiced an opinion. He never thanked time for the change in his disposition, though. He loved his father and missed him. If time could have done anything for him, it would have provided a couple of hours for them to be together and Trevor could have told him what he never got the chance to in life.

The other expression I hate is "better to have loved and lost than never to have loved at all," as whoever wrote it clearly had never been dumped by the one and only woman he'd ever met who could make him truly happy.

Tennyson may well have dreamily looked onto a field of poppies and remembered the tenderness of a wonderful relationship, shedding only a romantic tear to express his feelings of loss.

I look out on a corridor full of tobacco-smoking cons with dirty teeth and body odour and wonder where my dreams have gone. Up in smoke, or down the drain?

Maybe it was all just a case of easy-come, easy-go and other such clichés.

All I know is that life isn't what I'd hoped it would be.

'Hey, what you done with the new boy?' says Brian as he walks past my cell door. I've left it open so I can see the queue for the phone from my bed. Trev said to give him a call sometime and that is what I want to do, just as soon as I can.

'I think he's been taken care of,' I say, being careful not to give anything away about the 'care' being offered.

'Good work, Al. You're a star.'

The poor, misguided man. Brian thinks I've actually helped the lad feel comfortable. If anything the boy will now start to realise what he's in for. Not just twelve or so years for GBH, or whatever his crime is - it will be violence of some kind. He's not intelligent enough for fraud or perjury – but what his jail term will mean. It's not just a case of losing your freedom. In most cases you lose your dignity, in some cases you lose your mind. And occasionally people lose the will to live.

Outside, having a violent and sociopathic nature can mean you get exactly what you want, when you want it. It's all a bit different in here. The culture is very much survival of the fittest, but not the fittest in a physical sense. By the very nature of criminality the cons are likely to be maladjusted and therefore the people least likely to be able to cope with personalities so akin to their own. The boy will get taught a few hard lessons. Shame he didn't get them before it came to all this.

The phone is finally free so I count my call tokens to see if I've enough to call Trevor. He's given me his home number and every time I look at it I can see him sitting on his settee, wife at his side, drinking a cold beer or maybe just a cup of tea. Trevor told me he'd never been much of a drinker. He'd have two or three pints and either his bladder or his brain would give way and he couldn't cope with any more. Taunts of being a light-weight were wasted as being twenty-one stone and a former semi-professional boxer gave him a gravitas that most people respected. It was what got him into crime in the first place. Few were brave enough to say 'no' to him and so Trev became an obvious front man for a gang based in north London, at a time when his career had taken a nose dive because of a major head injury.

'Money just dried up,' he told me when we first got to know each other well enough to talk about why we were imprisoned in the first place.

'It started with small stuff, security and that. Then it escalated. I knew too much so if I tried to leave I wasn't allowed. They never actually threatened my family but suggested they would. The money was good, too. I was always going to leave after the next job, or at the next birthday. I didn't get a chance.'

We had a lot in common. Trevor and I often spoke about what we might have done. Maybe all cons protest that their intentions were otherwise but I think we both genuinely would have liked to have been good at something worthwhile.

'How's it going?' I say when I hear Trevor pick up the phone. It's so good to hear his voice even though he's only been gone a short while.

'Cushty, Al. Got my beer, dinner in the oven and the girls are coming over later.'

Trev loves his two girls. They are in their early twenties now but over the years were regular visitors, as children, to the prison. They weren't phased by his sentence, no doubt protected from harsh realities by his supportive and bordering-on-angelic wife.

In recent years they've both pursued careers in events management and design, encouraged from afar by their father who emphasised regularly how he didn't want them to end up like him. While they never uttered a word of judgement about Trevor, one assumes they didn't want to end up like him either.

I can't help but cry. I cover my eyes as Trevor talks about the job his brother-in-law had found for him and how his life is beginning again.

There's nothing I can see in my future that gives me the same hope. Not even the possibility of moving in with Trevor and his family while I get on my feet. That's his life, not mine.

'Hey, chin up, boy,' he says, hearing my snuffles over the phone. 'Don't let anyone see you like that. Not long and you'll be out, too.'

I wipe the snot on my sleeve and, keeping my face to the wall, to give my tears time to dry, I say my goodbyes.

Hearing all that hope has flattened me. Not that I don't want Trev to have it all, of course I do. But while his life shines, mine is in the shadows and the dark dog of despair descends and firmly places itself at the very place I hoped my own heart would soar and rise at the prospect of freedom.

Getting out doesn't seem such a great option. In fact it seems like the worst option of all.

CHAPTER TWENTY-SIX

The van stopped in a layby and its hazard warning lights went on. The driver, a plump woman of about thirty, got out and walked to the front of the vehicle.

She went back to the driver's door, pulled a handle to open the bonnet and went back to look at the engine. After a few seconds she scratched her head, kicked the front tyre and then climbed back into the van, leaving the bonnet open.

'What the fuck's she doing?' said Doc to Alan, who'd been holding the map King gave him and trying to identify where they were. 'We look bloody stupid stopping here,' he added.

Doc had parked his car – a stolen Vauxhall Zafira, chosen for the fact it was one of the most common vehicles on the road and not likely to stand out – less than one hundred metres behind the van they'd followed from the police station.

'Get out and pretend you're being sick,' said Doc.

Alan looked at Doc and didn't move.

'What do you mean, pretend I'm being sick? How do I do that?'

'Oh for Christ's sake, I'll do it,' said Doc, leaping from his driver's seat and making his way over to the side of the road. Bending over double with his face away from the van he made some convincing retching noises.

Just as Doc had stopped his play-acting, a passenger jumped out of the van. A younger woman than the first, wearing what looked like police uniform, looked around and spotted Doc by the side of the road.

As she started a slow walk towards their car Alan felt a wave of panic rush over his scalp, sending his nerves on edge. He wound down the window and called to Doc.

'Get back. She's coming,' he said as loudly as he could without shouting. He didn't want the police officer to hear.

Doc leant over to retch again, then stood up and wiped his mouth. Alan glared at him through the window, willing him to return to the car and get moving before they were both seen in broad daylight.

'Hi there, you OK?' said the young officer as she approached. She was blonde, petite and Alan thought she was very pretty for a policewoman. Most of the ones he'd had dealings with in the past were quite manly in their looks, which weren't helped by the unflattering trousers and flat shoes.

She handed over a small packet of tissues and a wrapped mint.

'Here, have these. Mints are really good for stomach upsets.'

Doc looked admiringly at the officer who was a good foot shorter than him. Alan turned away from the window and put his hand up against his face.

'Thank you. Must have been something I ate,' he said as he opened the mint and put it in his mouth. 'I feel much better now it's all up,'

'Good,' said the officer. 'I know what it's like – I'm ten weeks pregnant and am throwing up all the time!'

She laughed and was turning to walk away when Doc said: 'So where are you off to, then? Chasing after robbers?'

The officer smiled at him. 'No, just some routine police stuff. Because I'm up the duff I only get to do the boring jobs. We're nearly finished or would be if we could get the van to work properly!'

'Well you get to see a few motorways if nothing else!' said Doc, continuing his banter with an ease Alan couldn't understand.

'So is the other lady you are with a police officer, too?' he asked – at which point Alan thought Doc was being far too intrusive and possibly putting their task, to identify the route for their next job, in jeopardy.

'No she isn't. She's one of the security drivers. She does this run all the time. I'm here as support although I don't get to do much. It's just to have a uniform present in case anything goes wrong – which it has, although I'm not much use as a mechanic. We seem to be overheating so just getting some help.'

'Well, good luck with that,' said Doc. 'We're just off to see some family. Nice to meet you.'

The officer walked away slowly just as a recovery vehicle drove into the layby and parked between the Zafira and the van. Once confident the officer was out of earshot, Alan asked Doc what he thought he was doing.

'That was madness! What if they recognise you when we do the job?'

Doc raised his eyebrows to the roof and slowly looked around to meet Alan's stern gaze.

'She's just a constable and pregnant. Apart from the fact she's unlikely to be on this run when we show up, she probably can't even tie her own shoelaces. The other one is the driver. She didn't even bother to look at us.'

'So what do we do now?' said Alan, feeling a lump of phlegm settle in the back of his throat where it wouldn't budge. He coughed and made it worse.

'We sit tight. They won't worry about us now they've come over and said hello. Why would they think we're anything but ordinary people going about their business.'

Alan huffed and fidgeted in his seat. His jeans were itchy and a trail of sweat had started to form inside his knee.

'We can't follow a rescue vehicle,' he said. 'That really would make us look bloody stupid.'

Doc opened up the glove department and brought out a packet of cheese and pickle sandwiches and a can of coke.

'Let's share these while we watch what's going on. We're not far now. Just keep calm.'

By the time they'd got through half a sandwich each the recovery vehicle drove away from the van, which then pulled away into the line of traffic – seemingly repaired and roadworthy again.

'Looks like they're sorted,' said Doc, stuffing the remainder of his sandwich into his mouth. He went to speak again but Alan couldn't understand what he was saying.

'I don't know what on earth you are saying,' Alan told him.

Doc swallowed and then said: 'Let's get going. Mission nearly accomplished.'

Alan threw the rest of his sandwich out of the window, then

checked off the distance they'd already followed the van which was around forty miles. The final destination was expected to be within the next five to six miles – assuming the map was correct.

'What are we going to do when we get there? We can't follow them all the way?'

Doc breathed in deeply. 'We don't need to. We won't be following them all the way there on the job, will we?'

'No, I suppose not,' said Alan, thinking that he was unsure about what they would be doing anyway.

King had explained they needed to be sure of the van's route before any further plans were made. He'd given instructions for the two of them to make notes about the vehicle, its drivers and whether or not there seemed to be any support vehicles. They also noted where the van had stopped, which was at one service station where the driver came back with an armful of food and drink, and then again when it stopped in the layby.

Doc followed the van at a distance until it took a turning off the motorway.

'There, just as we thought,' he said, before speeding along a few more miles until he found a junction where he could turn round and head back to London.

'I think we've found the weak spot, anyway,' said Doc. 'That layby would make a perfect place to pull them over.'

Alan thought carefully about what Doc had said.

'There are a lot of people driving past a layby. Wouldn't we be better pulling them off after the junction, on a quiet road?'

'The job will be done so quick they won't know what's happened to them. And we'll be tooled up so people ain't gonna mess with us.'

Alan didn't feel so sure but refrained from expressing his concern. When the two of them got back to King's flat, Doc did all the talking.

'The job will be a doddle,' he said. 'Two women, pretty brainless. They won't put up a fight.'

King listened and then asked how and where they were going to pull them over.

Doc added: 'The layby's too obvious; too many people driving past. There are some small A roads off the motorway on the way to the final destination. I think somewhere along the St Hertford Road would be perfect.'

Alan looked incredulously at Doc. *He's pinched everything I said*, he thought.

'Good thinking Doc,' said King as he wiped round a mug with a tea-towel emblazoned with kittens.

'Do you agree, Al?' King said as he walked into the kitchen to place the mug in a cupboard, bringing another from the draining board to dry.

'Erm. Well the layby would be OK as we're going to be quick,' said Alan, casting a glare in the direction of Doc, who seemed to be deliberately avoiding his eye. 'But I guess the quieter option makes sense.'

'Well, in that case we need to sort the details. I'll call the boys to a meeting for seven tonight. Goose is out for the day and won't be back until late. I don't want her knowing what's going on. She won't like it if she sees the tools.'

Alan wanted to run from the flat and never come back. He kept getting a vision of the young, blonde officer and how scared she'd be at the sight of a gun. Not just for herself but the unborn baby. He calmed himself with the thought she'd probably had loads of training and that maybe she wouldn't be as scared as he thought.

Alan wanted to tell King how wrong he was to be doing what he was doing. What *they* were doing.

What the fuck am I doing with this lot? It could all go so wrong, he thought. They'd never mucked about with police business before.

'Now, Al. You are the main man in all of this. We're relying on you, and Doc of course. You won't let me down, will you?'

Alan felt something menacing about King's look. He knew what he was capable of and quickly agreed that he was up for the job.

'Yeah, sure. Just want to get it right,' said Alan, feeling faint at the prospect of being in the frontline of one of the biggest heists The Team had pulled off.

'Don't look so bloody glum, Al. This will make you your fortune,' said King, flicking the tea towel in Alan's face so the corner caught him in the eye, making it flicker and water. Tears ran down his cheek so Alan wiped them away with the back of his hand.

'Aww baby's having a little cry,' said King, pulling Alan over towards him in a mock sideways hug before slapping him on the back so hard it made him cough, finally releasing the phlegm that had settled in this throat from when they stopped behind the police van.

'Give Alan a lift home, would you Doc? Then I'll see you both here later. Don't be late.'

When Doc drew up outside Alan's house, he automatically

parked up and stopped the engine. Alan felt obliged to invite him inside.

'Beer?' he said, hoping Doc would decline. But he never declined and followed him through the front door and into a hallway strewn with children's toys.

'Where you been?' said Marie flying through the lounge doorway, holding Shane at arm's length. Even at a distance Alan could tell his nappy hadn't been changed for a while.

'Oh, you're here,' she said to Doc. 'I wish I'd known you were coming, I'd have got the house sorted.'

'You never bother for me,' said Alan, taking Shane and carrying him upstairs. 'Get Doc a beer while I change this one'.

Doc followed Marie into the kitchen and closed the door behind him.

'Have you told him yet?' he asked as she pulled the top from a beer with some difficulty before reaching into the fridge to pull out a half empty bottle of white wine. Pouring some into a glass – one of many she'd stolen from the local pub and so they had the measurement markets on the side – she said: 'Of course I bloody haven't. You think I'm mad?'

'You're going to have to at some point. You can't keep on pretending for the rest of your life. Is this how you want to be forever?'

Doc pulled Marie to him, spilling her wine down her front. She continued to drink from the glass as he undid her blouse to lick the wine from her breasts. She giggled and clutched his groin. At first she was gentle then as she heard Alan coming down the stairs with Shane, gripped harder until Doc gasped and let her go.

She was doing the buttons up on her blouse as Alan came into the kitchen. He looked quizzically at his wife.

'Just spilled some wine down me front,' she said, picking up a cloth and making a show of mopping herself up.

'Right,' said Alan. 'Do I get a beer, then?' he added, looking at the open bottle in front of Doc.

'Let me take the boy for you,' said Doc, pulling Shane away from Alan. 'Then you can sort yourself out with a drink, eh?'

'Thanks,' Alan said after some hesitation. 'Where's Shannon?' Alan asked.

'With Mum. They've gone to get their hair cut at Aunty Pat's.'

'So why hasn't Shane gone with them?' Alan asked, looking directly at Marie who avoided his gaze.

'Thought he'd like to see his Daddy,' she said as she turned her face away, making a show of drying off her blouse. Alan bit his lip.

Doc sat Shane on his lap and looked at the boy with admiration. Shane gurgled happily and reached for Doc's beer.

'A bit young for that, my lad,' said Doc. 'Daddy will teach you about beer when you're a bit older.'

Marie swung round from the sink where she'd gone to find a damp cloth.

'Yes, he will. Won't you Al?' she said, glaring at Doc.

Alan didn't say anything but went to the fridge and pulled out a beer for himself. He used his teeth to pull off the top, then grimaced. The metal ridges had caught the side of his mouth and he was bleeding.

Marie looked at the beads of blood appearing on her husband's lip.

Wipe your mouth before you make a mess,' she said, chucking him the cloth she'd just used to mop up the wine on her blouse.

'You in tonight? I need to go out for a bit?' she said looking at Doc who didn't respond as he was too busy playing with Shane.

'No. I've got work. We need to be back in the office by seven,' said Alan.

He always referred to King's flat as 'the office' in a bid to make his 'job' sound more realistic. He gave only the barest elements of information to his wife in the belief that the less she knew, the less she could talk about.

'What will you being doing that can't wait?' said Marie, visibly irritated.

'It's true,' said Doc. 'We've got a big job on. Lots to sort out.'

'Why do you always need to go out anyway? Why can't you just stay in with your kids like normal mothers?' asked Alan. He felt some strength at speaking out in the knowledge Marie would restrain her response in front of a visitor. He suspected he would get a mouthful when Doc was out of sight but felt it was worth the risk to have his say.

'You've no idea what it's like being a full time mum' Marie said.

'Neither do you,' Alan muttered.

'What's that supposed to mean? You're hardly ever here and when you are, you just put the kids in front of stupid films or read them stupid books. Why can't you take them for a burger like every other dad in the street?'

Alan looked at his wife and wondered if he could be bothered to reply. He was tired.

'I bring home plenty of money, don't I? If I didn't you wouldn't be able to afford to go out, anyway.'

Doc looked uncomfortable and stood up from his chair, placing Shane carefully on the floor in the corner of the kitchen. He started to cry.

'Now then, don't cry. Daddy soon have you feeling much better,' said Doc, looking directly at Marie who turned her face away and went to the fridge to fill up her glass with more wine.

'It's a good job you do, because you're useless at everything else,' said Marie, flouncing out of the kitchen into the lounge where the television got louder.

'Think I'd better go,' said Doc. 'I'll pick you up later'.

Once Doc had left, Alan's attempts at conversations were met with silence. He made himself and Shane a Spam sandwich and he went through the alphabet with him. Shane wasn't nearly as bright as Shannon at that age and had only managed to get to 'C'. It was the same with counting. Five was the maximum and that was with supreme concentration.

By the time Doc arrived to collect him, some three hours later, Marie still hadn't spoken to Alan and he didn't really care.

'I'm off, then,' he said on the way out of the house.

'Too right you are, tosser,' she said, loudly enough for him to hear.

CHAPTER TWENTY SEVEN

There was no defining moment, no point at which I knew my marriage was over. It was certainly well before I found out that Shane wasn't mine.

I knew deep down the boy wasn't of my blood but was happy to let it go. What difference does it make? I was brought up by men who weren't my father and one was OK at it. I knew I could do a better job. It wasn't the poor blighter's fault his mother's a whore. And I loved him.

Looking back I should have known we couldn't go on. It was the sinking feeling I got every time she came in through the door. The hoping she was going to be later home than she said. We occasionally tried talking about where we were, what we wanted. Or at least, I did.

Marie rarely responded. She'd just pull the quilt nearer to her side of the bed, making sure none of her skin touched mine, and then tell me she was too tired for talking. She was always too tired. But then she would be, being out most of the time. It wouldn't be from child-rearing as she always seemed to find someone else to do that.

'Why don't you just put up with what you've got,' she said on one occasion. 'Just stop trying to read more into things than there is. It gets on my nerves.'

I couldn't express myself at the time. It felt like she was holding back love and affection from me and that she was doing it to be cruel. Even when I told her I just wanted to be hugged or touched – like when we first met - she could barely do it and would just look at me with a contempt I felt was unreasonable. I brought home money, helped around the house, stayed in while she went out, didn't drink — and always tried to please.

None of it seemed to be enough. All I could feel were familiar feelings of rejection. I don't believe you should walk out on your family. I made a commitment and would have been happy to stick to it for the kids.

But how much daily rejection could I keep taking? I'd touch her softly on the shoulders or the back and she'd act like I wasn't there. She even came up with lots of reasons why she couldn't be affectionate – generally relating to something I did or said years before.

Once it was because I said blue shorts didn't suit her. Another time I'd upset her, she claimed, when I suggested she should do more with the kids rather than leaving them with other people all the time.

'They're your bloody kids, too,' she'd shouted. 'You do more with them if you care that much.'

Of course that was pure bravado as she must have known that Shane wasn't mine. Even if she couldn't be sure on dates, she could be pretty much certain on his build and colouring.

I thought it must all be my fault. Most things in my life are. I would go over and over where I'd gone wrong, blaming the lack of role models and poor self- esteem on my inability to make a woman happy.

I even learned to cook and every evening for months would try and make something for dinner as a surprise. When she did make it home before everything was ruined, she'd check out my offerings and then order a pizza anyway.

'You know I don't eat peppers,' she told me on one occasion after picking around in a spaghetti bolognaise.

She was happy enough with the peppers that turned up on her 'vegetarian feast' about half an hour later. I couldn't help but feel hurt to the core and vowed each day to care a little less.

It's easy to feel desperate when you're sad all the time. She didn't care I was sad. She was just hostile or angry. There were so many times she told me to 'pull myself together' or 'stop being such a miserable bastard.'

I tried to be happier, even though I wasn't. I'd take pills from the doctor to help me through the worst but there was always that underlying misery; the feeling that life could be so much better, but not for me. I'd been earmarked for the shitty end of the stick. A fact she managed to prove quite forcefully with some of her actions.

I asked her once why my toothbrush tasted funny and all the bristles were bent. She didn't tell me at first but after an argument said she'd used it to clean the toilet. That isn't love. It isn't even in character because she'd never cleaned the toilet before.

I can understand an affair, I suppose, although I haven't got the gumption for such deceit. I do, however, see how a man – or a woman – can be pushed into another's arms. Someone who thinks more of you than your partner does. Who finds you exciting and attractive and worthy of their time and energy.

It's a heady mixture and worthy of classification on the drugs scale. I've seen people survive addiction to heroin better than they have a heated, sexually-charged relationship. The consequences can be devastating not only to the individuals when the affair reaches its climax – apologies for the pun – but for all the connected outsiders who won't understand the veil of lunacy that has infiltrated their partners.

The excitement is alluring on so many levels and like so many occasions where pleasure is the only goal, the fall out is painful for more than just those immediately involved. The lovers will have injected life into the corpse of a passionless marriage while the cuckolds will feel a fatal blow to the integrity of everything they held true. Those who recover do so as walking wounded, diminished souls, while those who don't limp forward in mistrust and with a lack of forgiveness. There are no winners in affairs of the heart.

For me, the worry of all the lies and cheating would just bring me out in nervous ticks and a rash; even if I could find someone who would want me just for occasional sex.

When I hear about these men who cheat on a regular basis I wonder what it is they have about them? And how do they find the energy to chat up woman after woman, all to the same end? Doesn't it all get rather boring?

I suppose many men are programmed by their dicks and will do what it takes to get their next lay. When women are like that it surprises me although it shouldn't. My mother was happy enough to take on a team load of sexual partners. Even when it was for money she seemed to enjoy the whole process.

All I wanted was a cuddle; a hug, a kind word -the knowledge that someone was in your corner for the next fight.

Marie told me she was leaving me when I was on remand. It was a forgone conclusion I'd be going to jail but there were wide variations on what my lawyers thought I would get. It would all depend on whether or not the jury believed me.

If they did believe me, then I may have been looking at just a couple of years and would have been out on licence within months rather than years.

She didn't wait for the verdict. She came to see me the day before the sentencing to tell me she was leaving me and going to live with another man.

Without even blinking she mentioned in the same sentence that Shane wasn't mine and her life was now with his father.

'And he's going to take Shannon on as his as well, so once you're locked up you might as well forget us all. You're no good to us now.'

Marie didn't wait for a response or any pleas from me, although I'm not sure whether she would've got them.

I shouted out as she walked out of the visitor's room: 'So who's his father then?'

She didn't answer, but didn't need to.

I'd known all along.

CHAPTER TWENTY EIGHT

King's flat was bright. All the lights were on and he'd rigged up a spotlight above the kitchen table, where a number of pieces of paper were scattered – each with various drawings and notes in King's handwriting.

Tommy and Kevin were already in place when Doc and Alan arrived. King was wearing a suit and red brocade waistcoat, spats and a tie that just hung loosely around his neck, waiting expectantly for someone to fasten it in the accepted format. King paced around the tiled floor, holding either end of the tie and pulling it from one side of his neck to the other.

'Welcome, welcome' he said, in a manner that reminded Alan of an early visit to the circus on Mitcham Common. He was waving his arms at them to sit down and Alan half expected a herd of elephants and some mono-cycling clowns to appear from the larder.

King appeared to be in his element as the master of ceremonies. Alan noticed how different he was when his mother wasn't there.

'This is one of the most important weeks of our lives,' he said pompously, passing round the papers according to the instructions he'd written at the top.

'Once this job is over we'll be able to make a future for ourselves we've only imagined.'

He looked at each of them and Kevin, Tommy and Doc duly nodded. Alan kept his head down, studying the words he'd been given.

'Where are the tools?' said Doc, impatiently. 'We can't do this job without them.'

'Calm down, Doc,' said King. 'You'll get them in a bit. I need to be sure you know what we're all doing first off.'

King then explained how the job was going to be carried out, with Doc and Alan at the front and responsible for driving the van off the road and getting it unlocked. Kevin, King and Tommy would follow in three different vehicles, to pick up parts of the load and go off in different directions.

'We've got customers for two of the loads. I'll be taking mine straight to our friend Percy Virtue who will have a ready bag of money for us. It's amazing how helpful he has been recently,' said King, winking at Doc.

'Kevin and Tommy, you both have instructions of where you need to go. Don't hand anything over until you've got the cash. Then bring it back to me.'

Alan lifted his head to talk.

'Just wait your turn,' said King, who continued to give Kevin and Tommy their instructions as to what to do with the haul.

'But you're assuming this works,' said Alan, after waiting for a full minute to talk. 'It's one hell of a risk. What if the drivers are armed? What if they are being followed by police who see what's happened? What if we can't get into the van to get the goods?'

King's face dropped. He said nothing as he slowly walked over to a cupboard and pulled out a box. He lifted out two guns and pointed them, one at Alan's face and the other at his own head.

'Because, Alan, there's no room for mistakes or we're all dead. These little babies will make sure you get what you want,' he said, swinging round to the back door and pulling the trigger of one of the guns, firing a bullet through the door and shattering its glass.

Tommy and Kevin were cowering, Doc was grinning and Alan wondered what on earth he was involved with.

The bloke's gone mad,' he thought as he aimed to keep a cool countenance.

'You've done your homework. We know it's a woman who drives the van and the police don't take the job seriously enough to give her any decent back-up, other than a slightly pregnant junior officer. No-one outside The Filth know about the run or what the van contains. It's the easiest job in the world.'

Doc stood up.

'Let's have a look at one of the guns,' he said, lunging over to grab a weapon from King's hand.

'Absolutely not,' said King. 'These are lethal in the wrong company. Alan can have his on Tuesday and I'm keeping the other as security.'

Doc looked disappointed but cheered up as King went into further detail about the operation. Vehicles had been sorted for them all, apart from Alan.

'As the non-driver I'm putting you up front, Al. The success or failure of this project is down to you.'

Alan felt the familiar lump of phlegm reach the back of his

throat again. He knew it was pointless trying to swallow it. This time it could choke him.

'Well, we are The Team, aren't we?' said Alan, trying to dilute the effects of fear.

'You're a bright chap. Your quick thinking will make sure this happens for us and we'll be right behind you,' said King.

Alan found it difficult to sleep for the next few nights. He was pleased Doc stayed away from his house in the run-up to the job because he didn't want any slips in conversation to give the game away to Marie. She wasn't particularly suspicious as she didn't care that much about Alan's work, or how he made a living. But Alan knew she could have a loose mouth and little concern for the consequence of her thoughtless actions.

She did ask on a couple of occasions why he was so twitchy in the night and told him to sleep on the sofa. He did, not to obey her orders, but more to occupy his thoughts with books. They were the only constant in his life and the one thing that could help him escape from reality. Only he was finding that the more he read, the more he identified with the stories.

He'd picked up Sophocle's *Oedipus Rex* when shopping with the kids. It was in a charity shop for 10p and he reckoned it was a waste to see such a tome have such little value. Like others bought kittens or puppies to ensure they had a good home, Alan would rescue unloved paperbacks, promising to read them all as soon as he had a chance.

Reading this particular book was difficult, although there was a glossary of the more difficult words at the back.

Alan went over and over the prospect of the play where, in

ignorance, a king kills his father and marries his mother. He thought of King and Goose and whether that was the background to their own strangely complicated but unthreatening relationship – and thought also of the prospect of marrying his own mother. He hadn't seen her for years and didn't particularly want to, wondering if he'd even recognise her if she walked past him in the street.

The thought of his mother made him depressed so he put on the video of *The Shawshank Redemption*. There was something about the story that eased his mind, although he was never sure what. Maybe it was just the fact that the guy who was wrongly accused finally got his justice and made it to paradise. Either that or it was just a damned good film.

By the time the day of the job came, Alan was tired and listless. Sleepless nights had robbed him of the rest required for a calm mind and he was jittery. Black circles underlined his bloodshot eyes and his skin was pale and spotty.

'Jees, you look like shit,' said Doc when he came in through the door.

'Thanks. That makes me feel a whole lot better,' said Alan.

'You ready, then?'

Alan put on a dark anorak over his cable knit jumper and jeans and wrapped a scarf around his face.

'Will that do?' he asked Doc who was half hidden behind the large hood on his coat and a large pair of dark glasses.

'You got no shades?' said Doc, pointing upwards to his own.

'It's November. Not really sunglass weather?'

Doc sighed and pulled out another pair from his inside pocket.

'They ain't for the sun, you dick. No-one will see you if you're wearing these.'

Alan put them on and took them immediately off.

'And I won't see anyone at all, they're so dark.'

'Probably a good thing,' Doc said. 'Just put them on.'

Marie came down the stairs in her dressing gown, with Shannon following at her heels.

'Mummy, can I have pancakes for breakfast?' she asked with a slight lisp. Alan's heart swelled at the cuteness of his daughter.

'No you bloody can't,' Marie snapped and immediately the little girl's face crumpled.

Alan fired a fierce look at his wife and told Shannon he'd make her some pancakes as soon as he got home from work.

'Work, my arse. You don't know the meaning of the word.'

'Where's the boy?' asked Doc, diffusing the situation before Alan had a chance to engage in a full scale argument.

'Upstairs, playing with his toy gun and pretending to shoot people. Can't think where he gets that from,' said Marie.

Alan's chest rose and he took a deep breath.

'I don't shoot people.'

'Sure you don't. Yet.'

Alan couldn't understand Marie's sudden intuition although guessed she may have had information from a source other than himself.

'Come on Doc, King will be waiting for us,' said Alan. 'Goodbye my sweet,' he added sarcastically. 'Don't wait up.'

'Don't worry, I won't,' said Marie, dragging a crestfallen Shannon into the kitchen. 'You can have some toast.'

Alan and Doc drove off in the latest acquisition for The Team – a BMW sports car with enough acceleration to make Alan's head lurch backwards as Doc revved his way out of the estate road.

'Got some poke, hasn't it?' said Doc, reaching in to the inside of the door and handing over a gun to Alan as if it were a bag of sweets. 'Just like this little beauty'

'Christ. Is this thing loaded?' said Alan.

'Yup. So there's no messing with us today,' Doc laughed.

Alan felt the bile rising and mixing with a taste not unlike vomit. His throat closed and his heart sent pulses of electricity down both arms, rendering his hands numb. He could barely hold the cold, metal weapon without shaking.

'You've used one of these before, haven't you?' asked Doc.

Alan's mind went blank. The thought of any kind of violence unsettled him. King's punishments were bad enough but at least the victims had a high likelihood of easy recovery. A gun was something different. He thought of a hard, speeding bullet, shaped for easy entrance into flesh, flying its way round his blood and organs, destroying every bit of life support in a few seconds; wiping out everything valuable with no thought to its own power.

'Yeah, sure,' said Alan, tucking the gun into his waistband.

It's too late now, anyway.

Alan removed the gun then inspected it as Doc drove to their destination point – a petrol station a few miles away from the slip road onto the motorway. By the time they reached the roadside restaurant, he reckoned he'd pretty much understood how the thing worked.

King was dressed more demurely for the occasion, with an

oversized Crombie-style overcoat and slip on black shoes. He wore dark trousers and a white shirt with no obvious sign of disguise until he lifted the collar of his coat, which covered most of his face.

'Kevin has already called in to HQ with the message,' said King, explaining that Goose was on standby – in her capacity as The Team's Company Secretary – to take all calls co-ordinating the job. She thought it was a delivery project for some of King's "business contacts".

'The bird has flown the nest,' he added, which translated as the van had left the station in south London and was on its way to the incinerator plant.

'That means it should pass Tommy's look out in about forty minutes. He'll call in to say that the delivery has been confirmed, and then we can head out to the layby in good time to catch them.'

King went over the plan again. Both Kevin and Tommy would follow the van once they caught sight of it. They'd keep a distance until they got to where they'd planned to carry out the heist.

'Doc, you'll park up in the road in front of us. Once the van is close by, Kevin and Tommy will block it off with their vehicles and push it off the road. Then you go in.'

Alan's head was in turmoil. The thought of the pregnant officer filled him with dread. *What if the hold-up caused a miscarriage? That would be an unborn life they'd have on their conscience,* he thought.

'Alan. You are in charge of making sure we get them to open the doors. The sooner they do so, the sooner we take off with the goods and get the cash for them.'

King nodded to the gun.

'If you need to give it to them, give it to them, OK?'

Alan wasn't sure what King meant. Why would he want to give anyone else the gun? He didn't want to go any further, his intuition was telling him he shouldn't go any further but his body gestured his approval - and with a slight movement of his head his fate had been sealed. The weight of the gun felt too much. Not physically but metaphorically.

There wasn't much time to lose once King picked up the final message. They were all on their way to the point of no return.

'Put your glasses on,' said Doc as they followed Tommy and Kevin's cars which were both keeping a reasonable distance from the large, white and unmarked van that Alan recognised from their fact-finding missions.

Doc and Alan were both quiet as they turned off the motorway. Kevin and Tommy's cars were both in front and King was driving a few hundred feet behind.

'I'll find you. Don't worry if you lose sight of me,' said King. 'I'll know what's going on.'

The road was much quieter and, apart from the occasional car coming the other way, there wasn't much to be seen. All vehicles bunched together as they were stopped at traffic lights. Kevin and Tommy both waved at Doc and Alan.

'Stupid fucking idiots, what are they doing?' said Alan. 'Talk about attracting attention to themselves.'

'Don't worry about them,' said Doc. 'No-one will notice them.'

When the lights changed, Doc held back allowing the other cars to take their positions behind the van which seemed to be stalling.

Three miles before the agreed point, the van pulled out to the side of the road by a verge, black smoke billowing out of the bonnet.

The same driver jumped out of the front and went to have a look before looking around and trying to hail down Kevin in his yellow Ford Mondeo.

'Now what do we do?' said Alan.

Doc seemed distracted for a moment and then revved the car and raced forward to the scene, waving at Tommy to join them.

Kevin's car stopped in front of the van and Tommy's to the side. Doc pulled up around one hundred feet behind all of them.

'Now get out and do what you need to do,' shouted Doc.

Alan couldn't move. He was staring at the scene in front of him, his thoughts foggy with indecision. Sweat poured down the underside of his arms. He couldn't think what possessed him to wear a jumper for something like this.

'GET THE FUCK OUT!' screamed Doc, getting out of the car and going to the passenger side where he pulled Alan from his seat and pushed him forward.

'You've got the fucking gun, now use it! And keep those glasses on, you arse hole!'

Alan pushed the sunglasses up his nose.

'I can't see anything,' he shouted back, panicking.

'You can see enough, now get on with it.'

Alan thought of King and what he'd do to him if he didn't act on orders. He ran as best he could to the van where the driver was trying to engage Kevin and Tommy in conversation. King was nowhere to be seen.

'Open up the van,' Alan shouted, although it came out more as a high pitched cry. He pulled the gun from his waistband and started to wave it about at the driver.

'Hey, I don't want any trouble,' she said. 'Please just leave me out of this.'

The passenger door on the van opened and Alan was relieved to note that it wasn't the pregnant police officer who came out, but a small male officer with his hands up.

'Open up the van,' Alan shouted again. 'Then no-one will get hurt.'

'We can't,' said the police officer, his voice shaking. Alan wondered if he was a new recruit, or a special constable. He looked young.

Kevin and Tommy walked to the back of the van and pulled at the doors. An alarm started blasting out which pierced through the air. A BT van drove past and the driver looked out of his window at the scene. Tommy waved him on and raised his hand to suggest there was nothing wrong, while Alan hid the gun behind his back.

'You must have keys,' said Kevin to the woman, in a calm and collected voice.

'We don't,' said the woman who repeatedly looked around at the young officer who would just nod back to her, not uttering a word.

'I don't even know what's in there,' she added. 'It's all part of the security. I drive a dozen vans a week, all with different things going to different places.'

'You don't need to know what's in there,' said Kevin as the sound of distant police cars rumbled through the motorway bridge.

'Did you call them, you idoit?' called out Alan, visibly getting more and more frustrated that the job wasn't going as smoothly as everyone had planned. It didn't help that he could barely see who was who, and at one point mistook Kevin for the driver.

He moved to a position where he was standing to the back of the van holding the gun in both hands.

What the fuck do I do with this thing? They aren't taking any notice of it, Alan thought.

Doc came up behind Alan and pushed him forward.

'He's got a gun and isn't frightened of using it. Get the fucking van open you stupid bitch,' he said. 'And you can stop whimpering, or you'll be the first to get a hole in your head,' he directed at the officer.

The driver walked slowly to the van doors, her hands in the air. She was crying.

'I've been doing this job for twenty two years and not so much as had road rage, let alone anything like this.'

The sound of the police sirens got louder and as they did so, Kevin, Tommy and Doc started to run around the van. Doc pulled out a crow bar and hit the officer in the legs, sufficiently hard to force him to the ground. He then forced open the van doors and pulled out various boxes in different colours, labelled up as 'cannabis resin' or 'crack cocaine'. Some were marked up 'Ket' and others ' heroin'.

The sound of the sirens was behind them and police cars could be seen on the bridge road above them.

'Fuck, they're onto us,' said Kevin. 'We need to get outta here.'

Kevin and Tommy loaded their cars as quickly as they could, passing each other boxes and throwing them into the back and passenger seats. Doc joined them and had brought the BMW close to the van. When the sound of the sirens got too loud for comfort, Kevin and Tommy jumped in the drivers' seats and sped off.

Doc was still loading up while Alan was stuck in one position.

He was looking over at the police officer, still on the ground and not visibly breathing.

Jesus Christ, what have we done?, he thought.

Within seconds an armed response unit had pulled up. Only one officer got out of his car and stood behind it, calling at Alan with a loudspeaker.

'Put your gun down,' said the voice.

Alan froze and looked around him.

Who are all these people? He thought. *If they're here for me it's all a bit of overkill.*

He wanted to laugh.

'You have ten seconds to put the gun down,' repeated the voice.

'Fuck them', said Doc. He'd been hiding behind the open back door of the car and couldn't be seen by the response unit.

'Why don't you give me the gun?' said the van driver, whose composure had returned on arrival of the police.

'Come on, then no-one gets hurt.'

'Shut up you stupid bitch,' said Doc from behind his cover. 'You on a death wish or something?'

The driver ignored Doc and started to walk towards Alan. At the same time the loudspeaker urged him to give up his gun, which Alan was turning around in his hand. He caught his coat sleeve on the safety catch as he tried to remove his finger from the trigger.

'Just give it to the stupid cow!' screamed Doc. 'You know the deal!'

Alan couldn't see through his glasses to unhook the gun. He tugged at the sleeve at the same time as trying to throw the weapon to the floor. As he did so he fell backwards from the blast. He looked up and as he did so, saw what he could only describe as a slow motion movie following a bullet as it flew in a straight line and straight towards the van driver's head.

Before she fell to the floor Alan felt intense heat to the bottom of his leg. He didn't feel the pain of where he'd been shot until three police officers had him pinned to the floor, handcuffed and under arrest.

He didn't hear their words as he tried to tell them it was a mistake, that he'd got his finger caught, before passing out.

CHAPTER TWENTY NINE

I'd been in custody for two days when the Crown Prosecution Service added 'murder' to the list of offences.

My brief told me. None of the coppers had anything to say although they'd plenty to do the night I was told – mainly involving bruising where it wouldn't show.

'Your victim passed away overnight,' said the duty lawyer in a monotone. He seemed bored by my very existence and incapable of enthusing me with any feeling I'd get a fair trial. I couldn't afford anyone else.

'The statements from all witnesses give very strong evidence towards a cold blooded killing' he added – giving me little chance to defend myself.

'I suggest you plead guilty and hope for the lightest sentence they feel like giving you.'

I told him I'd got my sleeve caught, that I'd every intention of passing the gun to the police but he looked bored at my protestations of innocence. I suppose he's heard them all before and will do so again, from the very many people who can't keep their lives along the confines of socially acceptable behaviour.

He wrote a few notes and told me he'd see what he could do in terms of putting together mitigating circumstances. He didn't sound too hopeful and I thought I could hear the sound of the key to my cell being thrown away.

The lawyer, dressed in a pinstripe suit that shouted out his profession as if it were a uniform, told me the name of the driver was Julie Gill. She was forty three years old, divorced with two daughters; one at University and another still living at home, studying for 'A' levels. He seemed to enjoy giving me the information as if every detail was as personal to me as it was to my victim.

He was right if that was the case. All I could think about was the poor girl being alone, waiting for her mother to come back from work. Then being told some bastard – that bastard being me – had blown her life away. The crushing sense of inevitability has never left, the fact that one simple action – one that should never have happened and was not intended – rippled out to destroy so many people.

I wanted to go and speak to her, to beg her forgiveness, but was told it wouldn't be possible.

'I expect you are the last person they want to hear from,' he replied when I asked if it could just try and explain that it was an accident. That if I could do anything in the world it would be to turn the clock back and change the outcome. Failing that I would happily exchange my life for hers, which was obviously worth more than the miserable existence I was looking forward to.

That was then. Now there's something called 'restorative justice' where offenders get a chance to apologise to their victims before being sentenced. If I'd had that chance then at least they'd know I didn't mean it -that I was sorry, more than sorry; devastated beyond belief, in fact.

Some politicians think such a process is nothing more than a sideshow but I don't agree. Some bloke called Lord McNally almost got it right when he said people want to see a more central role for the victim. I'm sure Julie's family would say the same, they'd want her to be seen and heard, take centre stage. They must want to say something to my face– even if it's how much they hate me and want me to die a horrible death.

There's also the matter of how much prison costs. It's very expensive I know. Just think of all the food, lodging, heating, health benefits and clothing. Not to mention the various services such as psychiatry and counselling. It's almost a privilege to be here. It beats living on street corners or begging a living by working horrendous hours in horrendous jobs.

No wonder so many people re-offend. You can hear people question why the same prisoners keep ending back in court, often for small offences of theft or causing affray. What they don't realise is these people are in a system and because of it are institutionalised. They've been given stability, routine and a roof over their heads for possibly the first time in their lives. They don't want to leave that comfort and when released into society will do what they can to get back. Often they will steal a few cans of beer or swear at a policeman but when that fails to get them the custodial sentence they crave they will move up the sentencing ladder and commit a crime more likely to get them locked up. They don't care about the victims, they don't even register in their minds when planning the next socially unacceptable action. The focus will be on the outcome, not what they are doing to someone else.

Brian told me not so long ago that a prisoner called 'Bags' – on account of the amount of money they found stuffed into carrier bags throughout the entire living space of his camper van – faced up to one of his victims as part of his early release programme.

'He said it was one of the worst and most difficult things he'd ever had to do, even worse than identifying his brother after his motorbike accident,' Brian said.

'But he said it was like a moment of truth when he came face to face with what he'd done.'

He'd attacked a woman in her own home. He knew she was in and had targeted the house having seen her come back from a night out. She was on her own and all he could think of was getting a conviction for aggravated burglary – which would come with the prison sentence he craved.

She came out of her bathroom, undressed, to find Bags rifling through her jewellery box with the lights on and a knife in his hand. She screamed and to make the crime more realistic he pushed her down on the bed and threatened rape, unzipping his fly to make the scene more realistic.

Bags didn't want to hurt her but caught her with the knife, drawing blood and causing her to scream in such a primal fashion he was scared. He left her in such a state he knew she would call the police and then hovered around outside in the full knowledge he would be picked up as a suspect.

'Facing her again really stopped him in his tracks, it did,' said Brian who added he'd been Bags' liaison officer at the time.

'Within a matter of days he became a different person. He's lost the haunted, jaded look and has a sense of reason about him. He wants to do something to help his victim's family, prove that his life isn't a total waste of time. It was only because he was made to see things from someone else's point of view that his attitude pivoted. He'd never thought of it before.'

I may be cynical but it might have been helped by the fact the victim had received a whacking great pay out from the Criminal Injuries Compensation Scheme following the event.

She'd been given over ten thousand pounds for a scar that ran from the back of her ear and along the back of her neck, where Bags had caught the knife in the panic. She's grown her hair since the attack to cover the now faded red mark, and is planning to spend the money on a boob job – something she couldn't afford on her wages as a filing clerk. By all accounts she was thrilled with the compensation and after sorting out her feelings with the help of the restorative justice team, told Bags she believed everything happens for a reason and he wasn't to worry about what he'd done to her. She stopped short of thanking him but said that without him, her dreams wouldn't be able to come true.

I'm not sure Julie Gill's family will think the same. I don't suppose they'll pop in to see me one day and say: 'Oh it was great losing Mum. We got her house and all the furniture so never have to pay a mortgage or buy her any birthday presents and, thanks to the life insurance, we can have a good time.'

I'd still like to say sorry, though. I don't want them to think of me as a total bastard, someone who is languishing in jail without a thought for what happened, or how people have been affected.

I don't want to be thought of in the same category as someone like that Ian Brady. Nothing would make him repent and he has no care at all about the mental torture he's inflicted on innocent and otherwise ordinary people.

I read his book, *Gates of Janus*, and hate the fact we could be judged for the same crime. Murder is a powerful word but not all murders are the same.

Brady said he didn't think it would make any difference if he apologised to the parents of the kids he killed. He wrote: *'You contain me till death in a concrete box that measures eight by ten and expect public confessions of remorse as well? Remorse is a purely personal matter, not a circus performance.'*

Well, remorse is a personal matter but so are the feelings of those whose lives he's destroyed. He doesn't know what they were thinking when they heard or what it did to them. Or how other murderers, like me, feel about their crimes. I wouldn't hide the burial place of a child from their grieving parent. He did and I despise him for it.

It makes me think about Shannon and Shane. What would I do if they were taken by this horrendous devil of a man? What would I want him to say to make it better?

I don't think any apology would be enough so maybe he does know more than we think. There are some things you just can't say sorry for. But surely trying is better than not?

It's getting nearer my release date and I don't believe my freedom should be allowed. Julie will never return. She doesn't do fourteen years dead and then come back to life – like I've done with a jail sentence.

I've taken a life and I should give up mine in repentence. That's what Julie's family will think. It's what they should think, as I deserve nothing else.

I need to go and see someone in a day or so about getting somewhere to live, finding a job. Trev said I can stay with him but the authorities don't approve of putting cons back together on the outside. Not on an official basis anyway.

So I'll get a list of hostels and access to benefits to pay for them. I'll be told to sign on for work and will probably get someone to help me get a job, maybe in a supermarket or building roads. There's probably even a support group in case I find it all a bit difficult and need help finding a way of living a free life.

It all seems very wrong to me.

CHAPTER THIRTY

Alan woke up to see a police officer waiting by his bed and his leg in a plaster cast, suspended from ropes attached to a pulley system.

A door crashed open and a small woman wearing overalls and a hat not dissimilar to a shower cap pushed a trolley into the ward.

'Tea Mr Shoesmith?' she said. 'And how about for your visitor?'

'I'm not sure he's exactly what you'd call a visitor,' said Alan, trying to pull his weight up onto his arms but finding it impossible as the ropes slackened and tightened on his legs, pulling him around like one of those puppets you can buy on Blackpool Pier.

He half expected to find a piece of string hanging between his legs that he could pull, causing both his legs to shoot upwards towards his shoulders in one movement.

'Well, he ain't a patient,' said the lady in the overalls. 'So he's a visitor.'

'Point taken,' said the officer who took the offer of a cup of tea, in one of those pale green cups with embossed stripes around the top, refusing sugar but accepting milk.

'Same for you, duck?' she asked, handing over a similar offering with shaky hands.

Once she'd moved on, ignoring the old man in the corner, the officer told Alan he needed to ask a few more questions.

'We'll be holding you on remand as soon as the doctor gives us the all clear to move you. It's a superficial wound so no reason you need to be kept here for much longer,' he said.

Alan winced. It didn't feel like a superficial wound. The pain brought him back to reality quickly and as it did so, brought immediate memories of the job – and the shooting of the van driver.

'Is the driver OK? Is she badly hurt? I didn't mean to do it,' he said. 'It was an accident.'

'Yes, of course it was,' said the officer as he sighed quietly. 'I suppose you are going to tell me how sorry you are and that if you could just have one more chance you'll never do it again'

But I won't, thought Alan. *I didn't mean to do it in the first place.*

As he re-lived the last few moments of the job, before he was arrested, Alan's mind went into a spin. He couldn't deal with the facts of what had happened. It felt like a dream, like an instant moment in his life that had the impact of a million years of badness. *How can one stupid moment make such a difference to so many people?*

'We need to know where the others are,' said the officer as he leaned in to look directly into Alan's eyes. They were wide open and blinking furiously as if he were trying to blot out the vision before him.

'What others?' said Alan, genuinely wondering what the policeman was talking about. He'd forgotten everything about Doc, Tommy, Kevin and King.

As the officer continued to ask questions, Alan felt himself going into what felt like a trance. He could hear the words but they didn't make any sense. He remembered Doc shouting at him and Kevin and Tommy making off with whatever they'd got from the van. He couldn't remember seeing King anywhere.

'We don't want to play silly buggers, do we? If you can just give us their names and likely whereabouts then we can pick them up and they'll be able to take their share of the blame for what has happened.'

A hundred thoughts raced into Alan's brain at once. *Where are they? What has happened to them? They promised to keep me safe.*

'I don't know their names," he replied, remembering King's constant mantra that they were all in the job together and whatever happened, everyone would be OK.

'I think you do, young man,' the officer said in a voice that reminded him very much of his first telling off at school.

'I promise you, I don't. We met in a pub and agreed to do the job. I just went along for the ride,' said Alan, running through any ideas he might have on how to get hold of King and make sure he'd take care of Marie and the kids while he got out of the mess he found himself in.

'So you just pick up a gun from any old stranger and go about shooting innocent women with it, do you?'

Alan paused. He knew that wasn't the case but had to protect The Team. They may well have all been arrested by now.

'Have you found any of the others?' he asked.

The officer sat back in his hard, plastic chair. It bent too much for his weight and he had to steady himself.

'If we had, I wouldn't be asking you for their names would I?

Now, let's just get this done and then we can all get on with our day, can't we?'

Alan wasn't sure he wanted to get on with his day. He'd shot someone, been involved in a major robbery involving drugs and police, and now they'd shot him in the leg.

'If I had their names, I'd give them to you. But I only know their nicknames.'

The officer pounced on the snippet of possible information.

'So, what are the nicknames, then?'

Alan thought back to his schooldays, in a bid to find credible names to lend to The Team members. He remembered Parsley, called because his mother would make him eat the herb to ward off bad breath. Then there was Donkey, on account of his visibly large penis; Black Belt because of his success at karate and Mundy, just because that was his surname.

He repeated them all to the policeman, without the explanations, and he seemed satisfied they were genuine.

'Any idea where they would be now? What pub did you meet them in?'

Alan gave the name of a run-down bar in Shoreditch, the sort of place a group of would-be robbers would meet to plan a job anonymously.

Feeling some confidence that he'd gained the officer's attention he went into some detail about how they'd met after a football match, that they agreed to meet every Tuesday for three weeks to plan their job – and that it was all master-minded by Black Belt who'd had information passed to him by some police contacts.

'I don't believe for a minute that is true,' said the officer, his face reddening at Alan's suggestion that his colleagues might have to take some of the rap for the incident he was investigating.

'Well, it seems it was,' said Alan, gaining composure and resolve as his belief in The Team's loyalty rose within him.

The officer got up and as he did so used one of the ropes attached to Alan's leg for leverage. Alan yelped.

'So sorry,' said the officer sarcastically. 'Bet you'll be glad to get rid of that?'

He left the ward without saying anything else and Alan was left alone with his thoughts. He wanted to call Goose to see if there were any messages but couldn't see a way of getting his leg out of the contraption it was in – and he was aware that any contact should really be avoided.

'Any pain?' said the doctor who'd come into the room just as the police officer had left.

'Not pain as such, just throbbing.'

The doctor smiled. 'All quite normal. You are free to go. I'll call security.'

Within minutes Alan's wrists had been tied together with a pair of sparkling new handcuffs and he was pushed down into a wheelchair by a prison guard.

'I think I need a change of clothes,' said Alan, who noticed his trousers had been cut off him so he was only wearing his pants and a shirt. The guard ignored him as he used Alan's plastered leg as a battering ram to get out of the ward.

'And would you mind not doing that, it hurts,' he added as his leg bashed into a set of double doors on the way out to the ramp into the car park.

When the van arrived at Wandsworth prison another officer took over, having requested that Alan be released from the cuffs.

'Get yourself up and put these on,' said the officer, throwing a package of clothing in Alan's direction. He also handed him a set of crutches. 'You've got an interview in forty minutes.'

Alan balanced on his one good leg and leaned forward onto the crutches that were about three inches too short for his height. He watched as his possessions, the few he had, were taken from his old clothing and packed into a sealed plastic container. The officer concentrated on writing Alan's name, slowly, on the label attached to it.

'Take him through,' he then said to a female colleague.

'Cell 15 for you,' she said and marched quickly through the prison's corridors, followed by the clattering of Alan's crutches as he tried to master walking at the same pace with one good leg and two pieces of metal he had yet to become familiar with.

'What you been up to then, boy?' said a short, ginger man leaning against the door of Alan's new home.

Alan knew more than to tell him. It's a con's rule never to give any information away you don't need to, or doesn't have a value somewhere.

'This and that,' said Alan. 'Bit of armed robbery and stuff,' he added, thinking it might add a bit more gravitas to his presence.

The warder snorted.

'A bit more than that,' she said, looking at Alan directly for the first time since she'd set eyes on him. 'You'll be in for a while longer than most.'

Alan looked puzzled. He'd not come across any judgement from the authorities before. They would take him in, look after him and allow him to do his time.

'What do you mean?' he asked her.

'You really have got some cheek, haven't you?' she answered, lowering her head and keeping quiet as another warder walked towards them.

Alan was shown into his cell and told to wait until called for his interview. The room had been made up for a new prisoner. Folded blankets and sheets, a new bar of soap and a clean white towel with the prison motif stitched into the corner. Alan knew it would only be a short time before the towel would be grey with washing, scragging at the corners, and the soap would be collecting pieces of brown stain and sticking to the side of his sink, leaving a congealed ring.

He sat and looked around. One of his crutches struck the bare metal of the bunk beds and made a sound that was almost musical. He noted the light weight of the walking sticks and looking inside them, from the top, he saw they were hollow.

Any heavier and they'd be a weapon, he thought.

Alan found a way to sit on the bed so his leg could rest on the one chair in the cell. He'd just moved his crutches to a leaning position against the bedside table when a slim man wearing a short sleeved uniform shirt leant into the door.

'Alan Shoesmith I presume?'

'That's right,' said Alan, trying to shift up. As he did so, the warder came to his assistance.

'Brian Phillips,' he said. 'Although some call me Bony. Not quite sure why!' he laughed as he jokingly jabbed Alan with his elbows.

'I think I know why,' said Alan wanting to rub his ribs where

Brian's bones had made themselves known, but not being able to on account he was using one hand to balance while the other was contained under Brian's armpit. Alan didn't want to complain as he was trying to help. He was also the friendliest person he'd come across for some time.

'Come with me young man. It seems there are a few people wanting your company.'

One of the police officers from the hospital was sat behind a desk in an interview room. There were three others, two standing by the door. Only one was in uniform.

'Take a seat, Mr Shoesmith,' said the officer behind the desk. 'I'm Detective Inspector Carson and this,' he added, pointing to a plain clothed female,' is Detective Constable Petrie.'

Alan didn't say anything as he lowered himself into a seat. A man in a badly fitting suit sat next to him.

'You have a right to legal representation and so we've taken the liberty of inviting our duty solicitor, Mr Lawless, to join us. Are you happy with this or do you have your own lawyer?'

Detective Inspector Carson glared at Alan as he looked at Mr Lawless, not considering him for his legal ability but for the look of cynical disaffection he thought he displayed. The irony of his name didn't go unnoticed.

'That's fine,' said Alan. 'Whatever it takes to get this sorted.'

A deep sigh echoed round the room.

'You don't seem to be taking your situation very seriously, Mr Shoesmith.'

Alan looked around the room at the people considering him and felt a knot tighten close to the top of his throat. His stomach clenched and he was glad no-one had offered him any food that day.

'I am, sir. I didn't mean to cause any harm and I'm sorry I hurt someone.'

The detective stood up and as he did so swung his face into Alan's, spitting as he shouted.

'Any harm? Hurt someone? Do you not realise you have shot a woman?'

The blood in Alan's head drained below his eyes. What were his thoughts were replaced with vapours of horror, strangulated by fear and enveloped by every terror he'd endured either as a child or an adult.

'You are going to be charged with some very serious offences. Do you understand?'

Alan couldn't get any breath into his lungs. Spirals of heat whirred around his chest and he tried to stand up. As he did so one of the officers standing near the door came from behind him and pushed him down.

'Stay where you are!' shouted DI Carson. 'We haven't finished with you yet.'

As he described the injuries that led to the driver's death, Alan started to sob.

'I didn't mean to do it. It was an accident,' he said in a whisper but the officer spoke louder to cover his protestations.

'The fact you willingly acted on instructions to, what was it your colleague said, "give it to her" makes you a calculated criminal. Your actions were not those of someone making a mistake,' the officer shouted.

Alan looked to the duty solicitor who was writing some notes, which when he looked over, couldn't help but notice included a reminder to call his mother and a doodle of women's breasts. There didn't seem much point in saying anything, despite his inner voice repeatedly telling him to explain what had happened, and make them realise he didn't mean it.

They've got me so wrong, he thought as they concluded an evaluation of what happened that was so different to his own he began to think he was party to a case of mistaken identity, or on some kind of parallel universe.

Their idea of what he did was so at odds with what he knew to be the truth that Alan was sickened by the injustice of their judgment. He baulked at being called a "calculating criminal" alongside other descriptions such as "a psychopath".

'I would rather kill myself than hurt someone else,' he muttered.

'I think a lot of people would agree with that sentiment,' said DI Carson. 'But it's a bit late now, chummy.'

As Alan lay staring at the walls of his cell he willed himself to die in his sleep; for his nightmare to be over. For justice to be brought by a higher force.

But he dare not sleep.

CHAPTER THIRTY ONE

I've had quite a few visitors recently. They're encouraged when you're due for release. Trev came in this morning. He looked well. He brought me some cigarettes and a really nice cake.

The screws didn't like it when I said thanks, very loudly, for the file. It's such an old joke there wasn't really any need to break the thing apart. There was icing everywhere so I'd no choice but to offer it round. I reckon the screws ate most of it.

Trevor showed me his tag. He has to wear it as part of being out. He's on some kind of curfew where he can only go out during the day and has to stay in after eight in the evening.

'I really don't mind, it's only for a few months' he said. 'I've got time to get to work and the wife and I just want to enjoy some time together in the evenings.' He winked as if I should understand how great that would be. I thought of Marie and our evenings which were rarely shared or enjoyed. If I was in, she wasn't - and vice versa.

I envy him the companionship. He can provide for his family, get to see them and just do what normal people do. I couldn't help but think of my prospects and compare options.

Trev had said I could stay with him but that was before he got out. He didn't say anything at the visit and I'm guessing his new life is so different from being in here that I'd just be a constant reminder of the past. That's fair enough. What right minded woman would want a murderous villain living with her when she's just got her husband back? One she likes as well.

Goose came in the other day too. She seems a bit lost without King even after all these years and has recently been taking me under her wing a bit. She said I could live with her but I don't think that's a good idea. I've got a very limited opinion of her son and wouldn't want it to come out when under her roof. Goose is a good woman but she produced a complete arse of a child, who turned into a worse arse of a man.

I did get a letter from Zara but I've put her out of my mind. She's getting married and that's that. All my dreams of starting a new life with an intelligent, caring and understanding woman – one who knew my demons and happily accepted them into her life – were shattered the day she told me her news. I never saw her as the marrying kind. I didn't even think we would ever get married as such but I did see her in my future. I wish her so much luck it hurts but I couldn't stand by and watch her with another man, however much she might love him.

Then I've had various liaison officers, rehabilitation people and do-gooders trying to sort out my next steps. They see it as their mission to put right all the nastiness of the world and in the absence of full-time jobs or a fulfilling life have turned to poking their nose into other people's business as a form of social contribution.

One volunteer, an ex-Sergeant Major from the army with a voice that sounded like he was putting it on, suggested I take up some 'strenuous exercise' and regular visits to church once I was released.

He'd also worked out what benefits I might receive and produced a spreadsheet with suggestions on how I might spend them.

There was nothing for fags but he'd slipped in six pounds a week for gym membership. I don't know how much time he's spent with people who are only just hanging on to hope with the last thread of the skin that has already fallen off their teeth, but that was the last straw and I had to tell him to fuck off. Don't these people get any training? Did he not work out that I might want to spend six pounds on a few pints of something that will numb the heavy weight of guilt sufficiently to see me through to the next day?

Sally the Sodding Social Worker has been quite conspicuous by her absence but I found out she'd been on a walking holiday in the Lake District. I have visions of her frog-marching her children around Windermere and Keswick, all dressed in the best brands of rambling clothing including Gor-Tex shoes and professional sticks for the grown-ups, which would end up at the back of their under stairs cupboard as soon as they got home. She'd insist on calling it "The Lakes" and telling them the place is famous not just for the water but also forests and mountains. But she wouldn't call them mountains, she would refer to them as "Fells" and would probably bang on about William Wordsworth and *Daffodils* and the kids would just be desperate to get back to the television, or in the case of her 'exceptionally brilliant' thirteen year old, wanking.

Because even when you're very clever and have practically perfect parents, you just have to play with yourself when you're a teenage boy because it's all there is.

I wouldn't mind being that age again, only with a different path. Maybe Sally the Sodding Social Worker has got it right. Her kids might think she's a pain but at least they have a good chance of getting a few things right.

I've been in here fourteen years and all mainly down to poor childhood guidance which led me to the point of bad luck that got me into the biggest trouble of my life. So say the lawyers anyway.

The plan was easy in principle. I was to walk up to the driver, wield the weapon and shoot a few light bulbs out of the van to frighten everyone a bit. I wasn't going to hurt anyone.

But that stupid sleeve got in the way. The bullet hit her straight between the eyes. She should have died instantly according to the coroner. But she didn't. She screamed and twitched her way to a painful and unnecessary death.

According to the Judge I'm a callous and calculating sociopath. He wouldn't listen to me when I tried to tell them what I was really doing and thinking – not the police version of events. My solicitor was as useful as a chocolate teapot, going on about my poor upbringing and lack of family support as if that would turn anyone into a murderer. I might be screwed up but I'm not cruel. I don't want anyone else to feel my pain.

The Judge also said I did nothing to assist my victim but how could I when I'd been shot and I was flaying about on the floor feeling my own life drift away. Not only that, I'd been handcuffed.

Anyway, what do you do when you find you've blasted someone's brains out? Scoop them back up and offer them a plaster?

I didn't mean to kill her it. It wasn't my fault. But I soon worked out using the word "accident" just pisses everyone off and I'm better off calling myself a murderer even though I can't get my head round it.

King was supposed to sort me out when I leave here. But he buggered off to Spain with the proceeds of the haul, although I have heard he had a heart attack three years ago after sampling some of the product himself and getting a cocaine habit. If he's still alive I don't think he's going to bother about me now. He hasn't so far and Goose says even she doesn't know where he is. I believe her too, because I'm pretty sure she'd have followed him to the ends of the earth if she had the address. As for the wife and kids- she fucked off with Doc and both my kids call him Dad. It's only right that Shane knows him as a father because of course that is who he is. Maybe one day Marie will tell Shannon who I am and my little girl will know she has a biological father who adores her. I adore Shane too but guess I'll never see him again. I doubt he even knows I exist and that's a blessing.

So it pays to be philosophical. Extended captivity has allowed me to see what life is all about - what's important. Or at least realise that everyone will be dead in a hundred years, so nothing really matters.

'Hey, Al. Want a telephone token?' says Big Dave. I suspect he's run out of fags and wants to do a swap. He never has anyone he wants to talk to, but neither do I.

'No, mate,' I say as cheerfully as possible in the hope he won't turn on me for not agreeing to his request. I hear a shuffle as he moves on and can't help but feel relieved.

I talked to Brian yesterday and he said something about me getting out and how it will be my last chance to get a life.

Last chance! Ha… that's rich coming from him. He's going home for his tea with his missus. He'll be home by 6.35, like every other working day, and will be watching the same old tripe that all the cons are watching. What makes him any different from us lot, other than he has a pensioned position in the public sector? For that he has to contribute most of his working day and the majority of his mortal soul. Me, on the other hand, isn't expected to have a soul and is considered of no value to society. So I get my days to myself. Who has the last chance I wonder?

I've got fifteen "A" levels and four degrees. I started off light with sociology and media studies and have moved on to marine biology and pure maths. There is no use for them, but at least I understand futility. They should do a degree in that.

It's a funny old place, prison. It doesn't really matter what happens on the outside because you aren't part of it. It's long term Bed and Breakfast with evening meal and lunch thrown in – plus a bit of entertainment and some male bonding. At the end of each day it is home.

Prison isn't what you think it is. It really isn't that bad… you can be whoever you want to be. You can even go to the gym and come out fitter than when you came in. You can even exercise your brain, talk to Jesus, play pool or get a drug habit. There are choices, lots of choices. I won't get those on the outside.

The real prison is internal; the voice of guilt, the shame of past actions and the impact on decent, loving people. You don't have to be locked up to be incarcerated. My prison is my mind, filled only with the "what if?" and the terrible knowledge we can't turn back time.

I can't imagine what I'll do. There will be people waiting for my release date. No-one who cares about me but people who think

I haven't done sufficient time – so will be there to make my life as hellish as I've made theirs.

People don't know what they are saying when they say don't waste your time. They really don't.

You see it is difficult going from the inside, out. No time to think. And everyone needs time to think. Time... to... think

CHAPTER THIRTY FOUR

'It seems he managed to form some kind of sharp edged implement using part of the wire found in the mattress,' said a doctor, leaning over Alan and placing his stethoscope back round his neck. 'BP's stabilised. He lost a fair amount of blood but the damage is mostly superficial.'

'I don't know how he managed to do it without anyone noticing. He's not been under obs for a long while and seemed pretty stable,' said Brian, who'd been in the ambulance with Alan after he was found slumped in his cell, his wrists cut into jagged pieces of flesh with rivulets of blood coagulating on the cold concrete.

'We'll never get the stain out of that floor,' said Brian to Alan as he showed signs of coming round. The doctor had left, believing he'd played his part stitching up the wounds. The rest was down to the psychologists.

'Shit,' said Alan, after looking around the room and focusing on his surroudings. 'I'm still bloody here.'

'Course you are mate,' said Brian. 'What do you think you were doing? Only a few more days to go and you'll be out. Free to do as you please.'

'That's the problem.' Alan said as he raised his eyes to the ceiling, awareness coming back to him and the pain of gouging lumps of his own skin away from his blood vessels starting to beat through his arms and up into his consciousness.

'There's nothing free about being let out of prison with nowhere to go, and a head full of dread, remorse and self-hate,' Alan said, willing a tear that was forming in his lower eyelid to go back to its source, and dry up for good. The last thing he wanted was emotion getting in the way of his plans.

Brian was just about to say something when a young man in a tweed jacket worn over jeans and a polo shirt burst into the private room.

'Hey, you Alan Shoesmith?' he asked.

'You shouldn't be in here,' said Brian. 'This is a private ward.'

The man blinked a couple of times, shook himself as if he'd walked in through the rain and then moved forward steadily – holding out his right hand to shake.

'John Reed,' he said, moving further forward, with his confidence gaining momentum. '*World Newspaper*. I understand Mr Shoesmith has attempted to take his own life, is that right?'

'I wouldn't go that far,' said Brian, aware he was treading on dangerous territory. By nature he was an optimistic fellow and hadn't any dealings with the press before. Instinctively he knew he had to be careful. 'We're not at liberty to give the media any information.'

Alan looked at the lad before him. He was shuffling with a notebook in his hand and a pen in the other. He looked a bit like a waiter at a cheap restaurant he used to go to with Marie when they first met. He half expected him to take his order for chicken and chips with curry sauce and a half pint of cola.

'The thing is, the sister of the woman you murdered wants to know if it's true,' said the young man, directing his conversation towards Alan.

'Please leave this room before I have to get you thrown out,' said Brian, standing up from his chair in a sweeping movement. As Brian reached his full height, it had an immediate impression on the reporter who visibly backed away and resumed his nervous demeanour.

'Leave him, Bony,' said Alan, stirring more as pain and lack of anaesthesia kicked in. 'He's only trying to do his job. Yes, I did try to take my life. But life being the bitch it is wouldn't let me.'

Alan slumped back against the pillows and winced. *Why can't I get anything right?* he thought, as his dark gloom spread like mercury through a thermometer, rising and pumping into his soul and physically dragging him down into a blackness he wanted to envelop him, take him away.

'Is there anything you might like to say to Mrs Gill's sister?' said John, backing his way from the room as Brian moved closer towards him.

'Time to go sunshine, you've seen and said enough for one day. Now scarper before things get messy,' added Brian.

'Tell her I'm sorry,' said Alan. 'That if there was anything I could do to change things then I would. But there isn't so she might as well just go on hating me as much as I hate myself.'

Brian pushed John through the door and Alan could hear more questions being fired his way but he was too tired to answer. He looked around the room in the hope of seeing some drugs he could take or some implements he could use that would do a better job of slicing his veins than a few pieces of thin mattress wire.

'Now, we don't want to be hearing any more of that,' said Brian as he came back into the ward and took his place in his chair again. 'You've done your time boy. You made a mistake. A bad one, I'll give you that. But a mistake all the same, so it's time you picked yourself up and got on with it.'

Alan didn't respond. He closed his eyes and tried to picture what Julie Gill might look like now. Fifteen years on, probably a grandmother, maybe retired. Enjoying the fruits of her labours, if only he hadn't killed her.

'Try telling that to her family. I've been inside but they've been as locked up as me. Locked up in their world without their mother, sister, lover, aunt, daughter – all those things she was. I get out, they don't.'

Alan was banging his head against his pillow half in frustration and half in pain as the hospital pyschologist came in.

'Hello Mr Shoesmith. How are you feeling now?' said the soft-voiced brunette with hair that curled around her face and almost into her nostrils. She pulled the stray fronds behind her ears which Alan noted weren't even – just one of them stuck out while the other lay completely flat against her head. He thought it odd and wanted to ask if she hadn't thought about having an operation to correct it.

'I'm Doctor Miller, from the psychology department. I need to undertake an initial assessment before we can release you' she said.

Alan laughed and then he laughed again. 'So you ask me a couple of questions, which I will know how to answer to get the response I require, and you will deem me fit to leave your care?'

Doctor Miller looked uncomfortable and dropped her head towards her notes which, as of yet, were empty.

'We just need to ascertain your levels of depression and likely risk to yourself,' she added. 'We are trying to look after you,' she added.

'Levels of depression? How many levels are there? The "I'm a bit pissed off so I'll have a drink" level, then the "My wife has slept with another man and had his child so I feel like killing him" level or the "I've taken an innocent person's life and I can't live with that fact any longer" level. Well, mix up all three and add a bit of total hopelessness and absolutely nothing to wake up for and you've just about got me sorted. Can I go now?' said Alan, sitting up as far as he could in bed without being able to use his wrists. He made a mental note of how weak his abdominals had become since stopping going to the gym.

'Come now,' said Brian, ever the bridge over troubled water. 'You're feeling a bit down but you'll be OK. You always are, aren't you mate?'

'Do you think you'll want to try something like this again?' said the Doctor, looking busily for some guidance on what questions might elicit a response deemed acceptable by the authorities. All she wanted to do was the minimum and get out. Qualified for just a few months she'd never dealt with murderers before, mainly post-partum mothers and a few Alzheimer's sufferers – and the usual weekend quota of teenager drinkers who have their stomach pumped because they don't know the difference between getting drunk, and getting close to death. The hospital is obliged to assess their mental health which is often dubious but beyond the capabilities of their staff - as resolution is more likely to involve parenting rather than medical skill. What started out as a career helping people with clinical and circumstantial depression resulted in patching up, throwing up and chucking out.

Alan looked at her with eyes that creased at the side. Brian wasn't sure if it was a sign of anger or whether Alan was amused by another example of what he would consider to be authority's interference in how he occupies his mind.

'Well I've learned from my mistakes,' said Alan, smiling at the doctor. She smiled back and looked relieved.

'I'd find myself something sharper next time so it does the job properly. Maybe get a knife or the side of a lighter. Plastic can be good for these things. I would probably pick a better time, like in the middle of the night when the warders aren't so likely to find me. Then of course I could always get hold of some drugs and really make sure I'm going to wipe myself out properly. But that takes effort and consideration, both of which go out of the window when you are on the top level of depression.'

There was a silence during which Alan smiled a wide, tight smile at this audience which now included a stunned Brian who stared at him with his mouth open.

Brian coughed. The doctor blushed. Alan asked if she would like to ask any more questions and she said no and ran from the room.

'Not sure that's going to help you get out of here as quickly as we hoped,' said Brian, sitting himself down again and picking up a copy of *Woman's Weekly* that had been left in the bedside cabinet.

Alan sighed and settled back into his pillow.

'I shouldn't have said all that really. Poor girl was only doing her job,' added Alan, pretending to go to sleep.

Brian raised his eyebrows and carried on reading about how to make knitted English Bull Dogs in a variety of colours and wondered at the extremes of life you could see in just five minutes.

Just as he was moving on to an article about a man who likes to dress up in clothes he steals from washing lines, a doctor appeared to discharge Alan.

'OK, you can take him back now,' he said. 'He's been cleared.'

Brian was surprised to hear this and considered that Alan's problems had been dismissed as physical on the basis that nothing could be done for his mental health – or that at least no-one was prepared to do anything.

After shoving a piece of paper in Brian's hand, the doctor left and Brian shook Alan to wake him up. For a moment Alan didn't know where he was.

'For a minute there I thought everything was going to be OK,' said Alan, shuffling off the bed.

'It will be. It will be,' said Brian, holding him up as he guided him through the hospital and to the car park where a van was waiting to take them back to prison.

'All will be fine, don't worry. I'm here with you.'

For the first time in his life Alan felt he could actually trust someone. And it wasn't himself.

CHAPTER THIRTY FIVE

You're a long time dead, that's for sure. That's another strange phrase that people use too much without thinking about it, and it certainly opens up an enticing world of justification.

Of course we will all be dead a lot longer than we'll be alive and the dead, to the best of my knowledge and belief, no longer enjoy the benefits, or the horrors, of life. There's some doubt about that and I wish I had the courage to believe in another world where everything is splendid and the sun shines on all who trust.

Personally I will hedge my bets on that idea. Then if it comes true all good and dandy, but if I wake up dead and find out there's nothing more, I won't be disappointed.

The message in this particular cliché is that we should spend all our money, eat ourselves into a diabetic coma, get liver disease and palsy from excessive amounts of drink, cheat throughout all relationships, walk out on any job you find a faff and shoot police drivers who get in the way of you and a fortune – all of which can be easily substituted for the first part of the phrase to end on the gloriously positive note "for you're a long time dead"!

It was a bummer waking up in that hospital. I wanted to get away from everything my life has become. While I'm doing time I feel that I'm at least being punished. But very soon I will walk free, but still be bound by the fact I have to face up to my demons, those demons being the family and friends of Julie Gill.

My dreams are haunted by her children and grandchildren, chasing me with a gun they're keen to fire into my heart to ensure my swift and definite death. They chant phrases about their desires for my destiny, where hell is just a preamble to a much nastier infinity of pain and remorse. When I wake from these nightmares there's not much that changes in terms of how I feel. But I don't deserve to have any feelings, do I?

Goose came to see me again. I think Brian asked her to come in after my 'episode', as the shrinks like to call it. She's the only person who bothers now and that's probably only because she thinks I'm a link with her son. She says he knows he can't come back but I don't see why not unless he's done more than I know about. I've taken the wrap for the murder – he got away with the spoils and the drugs. Knowing him he got greedy and went on to bigger things although she told me she didn't think he'd do that. But then she didn't know him too well considering he's her own flesh and blood.

One of Trevor's contacts reckoned he'd blown the head off a nightclub bouncer with a sawn off shotgun after he'd found King dealing drugs in a West End club. By all accounts King had lured him into a passage to hand over what he had - but pulled out the weapon and cold-bloodedly shot him at point blank range in the guts. The story goes that he walked back into the club and tried to dance with a woman who spotted lumps of the bouncer's flesh stuck to King's hair. She picked a piece off and screamed when the blood stained her fingers. King ran but hadn't taken account of the CCTV cameras. It's likely he would have been spotted by any diligent police officer – he had a long enough record after all – and his number would have been up. My guess is he had enough self-preservation and money to get out of the country and stay out.

Because of the concern about my mental health it seems there will be some discussion at management level about my release. Brian has told me it's likely I'll be sent to some kind of halfway house where I'll get help in dealing with the outside world.

I wonder if they will tell me how to work a mobile phone, or a DVD player? When I came in there were no such inventions.

I've been on a computer awareness course as part of my rehabilitation. According to the teacher, who looked about nine and a half years old but seemed to work his way around a keyboard like an Irish dancer on ice, everything is done through the internet now. Even dating, would you believe?

What's happened to the days when you pick up a phone and talk to someone, or pop to the shops and get some milk and bread? This new life means you don't ever have to go out because somewhere there's a delivery man who can bring you your heart's desire at the touch of a button.

I read something about that Tim Berners Lee bloke who invented the web. How can you invent something like that? The article said he didn't want to take responsibility for everything the web can do and I can't say I blame him. It looks like an opportunity for more crime, if you ask me. There's a few in here who could make hay with the things they can do behind closed doors. Not just the criminally minded but the perverted and dangerous. If I could speak to my daughter I'd tell her not to go near the thing.

Maybe I'll be able to find her if I, firstly, stay alive and secondly, stay out of prison long enough, although listening to the other cons I suspect that might not be possible. Many of the 're-offenders' have committed some completely inconsequential criminal act, and because of their history come back here like a shot. It seems the recidivist is the underclass cultural reality for many single men – and it would be easy to believe their lives have more or less ended forever.

From what these young lads say, the police half expect you to re-offend and so place bets on how long you'll be free. Not too bad for those with a caring family, the likes of Trevor and his sort, but for the rest of us it is the halfway house. I just hope there are some decent folk in the one being organised for me and then maybe I'll be on my way to being re-integrated to mainstream society. It would be a dream to do something of use. It would never make up for what I've done but some contribution would be something, although I'm not sure the real world rehabilitates ex-cons, it just consigns them to the bottom of all social lists. They are the pariahs, the undesirables. No wonder so many prefer to return to be within the comforts of prison life, with its familiar settings and routines. Many seek to re-offend because the outside world is too confusing and complex for their liking. Trying to start a new life, trying to find a mate, are almost impossible with a criminal record.

Brian suggested I could help get on in my outside life with the help of technology and even suggested I find myself a new wife online. I couldn't help but laugh as I could just see my profile: "Depressive ex-convict, having completed nearly fifteen years for murdering an innocent woman seeks another such innocent so he can destroy her life with his lack of prospectsneing a stra, morose personality and exceptionally poor decision making qualities. A sense of humour essential."

Of course I could lie. I could say I've been working away and all my family died in a monsoon; that I spent three years as a Buddhist to heal myself and now choose to live a simple life with no assets as a tribute to the greater power within us all. It would explain the poverty, lack of car, no job and general look of malnutrition. I suppose a few of the older, more desperate, women might just go for it for a while. It wouldn't last though. Everything I know about the last decade and a half has come to me third hand. Even the drunks and druggies would see through me eventually.

I need to convince those with my interests at heart, or so they claim, that I am looking forward to a future, from the inside out so to speak. I can't kill myself in here as I don't have the resources – I've already proved that - and there are too many people who want to make sure that suicide doesn't happen. Even though it would save a fortune in taxes and give vent to those who think a life should be for a life. For the purposes of my argument, I agree with them.

'Yes, I'm here,' I shout out to one of the warders calling me to my next session with the rehabilitation team. This one is about personal care and social integration. If they teach me about contraception and sexual safety again I think I'll scream. Even if I could find anyone who'd be in the slightest bit interested in shagging an old lag like me I reckon my get up and go has definitely gone southward. As for contraception they should just castrate me. People like me shouldn't be allowed to have children.

The thought of being allowed to live a life outside the confines of prison seems unwholesome. Set free to do what?

I will have the ability to control my own life and have free will. I can choose where I live, what I do, who I speak to and what I think. My freedom ensures I can live life as others do and take any opportunities presented to me. All while Julie Gill remains dead.

That, I think, is taking liberties.

CHAPTER THIRTY SIX

A handful of photographers huddled outside the prison gates while two young women and three young men, one of them the journalist John Reed, waited.

When Alan made his way outside they were the only people to meet him, although he'd hoped Trevor might be there. A probation officer he'd not met before was supposed to be there but had sent a message to say his train was delayed because of a body. Brian had told him with some disgust, as if the offender had deliberately put everyone to major inconvenience by daring to kill themselves on a busy Monday morning when people were trying to go about their business.

'Bloody selfish if you ask me,' he said, while fussing around and making sure all personal effects had been packed. 'Should make the families pay for the disruption out of their estate. Might make them think.'

Alan noted that those who've never suffered with any kind of mental illness, have no way of understanding how futile the world is when you are in the midst of total despair. Causing inconvenience is not an issue as other people and what they care about is totally irrelevant.

'I doubt the poor body, whoever he or she is, went out with the intention of causing anyone any problems,' said Alan as he looked around his cell with a mixture of peculiar feelings. He wanted to push Brian away, lock the door from the inside and stay there until something happened, although he wasn't sure what.

Alan looked around at the outside world that had been a strange place for so many years, then put his hand into the second-hand trousers he'd been given on release. The ones they'd kept from his first day inside were too small although strangely seemed to have come back into fashion. The docket to take the dole office was there along with a travel warrant. He carried a small bag with the very few belongings he took inside with him – and the copy of *To Kill A Mockingbird*, which Brian told Alan he could keep.

'What does it feel like to be free?' asked one of the women, shoving a microphone under Alan's mouth while the photographers snapped far more pictures than he deemed would be necessary for their needs. The lights flashed over and over and made Alan feel slightly nauseous.

The sun was rising in the sky and his eyes darted around and watered, finding it difficult to focus in this natural and all-pervading light. As he went to put his hand up to shield his eyes one of the female reporters jumped back and let out a slight noise, not unlike a woman in the last stage of the birth process. It was guttural and clearly not something she intended to do.

'I won't hurt you,' said Alan. 'I just want to get out of here,' as he heard the female reporter talking to camera about the 'notorious murderer of Julie Gill'. For a minute Alan wondered who she meant.

John Reed came forward and in the absence of a prison warder was more assertive in his questioning which was on similar grounds to when he saw Alan in hospital.

'Are you going to see the Gill family? Are you going to say sorry to their face?' he asked.

Alan flinched. He'd not thought of what he'd done for a few days as his focus was dealing with the Resettlement Team, the various interviews for jobs he knew he wouldn't get, the discussions about where to live on a temporary basis and how to sign up for the dole, medical support, adult education and so on. There was so much to take in and throughout the entire previous night he'd suffered a major panic attack about how he was going to cope. Like a baby in a cradle, his needs were met. Not with milk or cuddles but a large dose of valium which ensured the warders had a quiet night, even if Alan didn't.

His mind had been opening up doors to various possibilities, showing him show reels of potential disaster, each one more terrifying than the first. The pictures in his head were graphic and colourful, a life more dreadful than he could imagine. Women and children tore at his flesh, demanding it be sold by the pound to make up for his terrible wrongdoings; men with blades for teeth gnashed into his chest, eating out his heart and spitting the shreds into his mouth and forcing him to swallow. Crowds of onlookers cheered as his testicles were tied up with string that was then attached to the hooves of wild horses as they were whipped and shooed into gorse-filled fields. Still none of it sated the desire for their own delivery of justice.

'Let me be,' said Alan, feeling his legs weaken with the reality of coping on his own. 'I've nothing to say.'

Lights were still flashing around him when a man walked briskly up to him and showed him a card, indicating he was a member of the probation service.

'So sorry I'm late. Some selfish bastard threw himself in front of my train. We were stuck for two hours while they scraped bits of him up into plastic bags so we could get on.'

Alan thought how seamlessly life goes on even when despair drives a human being to an untimely and gruesome end, one from which they can never return. *He'll be a long time dead*, was all he could think as the probation officer pushed his way through the crowd and towards a café just a few strides from the prison entrance.

'Here, let's get a coffee and we can sort out what's what,' said the man who finally introduced himself as Jeff Sellers and handed Alan a card with his details including 'out of hours' emergency numbers. Alan wondered what constituted being within hours before settling himself down at a chair and looking around at the other customers of the café, wondering if his probation officer would buy him a proper breakfast.

'Think I'll have the muesli and some fruit,' said Jeff as he looked over the plastic menu which sported a large, dried, stain of tomato ketchup on one corner. 'And a super fruit smoothie.'

Alan had been looking at the sausage, bacon , egg, fried bread, beans and chips but wondered if he'd have to pay for it himself from the discharge allowance he'd been given – something less than fifty pounds. He wanted to save at least ten pounds to get drunk later and hoped it would be enough.

'Um. The same. Thanks,' said Alan, unsure what muesli might be. He was mightily disappointed when he forced his marginally repaired teeth to chew relentlessly through what he could only imagine was a concoction of carpenter's waste, rabbit droppings and the insides of a machine that makes holes in paper; all covered in something that smelled like baby puke.

'Lovely,' he said to Jeff who seemed to be enjoying his breakfast far too happily for any real man, in Alan's eyes.

'Right, let's get you sorted out with the next steps, shall we?'

Jeff scraped the dusty remains of his bowl and waved to a waitress to bring him a peppermint tea before he pulled out a notebook.

'You'll be staying in Streatham in a hostel near the station. You'll need to report to me once a week and we can see where we are getting with jobs and the like. Anything you need to know?'

Alan wanted to ask him the meaning of life, is there a benevolent God, does an afterlife exist, does he really like eating that stuff called muesli and what on earth possessed him to become a probation officer.

'No. I reckon I'll find my way around soon enough,' said Alan knowing full well that he hadn't a chance of finding his way around anything any time soon.'

'It's great you are so positive,' said Jeff as he asked for the bill and wiped his mouth on the paper napkin: unsuccessfully as he left the remains of a dried cranberry on his chin.

They were just getting up to leave when the door flew open and in rushed a short, spiky haired girl followed by a taller but equally spiky-haired girl, with bleached blond hair and enough metal through parts of her face to fill an entire jewellery box.

'Al… you're there! I thought I'd missed you,' said Zara, breathless and looking a little larger than normal.

Alan took a minute to compute the information in front of him.

He knew the face, knew the voice, the hair. He even recognised the strange feeling that the person talking cared about him, understood him.

'Aren't you going to say anything?' she asked as she came up close and grabbed Alan's hand. She stood on tiptoe to kiss him on the cheek but couldn't reach, particularly as Alan stood stock still as if in a competition to see who could stand in one position for as long as possible.

'This is Wendy, my wife. We're having a baby.'

Jeff gestured to the two women to sit down.

'We were just going but can I get you a cup of tea or something?' he said, looking towards Zara's swollen belly. 'When's it due?'

Zara slumped down on a seat and said she'd love a cup of 'builder's tea, nice and strong. Two sugars.'

So the world isn't that mad. People do still drink tea,' thought Alan, as Jeff went up to the till area to place the order. He was finding it difficult to process the rest of the detail of his encounter. Memory cells sprang into life and pieces of a long forgotten puzzle folded into each other and brought back a time when Zara was the love of his life.

'I've heard a lot about you,' said Wendy, pulling up the chair next to Alan's. Her long legs folded under her to leave sharply angled knees jutting forwards as she wrapped her booted feet around the chair legs.

'I thought you were getting married?' said Alan finally, after what could have been an awkward silence although no-one seemed to notice other than him.

'I *am* married, look' said Zara, extending her ring finger on her left hand to show a thin, silver band and a tattoo of a W above it.

'I mean properly married. To a man,' he said, looking at Wendy and frowning. 'If you're having a baby you should be marrying the father.'

Both the girls laughed and looked across each other, holding hands as they did so.

'Oh Alan, you've been inside too long! I told you about Wendy last time I came to see you. I said we were getting married.'

He thought back. He recalled the conversation. The devastation it caused when Zara had announced she was in love, that she was moving away and planning her wedding. That she wanted children and couldn't wait to start a family.

His world had fallen apart and every dream he'd had where he'd shared that life, where he was the provider and the gatherer, the protector, the lover and friend, shattered like a chandelier falling onto a granite floor. Alan had been picking up the shards of lost hope from that day, eliminating his fantasies and rubbing out the images he'd held so dear; those of Zara and him together forever. His 'Get Out of Jail' card and a final prize after a crap life.

'You didn't use names. Or genders,' he said, trying not to sound too petulant.

Jeff brought four teas and Alan was pleased to see they were all as Zara had ordered. He wondered at that point if the probation officer forced himself to eat and drink disgusting things by way of a deep rooted need for self- punishment. *Perhaps he's a Catholic*, Alan thought.

'Well, silly you for making assumptions,' said Wendy.

'I thought you knew I was gay. My dad reckons it's obvious, what with the short hair and my love of army clothing,' Zara said as she rubbed her pregnancy bloom in a clockwise motion with her small, wedding-ringed hand.

'I've never seen you in army clothing,' said Alan thinking that he'd never seen her in a dress either. But few of the women he knew wore dresses. Marie only ever wore leggings or pyjamas.

Jeff coughed and introduced himself, being carefully polite not to be obvious about his role as a probation officer.

'I'm Jeff - a friend of Alan's,' he said. 'How do you guys know each other?'

Alan flinched at the use of the word 'guys'. In his mind it barely worked for men but was wholly inappropriate for women. Plus it sounded far too imitation as if being said by someone who was trying to pretend to be at one with themselves, if only they knew who they were in the first place.

Zara looked at Alan and winked.

'We worked together for a while,' she said, 'before Al went to prison.'

Alan had wanted to ask the same question. Why was she here after all this time?

'I read about you in the papers,' Zara said, looking sideways at Jeff and then raising her eyebrows at Alan. She didn't want to give too much away.

'I've been in the papers?'

Jeff coughed. 'Did you not see the articles about you? I'm surprised you haven't been made aware, if only for your own safety.'

'Anyway, I was worried about you,' Zara continued. 'I found out you were due for release today and wanted to be there to meet you. But some twat threw themselves under a train so we were delayed.'

'We want to invite you to live with us,' said Wendy. 'To play a male role in our son's life,' she added.

Alan swiveled his head to face the woman who'd already changed every perception of his recent past and was about to change every perception of his future.

'Well, say something,' said Zara after a pause more pregnant than she was.

'What can I say when I don't know what you mean? I can't add anything?' said Alan, looking at first to Zara and then to Wendy. He stopped once to look at Jeff but couldn't fathom his role in this bizarre unveiling of opportunity.

'I've loved you from the day I met you,' said Zara. 'You know that. And if I wasn't gay I'd marry you tomorrow. I can't think of anyone better than you to help us bring a child up.'

Wendy leaned forward and touched Alan's knee. An act that nearly made him fall off his chair, so long it had been since anyone of any sexuality had touched him other than by accident or for medical reasons.

'Zara has told me so much about your life, what has happened and the injustice of it all. We want to help you start out again and we know that you will help us protect our son from all the things you know to be bad.'

Wendy went on to add that she had a good job as a computer game designer, it paid well plus Zara had been left some money so they could afford a deposit on a large house in Crystal Palace, near the triangle and close enough to parks for the baby and the train connections for commuting to London.

'We've three bedrooms so plenty of space. You can stay as long as you want,' said Wendy.

'Forever if you want,' added Zara.

'Well I think that beats anything the Resettlement Team can offer you,' said Jeff. 'We can sort out your probation for that area and any further support you might need.'

He couldn't help it, he had to let the tear drop. The one he'd been keeping dry and behind his eyes for as long as he could remember. From before he was beaten by Wanker, all through school and the bullying- and beyond the indignities of betrayal, failed suicide and crippling guilt.

'I might have to think about it,' he said, trying to maintain a sense of maturity. He couldn't accept that these people wanted him in their life and even though it formed part of his wildest dreams he knew he didn't deserve such luck.

'I'm not sure I can make a decision until I know what it means.'

'You take all the time you need,' said Zara, hanging on to her bump as she pushed herself up from the chair. 'Look, I've got you this,' she added as she pulled something out of her satchel. It was a mobile phone.

'It's got my number already in there so all you need is to press this,' she said as she showed him how to dial. 'You'll need this, too, it's the charger.'

Alan had seen the occasional mobile phone among the warders, social workers and lawyers but never possessed one. They'd not really been invented when he went inside. He looked at it as a biologist might inspect a new kind of bacteria.

'It won't bite you,' said Wendy. 'It's all quite safe!'

He pressed the button and Zara's phone rang. She automatically picked it up and answered, without thinking.

'Hello? Who is that?'

'It's me, idiot. Of course I'll come and live with you,' said Alan, salty bubbles of blue-tinged happiness rolling down his cheeks, stopping only to fight the stubble that still remained despite an early morning shave. 'Although there is one condition.'

Wendy looked nervously at her partner. 'What's that then?' she asked.

'I get to read him books of my choice and you won't mind.'

'It's a deal' said Zara, reaching across to hug Alan and then wincing. 'Jees,that hurt. It's the third pain since I've had that cup of tea,' she added.

'When's the baby due?' asked Jeff.

Zara winced again.

'Three days ago.'

CHAPTER THIRTY SEVEN

Birth is just the most amazing thing, although of course it is the first step towards death. Both are understandable and the essence of living, it is just the bit inbetween that is tricky.

I missed Shannon and Shane coming into the world and wished I'd been there - for Shannon, anyway. To see your own creation take its first howl isn't something that happens every day. I missed my chance first time round but have got a very close second best with Zara's baby.

It was difficult watching her in pain and it didn't help that Wendy was wailing in tune with Zara's cries, although I have to say she was amazingly calm about the fact something the size of a bowling ball was coming through a gap not much bigger than the diameter of a hosepipe. No wonder she bit Wendy's hand at the crucial point of no return.

But for all the blood and guts I wouldn't have missed it for the world, watching that baby's face appear— not unlike a Hieronymus Bosch picture – turning from a deep purple colour to a vibrant pink as soon as his lungs took in their first oxygen.

The little lad had just left the warmth and comfort of his first home, then got snared up in his own life force – the umbilical cord - so it was no wonder he was feeling a bit strangulated. The first breath was a big shock, you could see it in his eyes, and as he was pulled out of the cosy cavern where he'd lived in safety and comfort for nine months he let out a huge scream, mustering as much energy as his tiny body would allow.

I can't blame him for shitting all over the midwife the minute she picked him up. They're going to call him Freddie. I'd hoped for Alan but it isn't such a cool name and it could cause some confusion.

It was amazing to see him swaddled and suckling, naturally taking to the breast as nature intended. Marie wouldn't even consider it. Poor kids were put straight on the bottle. It all seems so wrong when you watch a baby routing for his mother, keen to take what her ducts are ready to deliver.

What sort of a world will envelop his life? There he is all new and shiny, having been born to two mothers, with a donor father, and an incompetent, fucked-up ex con as his father figure. Whatever my faults, I'm going to do my damned best to get it right.

It was a shock to find out that Zara's gay but once I processed the information it made me feel better, in a way. When she told me she was getting married I just assumed she'd found a decent bloke. One very different from me who could look after her, love her properly and provide a life that would keep her away from harm and poverty.

But to love another woman means I was never in the running. No man could get her, not the best man in the world, and so I have got something close to perfection with this arrangement. Wendy is a good partner. I don't really understand the whole 'scissor sister' act, which they had to explain (it all sounds very unsatisfactory to me but whatever turns you on – literally) but if it works for them and they are happy then they've come a lot further than many people in conventional marriages.

I'm surprised at what works and what doesn't when it comes to two people getting along. There are few people I've seen who would stand up as ideal examples and even if they do in public, probably have some dark secrets they hide behind their suburban closed doors.

Take Mr and Mrs Parsons who used to live near my parents. They were married in every public sense. They went to church together, he cut the grass every weekend in the summer and kept his car nice and clean. Three days after their Ruby wedding anniversary her sister turned up and confessed she'd been sleeping with Mr Parsons for over twenty years and couldn't live with the lie any more.

He denied it of course, but the sisters compared a few facts – some of which they wrote on a large sheet and posted on the roundabout near Crickley Hill roundabout – and ceremoniously threw his possessions onto the driveway for him to nervously collect over a period of three of four days. The sister moved in with Mrs Parsons and seemingly enjoyed more frivolity and humour than had ever been enjoyed openly by the married couple.

I want Freddie to understand love. To know he is loved and wanted and that people around him will give up their own lives for his benefit. His biological father doesn't want to know anything about him and that will be his loss. He's brought a life into the world that will carry his genetic make-up around with him, reproduce it if he is lucky and never be able to turn round and call anyone his father. Not in a real way.

They say blood is thicker than water but my water is thickening up nicely for this lad. He may never be able to call me his father but if he calls me 'Dad' that will be a total honour.

It all makes me think of my own children. Shannon will be grown up now and probably doesn't remember me. Shane was never mine in terms of blood but I still loved him. I still do but I know I have no choice but to move aside for Doc; if he's still there, of course.

I looked around when I first got out but Marie's moved, maybe with him or maybe not. He could have gone the same way as King although I heard he'd gone straight. With the amount of money he'd got from the raid on the drugs van he could afford to. That's if he avoided the temptation of doing more.

That's the criminal's downfall, greed. If you can do just one, big, job and get away with it you could probably live on the proceeds quietly and happily, pulling on the cash reserves when circumstances required. But few people are happy enough with their lot. If it was easy come, then they want more not realising that the 'easy go' part of that phrase is there for a reason.

I'd like to think I would have stopped if the job had gone to plan. If Julie Gill wasn't dead and I'd got my share of the profits. But I know that would have been unlikely. King would want more and I'd have to take part in it or face the consequences. If I hadn't have been caught he would have dumped me in it at some point, to save his own bacon. He might have escaped punishment and be living some bloated, expensive existence in a sunny country far away, but is he likely to be happy? Happiness, surely, has more to do with the achievement of small goals - of seeing your family happy and healthy. Bringing a new life into the world and knowing you'd do anything to keep it safe.

Ronnie Biggs, the train robber, couldn't even be there when his son was killed in a road accident. He'd been on the run for so long he had to leave behind everything – all the things that I'd consider far too precious to give up. How could he bear to sit in Rio knowing the mother of his child was weeping for their lost son? In the end he ran out of all the money he stole and had to live on nothing but his wits and notoriety. People called him a friend and he may well have been fun and generous but not exactly someone anyone could trust. He walked away from everyone who loved him, and for what?

I'd just like a job - one where I can make a difference. Where I can say 'I did that' and be proud of it. I don't care if it is sweeping the streets, picking up rubbish or wheeling people and things around hospitals. It beats going to bed at night worrying that sleep won't come because of all the shit in my head, visions of great wrongs and points in my life where I could have made a different decision. I know there's no going back but sometimes it helps to think there might be a way of putting things right.

If I could just find a way of doing something that was useful to someone else. I've been out for more than six weeks now and I know it sounds ungrateful but despite great things landing in my lap, everything seems easier in prison.

It's a hard world keeping on top of what's important. Freedom comes with some incredible responsibilities – often brought about by what other people hope you will become. In this case I've been trusted to be a friend, a father and a stable citizen.

I just hope I can live up to the expectation.

CHAPTER THIRTY EIGHT

'Can I ask who's calling?' said Wendy, having picked up the house phone while simultaneously rocking Freddie in her arms. He'd been suffering colic for six weeks, more or less since birth, and wouldn't settle.

'It's someone called Tessa Charlton on the phone for you, Al?' she said, placing the now quietened baby into a wicker basket on the floor next to the television in the front room. A tabby cat walked up and sniffed the milky breath of the baby, turning tail when Freddie started to cry again.

'Who the hell is Tessa Charlton?' asked Alan, picking up a dirty nappy from the dining room table and folding it into a small, pink, plastic bag designed to disguise the odour. Alan had considered reporting the company who made them under the trade descriptions act. 'God, these things just make the shit smell like shit covered in cheap perfume.'

He walked over to the phone and picked it up, holding his nose. He forgot to let go when he spoke.

'Heddo,' he said, releasing the grip on his nostrils as Wendy roared with laughter at him. 'Yes, it's Alan speaking.'

There was a silence and Alan's face frowned. He looked around the room for a piece of paper and a pen.

'Yes, I can write this down. Tuesday. 11am. OK.'

He put the phone down into its cradle and looked at it for a while, his eyebrows almost meeting in the middle.

'So, going to share?' said Wendy as Zara came yawning into the room, dishevelled with not quite enough sleep to satisfy her weary mind and body.

Alan jokingly waved the nappy sack under Zara's nose, which wrinkled automatically at the pungency.

'Eeugh, that's gross,' she said. 'I love him very much but Freddie can do some really stinky shits.'

'It seems I've got an interview,' Alan said.

'What for?' yawned Zara, as she slumped onto the settee, narrowly missing the various toys littered across it – none of which had been of any interest to the new born whose life revolved around sleep, milk and crying.

'I'm not sure I know, to be honest. Something the probation service has set up by the sound of it.'

'Didn't you ask?' said Zara, shuffling her way into a lying position, pushing a plastic dog with electronic eyes and a large, stuffed, giraffe onto the floor. A gurgle came from the basket and the three of them looked around, stunned by the realisation that Freddie wasn't crying. Wendy mouthed the word "yes" and punched the air. A leg kicked its way out of the basket, swiftly followed by an arm and then another arm. It seemed the baby was fascinated by its own ability to move.

'Well, I'm not going to get it am I? Every time they see my record I get turned down. It's just a way of pretending they are getting me into a normal way of life. They'll give up eventually,' said Alan.

'Don't be like that, Al,' said Zara. 'Have some faith.'

'Yeah, sure,' said Alan. 'Like God has some master plan where I come out of prison, spend a few weeks being a good boy and then everything is forgiven. I no longer have to stretch out a meagre existence on government handouts and the goodness of my friends and am almost instantly promoted to the job of my dreams where my experience of spending far too much time on my own with far too many dysfunctional people will come into great use.'

Zara sat up and threw the stuffed giraffe in Alan's direction.

'What have I said to you about being so bloody negative,' said Zara. 'You're bright, you're funny, you're kind. You can't be defined by your actions any more.'

Wendy added: 'Miserable git,' at which point Alan picked up the giraffe from the floor.

'You've got some neck,' he said to it and the girls laughed, keen to keep up their support.

Five days later Alan was sitting in the probation office waiting room. It wasn't his usual office, where he went to meet up with his resettlement officer, but where he'd been asked to meet Tessa Charlton. She didn't give him any idea of what the meeting was about so he played with scenarios in his head, exaggerating the boundless possibilities he thought up for himself.

'I just hope it's not going to be another wasted meeting with a do-gooder,' he'd said to Zara. Only two weeks previously someone from Age Concern had asked if he'd be happy to take a few of their pensioners shopping on a regular basis. Alan explained he couldn't drive and even if he could, he didn't have a car.

'She curled her lip at the same time as saying what a shame it was I couldn't help out as it would make such a difference,' he'd said when he got back. 'Well it would have made more of a difference if she'd checked out who was suitable for the work in the first place instead of making assumptions.' He'd seen the woman drive out of the car park in a new Jaguar estate which Alan reckoned cost more money than all the wages he'd ever earned in his entire life.

'I'm here to meet Mrs Charlton,' Alan told the receptionist when he arrived, twenty minutes early. The woman behind the tall desk looked up with a bored expression.

'No-one here with that name, love,' she said, concentrating on a notepad in front of her.

'Well, she said to meet here - Bridge Street. 11am.' Alan was trying to keep his patience with the receptionist who was making notes on her pad which, on closer inspection he could see was a shopping list, which included 'cat food, milk, Tena pads.' He guessed she lived on her own.

'That's the place. What's it about?' she asked as she lifted her head and gave him a look that suggested she really couldn't be bothered with him.

'I don't know. That's why I'm here, to find out,' said Alan feeling his muted temper rising. He rarely got cross but suspected this woman treated everyone who came in with the same contempt, all because she judged those within the criminal system to be somehow devoid of feeling, or the need for respect. He wasn't angry for himself but for all those people who didn't deserve the wrath of the public.

'Just a minute,' she said, picking up a phone. 'Chap here looking for Mrs Charlton.' There was a short silence. 'Oh. OK.'

She put the phone down, looked at her note pad again and got up from her chair, ignoring Alan's need for an answer. It was all he could do to stop himself saying something extremely rude, particularly when he spotted she'd been sitting on some chocolate which had melted onto her beige skirt; in just the right position to make it look like she'd had an unfortunate accident. It made him feel a bit better about her attitude and for a minute he wished he could be there when she realised she'd been going about all day looking like she'd shat herself.

After what felt to Alan like a lifetime of waiting the woman told him that Mrs Charlton would be arriving shortly.

'She's set up the meeting with one of the officers here. She's not one of us.'

Alan felt even more nervous. *What does this woman want?*

Eleven o'clock came and went and Alan was just about to leave the office when the door flew open and a dishevelled looking woman tripped in to the room, nearly landing on his lap.

'God, I'm all over the place today. Trains delayed, now it's raining and I'm soaked,' she said, flicking her arms so little splashes of water landed on the floor and some of them on Alan's hands.

'Oh, sorry,' she added when she saw what she'd done. 'You must be Alan. I'm Tessa,' she said as she offered her hand to shake. Alan stood up, took hold of her wet, but inviting, hand and said he was pleased to meet her. Even though he wasn't sure that was the right expression, considering his anxiety and desire to get to the bottom of her interest in him.

'Is the Conference Room free?' Tessa asked of the chocolate-bottomed receptionist. Alan was pleased to see the sneer of contempt was universal and not just for him.

'Did you book it? If not then you'll have to find somewhere else.'

'I think Mr Finchley booked it for me,' said Tessa, unbuttoning her coat and shaking the remaining drops of rain onto the floor. 'Could you tell him I'm here, please.'

The receptionist glared at her before picking up the phone.

'Visitor for you.' She was about to bang the receiver down when she placed it back to her ear. 'Yes, that's right.' Again she seemed keen to get the conversation over but was forced to keep her ear to the receiver. 'Yes. For three people. I can count.'

Realising her ambition of getting off the phone using the smallest number of syllables, the receptionist indicated to Tessa and Alan to follow her. They did so, both raising an eyebrow in the other's direction, in mutual mirth at the woman's manner.

Once in the room Tessa invited Alan to sit in a seat at the end of a long table. The receptionist was hurrying out of the room when Tessa asked if coffee had been ordered. A succinct and barely audible 'yes' was muttered as the door closed, catching the edge of the chocolate stained skirt, forcing the woman to re-open the door and release herself.

'Well, that was embarrassing,' said Tessa, pulling herself up into a chair to the left of Alan and placing a pile of papers in front of her. 'I suspect she has difficulty enjoying life, let alone her job.'

Alan smiled but felt the corners of his lips twitching. It reminded him of when he had a load of dental treatment and the nerves in his jaw gave way to the point he couldn't control what his mouth was doing. He jogged his leg up and down and pulled at some skin around the edges of his thumbnail. He'd always done that when nervous and the skin had scabbed and left scars. If he went out in the sunshine for any length of time they would turn bright pink and highlight the damage he'd caused.

Alan looked around the room and tried to work out from the various posters and bits of writing on large pieces of paper on an easel what went on in the Conference Room. Words such as "recidivism" and "restoration" appeared next to lists of statistics, one of them relating to a project called "Breaking The Cycle". Alan saw a pamphlet on Community Justice Panels and wondered how much of it was doing any good.

A tall man wearing faded and overly large corduroy trousers and an un-ironed shirt flustered into the room. His fringe was waving in the air making him look like a cartoon character.

'Dan Finchley. Pleased to meet you,' he said to Alan who, in response, thought it very unlikely he was pleased to meet him unless he'd muddled him up with someone worthwhile. Not many people would claim they are pleased to meet a murderer.

'Hi there, Tessa. How are you?' He added. She stood up to greet him with a slight kiss to one cheek – a habit Alan noticed was common place since he'd come out. People didn't kiss strangers in the 1980s. Not that he'd seen, anyway.

'Has the wonderful Tessa told you why we've asked you to come to this meeting?' said Dan as he unsuccessfully pushed his fringe back, revealing a receding hair line and the scars of a man who once had an eyebrow piercing.

Alan shook his head and looked down at his hands. He'd made his thumb bleed.

'Well, over to you my dear,' said Dan as he leant back in his plastic chair, making it creak with the strain of supporting his exceptionally long back. He put his hands behind his head, revealing sweat stains and some midriff where the shirt no longer met the waistband of his trousers. Alan could just see the upper edge of what he assumed were brightly coloured boxer shorts. 'Has the coffee arrived?'

Tessa started to move some papers about as Dan shouted out from the door of the room at the receptionist. 'Deirdre! Deirdre can you hear me? Three coffees please.'

There was no obvious answer and Dan sighed deeply as he settled back into his chair. Tessa looked intently at Alan to the point where he couldn't hold her eye contact. His stomach churned and he thought briefly about running away. But curiosity got the better of him.

'We've been looking at your resettlement reports and also your history of social contribution during your years of imprisonment. You've shown yourself to be a man who accepted justice and also took the time to acknowledge your part in crime and what contributed to your actions,' she finally said. 'The probation office tell me that you haven't yet found suitable employment although you have stable living accommodation, is that right?'

Alan wanted to laugh at the concept of "stable living accommodation". It made him sound a bit like the baby Jesus – no crib for a bed, and all that stuff.

'That's right,' he answered, trying to wipe the blood from his thumb on his trousers 'It's not that easy for a convicted murderer to get work I'm afraid.'

Tessa shivered and looked out of the window. She was biting her bottom lip. Dan asked her if she was OK just as the coffee arrived. It spilled into the saucers as Deirdre banged the tray on the table.

'No biscuits today?' said Dan in a voice that helped lighten the mood. Alan had felt a shift-change in the atmosphere just after he'd mentioned that he was a murderer and was glad of the lift. Dan pushed the cups in front of each of them but Alan thought it too risky to try and lift his, given how much he was shaking.

Tessa shifted in her seat, coughed and focused on some papers in front of her. Dan took up the reins of the conversation, giving her time to compose herself.

'There have been some excellent programmes running throughout the South East over the last couple of years which aim to bring offenders into the community and allow them to use their experience to help prevent other people making the same mistakes. Tessa runs a charity that helps educate and train released prisoners so they can be part of this system.'

'So what's that got to do with me?' said Alan.

Tessa spoke. 'Your history suggests you would provide an excellent point of contact for young people getting involved with gang culture. Our charity would sponsor you through your training and provide a small wage until you are fully qualified. At which point we would encourage you to work with the various agencies as a professional advocate for vulnerable teenagers.'

Alan took in the information but wasn't sure what to make of it. So far his job prospects had been as a part-time window cleaner, a delivery driver and a hospital porter. All of which he'd have been happy to take but wasn't given so much as a rejection letter, let alone an interview. His CV was sufficient to put anyone off even speaking to him, so his chances of employment were as slim as a butterfly's eyelash. His pulse raced at the thought of doing something worthwhile, being a part of a community. It occurred to him that all that time in prison might not have been a waste, not if he could use it and stop others ending up like him.

'God,' was all he could say. His mind's eye went back to points in his life when someone to help at the right time might just have made a difference; literally the difference between life and death.

'So why me? There must be hundreds of people better suited to this?' said Alan looking first at Tessa and then at Dan. He was looking for clues as to how they'd decided to give him hope, change his fate.

Dan nodded and looked at Tessa. 'Best you explain,' he said.

'I set up the charity ten years ago before restorative justice was so widely accepted. It aims to put offenders in touch with people they've impacted and allows them to try and do something to put things right.'

'I can't put things right, I killed someone,' said Alan, his hope diminishing as he spoke. 'There's no going back.'

Tessa shifted in her seat. 'No there isn't any going back. But there is going forward. I heard about your suicide attempt. There's no point wasting your life, too. If you do something good with it then you can help address the balance rather than just making more people suffer.'

Alan's chest starting heaving and he thought he might sob. The chance to do something, anything, that was deemed worthwhile would help him get somewhere in terms of his remorse.

'If I thought I could put anything right I would do it straight away,' he said, looking up as a tear ran down his cheek.

'Then it seems like we have a deal. I'll sort out the paperwork with Dan and we'll get back to you very soon.' said Tessa, hesitating. 'I'm glad you're on board. The news will make my family very pleased.'

Alan wondered why her family would give two hoots about him as she started to pack away her papers.

'Really?' he said. 'I can't see why. I'm just some old lag who's spent a long time in prison for making a very big mistake.'

Tessa turned to him and paused, biting her lip and letting her breath out slowly.

'I set up the charity a few years after my sister was killed. We couldn't stand the bitterness and anger. We wanted to do something positive in her name.'

She stood up and faced Alan straight on.

'Her name was Julie Gill.'

CHAPTER THIRTY NINE

Martin Luther King made a lot of sense. It was him who said *'Darkness cannot drive out darkness; only light can do that. Hate cannot drive out hate; only love can do that'.*

I didn't understand what he meant when I first read that. It's taken an awakening of my soul to really get it. That and a quote from a guy called Lewis B Smedes. *'To forgive is to set a prisoner free and discover that the prisoner was you.'*

Thanks to the immense strength of Julie Gill's family, I'm the prisoner who has been set free. Their understanding and compassion, borne out of intense grief and anger, has released me into a world that might just benefit from what has happened. Only a tiny bit, maybe, but that little seed of a difference can grow.

The Gill family hasn't always wanted to forgive me. I've learned that it's been a long process – one that started with murderous intent. Tessa told me they all had a pure rage, intense and very physical - great heat would rise in their bellies, exploding in their head and making them all realise they were capable of killing.

'That thought was incredibly frightening. We all started to understand how people can do things as a reaction to something they think is out of their control,' she said.

'Julie was dead and we wanted you dead too. We wanted revenge, public justice. But in the end none of that would bring her back.'

At first they'd have happily seen me hanged, drawn and quartered; locked up with the key thrown far, far away. But Tessa said that after a year it was like swallowing arsenic and expecting someone else to be poisoned.

I've been talking to the family a fair bit over the last year, since I signed up to work with the Julie Gill Restorative Justice Charity. It aims to stop people in the wrong tracks, get them to understand the impact of what they are doing. I see myself in so many of the young people I deal with as part of my job.

Young Sean Campbell is a good lad. His dad died when he was six and his mother tried her best to keep things together but depression got the better of her, then drink and drugs took their toll too. Sean was fostered at the age of nine but one of the older boys raped him so he was sent to a care home, where he spent most of his formative years frightened and alone – believing no-one loved him.

He would steal, fight, assault and then drink or smoke cannabis to numb the effects of his actions. He came to us on referral from social services after he stabbed a pregnant woman in the stomach with a Stanley knife. Thankfully she wasn't badly hurt but was particularly keen to meet her attacker to get him to explain why on earth he would do something so random and, in her view, so cruel.

'I was jealous,' he told me after many meetings, the first of which he would just sneer and look into his lap. 'She is beautiful and her baby was going to have her as a mother. I wanted her to be my mother.'

That might sound ridiculous to anyone not living inside Sean's head but for him it was a reality, a torture against his feelings of loss. Once his victim learned his story and of his remorse, which came quickly after the recognition of his motivation, she accepted his apology and offered forgiveness. It made all the difference to him and I could feel my ability to bring these two people together make some kind of retribution, not only for my own crimes but those Sean may have gone on to commit with a full stop at the end of his sentence.

He is now working for a supermarket and spending his evenings getting some basic qualifications. His ambition is to be a nurse so that he can help people who have been hurt or injured, or are suffering from illnesses.

'I want to put something back. My way of making things right,' said Sean.

It might sound too easy and those who live in mainstream society could believe that all interventions work. Well, they don't. Many criminals don't give a toss about what they're doing, or at least they don't until they are forced to think about it. You have to dig deep but when I've done that with our clients – I still find it strange calling them that –many people who have committed serious crime are sorry for what they've done. Mainly because they don't want to be like that, but they don't know any better. Of course they don't always admit it publically – I know I didn't.

Tibetan Buddhists have a ceremonial instrument made from the hollowed out thigh bone of a criminal. Blowing through it as part of a ritual is supposed to cleanse the karma of that individual. It's an interesting thought and it shows that all societies and all types of people look to balance out wrong with some kind of right. Maybe what I do is its own ritual, and at least no-one has to give up a leg to find a way of moving on.

I've been given a lucky break which I don't deserve. Julie's family tell me that while they can never forget what I've done they will keep forgiving me all the time I am stopping other people from following in my footsteps. Whether they are right or wrong they believe that catching young offenders and making them face up to the consequences of their actions may just, possibly, save another victim from Julie's fate. I really hope so because I am giving it all I can.

What I've been giving is my time. It's all I have to offer and with the right guidance I can be sure whatever days I have left in me are put to good use.

I'm also hoping I can be a good role model to Freddie who is surrounded by loving adults and people who want him to grow into the best person he can. When the time is right he'll learn about my past, and hopefully learn from it. I don't want him to waste his life, his time, or that of anyone else.

The Julie Gill project is a good one. It's turned something very horrible into a positive outcome. Of course we would all prefer the motivation behind it to have never been there, for Julie to still be alive and her family to be enjoying her company. But that can't be so. No amount of guilt or remorse changes that.

What can be so is a whole raft of support systems for vulnerable people. Those children whose parents think having a baby is for benefits, not for life. Those who treat their offspring like dogs, or dolls, and have no thought for guiding them into positive environments.

It's been hard turning things round. I spent a lot of time feeling sorry for myself - thinking that if I'd had a different start in the world I'd be in a better place, or had I not met The Team I'd have spent my time doing something more worthwhile. But I've learned that the difference between being a criminal or a public servant is purely a matter of perspective.

Tom Robbins said: *'It's never too late to have a happy childhood'* which, at first, I thought was a load of psycho shit.

But the truth is, he's right. Whatever has happened in the past is only retained by images in the brain; our own memories. We might see those pictures and thoughts as truth but they're only personal to us, in our own heads.

You can't love yourself if you keep blaming your actions on others. I learned to accept responsibility for my own bad choices and looked at how to parent myself. Robbins calls it 'remedial parenting' and you use the voice in our head to coach you through the day.

I dumped the inner critic because of the consideration I've been given by others. Instead of talking to myself like a piece of shit I try to value who I am as I would a neighbour, a friend or a member of my family.

Negative thoughts would hijack my mind, but what good was that doing? I know I'm not perfect but if I walk backwards forever, I can never move in the right direction.

I've done my time and by doing so have learned that time, as Einstein said, is just an illusion.

It's what you do with that illusion that's important.